Sunset Daydreams

The Wolves of Woodbine Hollow
Book 1

L.B. Benson

EMERALD MOON
PRESS

*For anyone who questioned their dreams but did the damn
thing anyway.*
xo, LB

Also by L.B. Benson

ANDROMEDA'S ACCOUNT

The Bartered Soul
The City of New Aphros
Andromeda's Vengeance
The Northman's Lullaby

———

THE WOLVES OF WOODBINE HOLLOW

Sunset Daydreams
Neon Elegies

Sunset Daydreams

By L.B. Benson

Wolves of Woodbine Hollow
Book One

First print edition July 2024

EBook ISBN 979-8-9896350-1-6
Paperback ISBN 979-8-9896350-2-3

Cover design by Tyler Evelyn Rood
Illustrations by Marta García Navarro

Edited by Kelly Hammond
Pickles Publishing

Content Warning & Author's Note

Sunset Daydreams is an adult paranormal romance that contains mature content. It is intended for readers over the age of 18.

To view detailed content/trigger warnings, please visit the author's website: https://lbtheauthor.com or scan the QR code below.

Chapter 1
Shane

Though the late summer breeze offers little relief from the heat of the season, the wind against my face is as close as I can get to running free through the woods. No matter the weather it always reminds me why I prefer my motorcycle over other modes of transportation. It's been a long week and I'm itching to take the edge off the call of tonight's full moon with a cold beer and shower to rinse off the scent of the shop. Rounding the corner, I spy the familiar form of my neighbor strolling toward our building from the subway exit. She wears headphones and struggles with a framed canvas and tote bag as she fumbles for her keys.

I back my bike into the spot in front of our building, killing the engine and preparing to ask her if she needs some help, but she doesn't look over as she yanks the door open and slips inside. I have to admit that I'm disappointed. This would have been a prime opportunity to talk to her. We only cross paths occasionally and haven't shared more than cordial smiles and pleasantries in the six months she's lived next door.

I hurry into the building, thinking I might catch her by the mailboxes, but she's already a flight up. Taking the stairs two at a time, I catch up to her near the top of the second flight, hoping she doesn't see me chasing after her.

"Need some help?" I raise my voice to be heard over whatever she's listening to, while trying to not sound too eager.

I'm rewarded with the canvas swinging abruptly toward me as she spins on her heel, long hair swinging. Almost taking a three-foot wide canvas to the face isn't how I expected to end my week when I locked up at the shop. But here I am, standing across from my beautiful neighbor, who clings to the cloth-wrapped wooden frame that nearly took my eye out.

I smile down at her, not remotely upset about the change of plans.

"Shit!" Realizing she didn't just bump into the railing, she hastily pulls at her headphones which are now tangled in her hair. "I'm sorry! I didn't even hear you back there!" Finally freeing her hair, she gives an adorably awkward wave and the canvas slips from her grasp. I grab it before it can plummet down the narrow stairs with what I can only imagine is an idiotic grin plastered across my face.

"It's fine. No harm done," I answer holding it out to her. If I moved a bit too quickly, she didn't seem to notice. My fingers are still slightly greasy from work, and I cringe inwardly at the marks they leave on the clean, white surface. "Fuck." I pull my hand back and rub it on my equally greasy work jeans.

Great, now *I'm* the one who's sorry.

"No worries. If I hadn't tried to knock you down the stairs you wouldn't have had to grab it. The marks will get covered with paint anyway. Like you said, no harm done." She smiles, still trying to balance her belongings without dropping anything else.

Standing awkwardly on the landing in front of our doors, I search my memory for the day she moved in, trying to remember when she told me her name in the hallway amidst a flutter of boxes and plants and movers.

It was something unique. With a C or a K, maybe?

I try and fail just as miserably to keep my gaze from roaming over her, admiring her toned legs bared by baggy cutoff shorts. She gives a little snort of laughter when she catches me, and offers a sideways smirk when my gaze returns to hers.

"Well, have a good night!" She gives another little smile, turning to unlock her door while I stand there like an idiot in the muted glow of the overhead bulbs.

"Are you an artist?" I blurt, louder than I intended. I mentally kick myself. Like the canvas isn't answer enough, Shane. But I'll use any excuse to keep talking to her now that we've started. I hope she'll mention her name again so I won't have to admit I can't remember it.

A little chuckle escapes her, and she cuts her eyes over her shoulder with a sly smile, as if she knows what I'm doing. Once she has her door open and the canvas propped inside, she turns toward me again, arms crossed over her chest. "I am." She glances at the canvas as if to say *Obviously*, then rakes her narrowed blue stare over me, brows raised in amusement. "Are you interested in art?"

I'm interested in you, I think. Hoping to mask that interest, I run my fingers through my hair and lean my hip against the railing of the landing before answering. "I wander by the galleries near my shop sometimes."

She hums a little noise of approval. Looking down at my left hand, she nods toward the motorcycle helmet I hold. "And your shop? You work on motorcycles?"

"Yeah, it's down near 84th and Ironwood."

"Well, if you ever make it to Red Lark Gallery on West 82nd you should stop in to take a peek. Some of my work is on display there, but I have my first solo exhibition in just over a month." Her eyes and smile sparkle with excitement. I've hit on the right topic.

"Maybe I'll do that." It's the opposite direction from my drive home, but if I can use it as an excuse to invite her to ride with me sometime, I'll make it a priority.

"Great, well...goodnight...?" The way she draws out the last word into a question and bites the inside of her cheek is a relief.

She can't remember my name either.

"Shane. Shane McKinley." I start to extend my hand but hesitate, remembering the dirty handprint on the canvas and cursing myself for not scrubbing them harder before locking up tonight. I just wanted to get home; I didn't think I'd be trying to make a good impression on the pretty woman next door.

"Kaycia Durand. Don't worry about a little grease," she replies, holding her hand out to take mine. Colorful bits of paint dot her fingers. "I've got my own oil stains."

Heat simmers through my blood when our skin touches, sending little lightning bolts up my arm and straight to my gut. I have to fight to keep from sucking in a breath at the sensation.

"Nice meeting you again, Kaycia. I'll see you around." I release her hand, trying to keep my voice even, and pretending I'm not affected by her nearness.

"I hope you do, Shane." With a final quick smile, she steps into the dim interior of her apartment. The door closes with a click and then the tumblers of the locks follow suit.

Hearing the second lock click into place, I blow out a deep exhale, then unlock my own door, directly beside hers, and flip the switch to illuminate my waiting loft. I think Kaycia's apartment is a mirror of mine, but I never took the time to snoop around after the old tenant moved out. Our kitchens share a common wall, then mine opens to a large, shared space for sleeping and living. It's a small, quiet building with our apartments sharing the uppermost floor that was once an attic or servants' quarters before developers tore through and remodeled the building and surrounding block. I've lived here for five years, and Kaycia is much more enjoyable to live next to than old Mr. Rexrode ever was. She keeps to herself and is quiet, for a human—she can't help that my senses are heightened so that I hear her music drifting through the walls in the evenings.

Tonight was a pleasant surprise. On the odd days we run into one another, I can barely drag my eyes from her, watching her smile at the other tenants in the building or strangers passing by on the street. Until today I've only ever given a nod in recognition, not sure how to strike up a conversation or if one would be welcomed. I'll take a bump to the face any day if it gives me an excuse to speak with her again.

Dropping my helmet on the entry table next to the pile of junk mail that's collected this week, I shrug out of my jacket and unlace my boots, putting both in the tiny closet by the door. Then I snag a beer from the fridge and head out onto the balcony to watch the sun set and the moon rise.

It's taken nearly a decade for me to become comfortable enough to be under the full moon without giving in to the urge to shift. I used to stay inside with the curtains drawn, prowling darkened rooms, wallowing in my memories. Now that I'm older, I spend these nights sitting on my wrought iron balcony toasting to the moonlight and wondering what my old friends—and enemies—are doing now. It's nearly impossible for me to shift in the city without causing a stir. Wolves don't typically stroll down city streets or dig for leftovers in alleyway dumpsters. When I had to flee my home, I hurdled into the unknown, assuming a city would be the safest place for me to hide.

For years, I stayed a step ahead of anyone who may have still tracked me, moving from one major city to another to remain anonymous in the crowds of other people running from their pasts. No wolf would voluntarily live amongst the concrete, metal, and brick, so luckily no one familiar has crossed my path in years.

Finally, I decided to settle in Argent. The city of towering glass and silver skyscrapers is now home. I shelled out the deposit on this place, saved up to open my shop, and haven't looked back.

Well, not often at least.

Still, the only place I'm fully confident I can shift without fear of being discovered is my vacation cabin in Snow Fern Tarn a little over an hour outside the city. Thinking about the cabin and its surrounding woodlands, wildness rises and prickles under my skin. The sensation swiftly overtakes the pleasant hum of longing I felt when I touched Kaycia. My wolf is aching to shift and run. I need to make a trip out of town soon.

As the light of the day fades, the breeze finally offers relief from the summer heat. I lean back in my chair, relaxing into the cushion and taking a deep swallow from my icy beer bottle. While the evening is beautiful, I find myself less interested than usual in the sun sinking behind the neighboring building in its orange and pink glory, and far more interested in the soft yellow glow of the windows just barely visible through the leaves of a lemon tree on the neighboring balcony.

Kaycia has managed to create a lush little green space

on the balcony a few feet away — potted fruit trees, a riot of colorful flowers, and collections of fragrant herbs cover nearly every inch of her balcony, cocooning a table and chair hidden in the foliage. I've never seen her sit at it, but we don't usually keep the same hours. Her sliding door opens and a hint of music drifts on the breeze, mingling with the sounds of traffic and other melodies of the neighborhood.

I don't stay long enough to listen. I've made enough small talk tonight. With the shift so close to the surface it's harder for me to concentrate, and Kaycia isn't someone I want to make a fool of myself in front of. Silently, I slip out of my chair and slide through my door before she steps into the twilight.

Chapter 2
Kaycia

Did I seriously just knock the hot guy next door in the face with my fucking canvas?

I blow out a loud sigh and bury my burning face in my hands when my back hits the wood of the front door. Which I just shut and locked. Also, in his face.

Smooth, Kaycia. Very smooth.

I know that I shouldn't walk around with my headphones on, it's one of those safety tips everyone harps on, but I was on my street and in my building, so I didn't think anything of it. I'd had one pushed off my ear the whole walk from the art store and on the entire subway ride. I just wanted to enjoy the song instead of the incessant street noise. Now, I've been reintroduced as the clumsy, airhead girl next door. But, at the very least the incident was an excuse to reintroduce myself at all, right?

I wouldn't have been a sweaty mess lugging the cumbersome canvas through the streets back home. It would have fit in my back seat. I realize how spoiled I was living somewhere with ample parking and only slightly horrible traffic.

I miss my car. I miss the convenience.

Nope. Stop it.

If I were back home, I wouldn't have a cute neighbor to almost knock down the stairs. I probably wouldn't even be worried about a canvas or painting, either.

It's been a rough week. Okay, several rough weeks. But I refuse to let a few bad weeks make me rethink my entire move to Argent. I already wade through enough negative bullshit whenever my parents call or text to check in. I'm not adding to it myself.

I spent twenty-six years of my life living the way they thought I should. I'm not going to let my own intrusive thoughts derail me when I'm finally following the path that *I* chose. That I dreamed of for so long.

Even if I really miss green spaces.

And wildflowers.

And the countryside.

And stars.

The aspects of that life that I *don't* miss are far more numerous than those I do.

I've only been here six months, I keep telling myself. *I'm sure I can find a balance.*

I'm certain of it.

Positive.

Dropping my keys in the basket by the door, I slip my shoes off and carry the new canvas to my easel where I prop it against the base and smile at the oily smudge from Shane's quick hands. If he hadn't grabbed the canvas the frame probably would have cracked on the way back down the stairs and I would have had to make the trek with it again tomorrow. I shudder at the thought of carrying another oversized canvas on public transit. But my smile returns when I think of how Shane clearly couldn't remember my name any more than I could his. He'd almost seemed nervous about it. In my defense, the day I moved in was so overwhelming with boxes and movers that I barely noticed him stick his head in to introduce himself.

I've definitely noticed him since.

Shane keeps a reliable schedule, and I often hide behind the plants on my balcony to watch him take off on his bike while I sip my morning coffee. I never thought I would be into a guy who rides a motorcycle, but something about watching him throw his leg over it makes me rethink that. So does that sideways grin he gave me, and the hint of sadness in his eyes. I can occasionally hear guests through our shared wall, but he's quiet otherwise. It seems we both keep to ourselves.

Maybe that can change now that we had our official reintroduction. Maybe I can get up the nerve to make the first move.

I grab a wineglass from the cupboard and fill it halfway with chilled pinot grigio before flipping on a few lamps, pressing play on my speaker to listen to some music, and heading to the balcony. It's a nice night. Warm, but not as bad as during the heat of the day in the concrete laden city.

I love watching the full moon over the buildings, even if I miss being able to see the constellations I could observe outside Summerville. I've tried my best to recreate some kind of natural oasis amidst the sidewalks and steel so I feel more at home, but I'm still getting settled.

Stepping onto the iron balcony, I hear the swish and click of Shane's matching sliding door, but the traffic and laughter on the sidewalk below swallow up any other noises that might drift from his way. Too bad. Maybe I should have asked him over for a drink. It would have been an easy thing to do instead of dashing into my apartment. Sighing, I sip my wine, the glass already coated in cool drips of condensation.

Maybe you should focus on your next project to get ready for your exhibition instead of daydreaming about your neighbor, I scold myself. But then again, having a friend—or more than a friend—could make things less lonely. Could even be a source of new inspiration.

Whether it was luck or fate that brought me to Argent, I'm happy to be here instead of the small town I grew up in. Back in Summerville I'd become frustrated with only being able to paint when I could squeeze it in after work. When my day job was restructured, offering me more work with no additional pay, I'd had it. It was the push I needed to get up the nerve to send my portfolio out to galleries in several cities hoping for a break.

Kelly, the owner of Red Lark, reached out with enthusiasm, offering to show a few of my pieces. I shipped them, and within a few weeks, I'd put in my notice, sold nearly everything that wasn't easily loaded in a moving truck, cashed out my savings, and said goodbye to everyone and everything I'd ever known to finally pursue my art full-time.

Kelly's assistance has helped me get my name out and make a few small sales. Having my first solo exhibition in the city could make big waves for me, even at a smaller gallery. The networking opportunities and potential for a residency have pushed me to focus on my work instead of my personal life, perhaps to my detriment at this point.

But it might also be the thing that finally proves to my family that quitting my secure office job was worth it, and that art is a viable career. I've always painted, and when I was young my parents indulged my hobby, but even though I've sold a few paintings they refuse to see it as a "real job".

My parents' judgment haunts me. They reacted poorly to my decision to move and think I'm selfish, foolish, naïve —even if they haven't said it directly. The little jabs, snide remarks, and incessant warnings about the dangers of the city spoke volumes when I told them my plans. As did their repeated questions asking why I would give up security for something so silly? Why couldn't I grow up and just settle down?

But settling is all I've ever done.

I was sick of living my life for someone else. Always wondering 'What if?'

While I'm excited for my opening at Red Lark, nothing makes me prouder than the fact that I took the risk to come to Argent on my own. That I finally put myself and my dreams first. I have to remind myself of that every time homesickness squeezes my chest. I can white-knuckle my self-doubt, but I'm finding that loneliness is a companion I'm struggling to manage.

Sometimes you can be happy and sad at the same time.

Taking another sip of my wine, I shake my head, clearing any tears blurring my vision. I refuse to cry when I'm doing exactly what I want. What I dreamed of.

I consider texting my best friend back home, but when I grab my phone to check the time, I realize it's dinner time there. Meg's probably getting her kids fed and then ready for bed. No time for my whining right now.

What I need is a friend in the city. Someone who isn't related to the gallery or work. Maybe it *is* time I crawl out of hiding and finally ask the cute neighbor for a drink.

Chapter 3
Shane

"Wanna grab a drink tonight? Jamila's off and wants to get out of the house," Raquel asks, packing sockets back into their places at the end of the day. I glance over my shoulder, still scrubbing my hands in the garage sink, in time to catch her wry grin. I know exactly what's coming out of her mouth next. "Maybe you can invite that cute neighbor you've been pining over?"

Raquel De La Rosa is my only employee and a close friend—another lone shifter in the city. Lucky for her, *her* animal side is far easier to slip into in the urban environment unnoticed, even if she's been known to cause trouble in her mischievous raccoon form. Her partner, Jamila Wilks, is human. They've been together for years, and Jamila has become unfazed by our kind. Raquel shares my affinity for motorcycles and stumbled across me when I was opening the shop. After circling one another and sniffing out our animal sides, she admitted she was hoping for a job. The rest is history. She and Jamila are as close to a pack or a family as I have now. Jamila works at a collection of low-key bars all run by the same hospitality management company, and Raquel sometimes drags me with her to hang out at them when J's tending bar. Otherwise, we try to have drinks or grill on the rooftop of one of our buildings once or twice a week.

"I don't feel like going out," I reply, receiving a dramatic eye roll and a muttered, "Surprise, surprise," from Raquel. I ignore her and add, "But you're welcome to come over to my place. We can order takeout. I'll call Max to join." I finish locking the metal rollup door and close the office just as she's ready to flip the lights off.

"Sounds good—we'll be over in an hour."

Waving goodbye as Raquel revs her bike and darts into traffic, I text Max, another stray shifter I've befriended since living in the city. He works in one of the high rises downtown as a graphic designer by day and plays gigs around town at night, so his hours are all over the place and I never know if he'll join us. Before I hop on my bike, I take a mental inventory of the inside of my fridge and decide to head to the corner store once I get home. I should have plenty of time before Raquel and Jamila make it over.

Balancing a case of beer in one hand and my helmet, mail, and keys in the other, I climb the stairs to our landing. Soft music filters from under the door of Kaycia's apartment when I reach our landing, folksy and melancholy. It's been a little over a week since we formally reintroduced ourselves and I haven't seen her since. I hesitate for a moment, considering whether I should knock and ask her to join us. Glancing down at my greasy jeans and sweaty tee, I decide to wait until I've washed off the grime from my work day, heading into my apartment alone. I deposit the case of beer in the fridge, shed my clothes, and turn on the hot water for a quick shower. Maybe I'll pop over once I'm dressed.

Steam drifts from the open bathroom door as I dry off and wrap a thick cotton towel around my waist. Just as I start to wipe the fog off my mirror, a sharp knock at the door echoes through the loft, surprising me.

Damn. Raquel made good time today, I think, before shouting through the quiet apartment, "Come on in!" My wardrobe is across the loft near my bed, so as I stroll out of the bathroom in only my towel I chuckle, remarking, "Couldn't wait to see me again, huh, Quel?"

"Oh, shit—I'm sorry!" a woman squeaks.

I freeze when I come face to face with Kaycia. I can't fight the urge to inhale deeply, her scent heavy in the humid air.

Well, this *is unexpected.*

I let a slow smile spread across my face when her cheeks flush and her eyes drift down my chest, then lower to the knot of my towel before they widen and snap back to my face.

"Hey, neighbor. Need something?"

Good. I sound in control.

My thundering heart and the flip-flopping heat in my belly say otherwise, but my voice remains steady.

"I am so sorry, Shane!" She stutters and covers her face with her hands. "You said come in! I didn't know you'd be indisposed. I just—" She trails off, tossing her hands in the air helplessly, as she turns her back to me.

I hold in a laugh, but as she turns, I realize she's wearing nothing under her paint-splattered, cut-off denim overalls, the curve of the side of her breast revealed when she moved. I exhale forcefully and avert my eyes.

Control, Shane. Control.

"It's no problem. I thought you were someone else. What's up?" I ask again, making my way toward my wardrobe to grab something to put on, trying to maintain a casual tone. I definitely need more than a towel between us.

"Someone you walk around naked in front of?" she asks, glancing over her shoulder when she hears the wardrobe door click shut. She quickly looks away again, but I catch the barest hint of a smile.

"Kaycia?"

"Yeah?"

"Did you need me for something?"

"Oh! Yeah! Sorry, the heat is melting my brain. I think my air conditioner is broken. I tried maintenance but no one is answering. I wasn't sure if you were having any issues?" Now that I'm wearing jeans, I toss the towel in the bathroom and stand beside her, pulling my t-shirt over my head. I fight a grin when I catch her eyes flick over my body, now fully clothed.

"Everything's working fine here—but let me come over

and look for you. If I can't figure it out you can hang out here until Martin answers. Give me just a minute." I grab my phone from the counter and text Raquel to come in when she gets here, then shove it in my back pocket and follow Kaycia to her apartment.

Entering Kaycia's place is like walking into a jungle. No wonder she's covered in a thin sheen of sweat—the A/C is definitely on the fritz. But it's more than just the warmth; almost every spare surface is covered in plants, just like her balcony. It's like she's living in an artfully designed terrarium. I stand for a moment admiring the comforting lushness, such a contrast to the cool brick and iron of my own loft. When I look past the greenery, I spy her artwork. Bold colors and gold leaf outline human figures woven into skies at various times of day. The half-finished painting on the easel is an indigo night full of golden stars that causes me to struggle to pull my eyes away, trapped by the longing for a clear night sky.

"Are these yours?" I ask in awe. I cringe inwardly—*of course, they're hers, you idiot.* The canvas with my finger-prints from a week ago is propped next to the easel making me smile at the memory.

"They are! I've got just a few more to complete before I have enough for the exhibition," she replies, fanning herself where she stands beside me. "This one has been giving me trouble, but I'll figure it out."

"They're beautiful," I tell her. I'm not just saying it either. Something mystical leaps from the canvas and, though I would never have thought I'd say it, moves me. "Who's your muse?"

"Anything beautiful really, but mostly nature. Goddesses, flowers, the sky." She shrugs and smiles up at me despite the sweltering temperature. "Or at least the skies I used to see. I'm not from a big city. We used to be able to see all the constellations on clear nights. My dad liked to point them out to me when I was little. Some of my other pieces are brighter. I painted one inspired by the wildflowers I missed this spring. I miss them almost as much as the stars."

"I miss them, too."

Shit, shut up.

I clear my throat and change the subject. "So, the A/C?" I look around, turning my attention toward the thermostat and closet where the unit is housed and away from the memory of open skies.

Chapter 4
Kaycia

Thank all the gods that I have the heat of my apartment as an excuse because I think my cheeks are still burning from walking in on Shane in a towel. I knew he would have a nice body. He's tall and lean and his face alone is chiseled, so it shouldn't have surprised me to find that the rest of him is similarly sculpted, right down to the vee at his hips. But seeing him still glistening from a shower with his blond hair damp and hanging tousled across his forehead made me itch for a paintbrush or sketch pad. Or the knot of his towel.

I'm still thinking about it, staring at his back in his slim-fitting black tee as he inspects my thermostat. It was cute listening to him ask about my art, but he clammed up after his comment about missing things, piquing my curiosity. He's remained silent ever since, fiddling with the thermostat and whatever is in the closet next to it.

"Do you want a drink?" I ask, pulling my bottle of wine

from the fridge. It's all I can do to not press the chilled glass against me, but I'm extremely aware of the fact that I'm not wearing anything under my overalls now that I have Shane alone in my apartment.

"No, thanks. I think that should fix it. I heard it kick back on. It was the condensation line, but the backup should be cleared now." He pulls his phone from his back pocket and scans it before tucking it away again. "Like I said, I've got some friends coming over..."

"Oh. Okay." I hope the disappointment doesn't bleed into my voice too pathetically. I'm an independent woman living on my own terms. I shouldn't be so downcast because someone else has plans and I can't seem to put myself out there to make my own. "Thanks for the help. I guess I can get back to work."

I put the bottle back in the fridge as my own phone starts buzzing. I silence the call, not remotely in the mood to hear from my mother right now.

"You could come over if you want. Let the apartment cool off for a bit. You can bring your wine," Shane offers with a nod at my heavy pour.

"Are you sure I won't be imposing? I'm not crashing a date or anything, right?"

That was nonchalant, Kaycia, not at all prying into his relationship status.

"Definitely not. Raquel is bringing her partner Jamila, and unless something has changed dramatically between Max and me without my knowledge, we are firmly in the friend category." He crosses his arms across his chest and gives a sideways smile from where he leans against the wall. "I admit he's good-looking enough, but not really my type."

"Oh, and what's your ty—" My phone buzzes again, cutting me off mid-quip. I sigh with resignation. "Sorry, let me get this real quick or she will never give me peace tonight."

Shane nods as I answer the phone, hazel eyes surveying the apartment as I pace clutching my wine glass. Clearly, he's planning to wait for me to answer his invitation. My skin tingles when I catch him watching me, and my breath hitches when his eyes flick toward my bed then back to my face. Clicking the answer key, I squeak higher than I expected, "Hi, Mom. What's up?"

Shane's breathy chuckle, quickly covered by a cough and cleared throat, has my cheeks heating. I force a couple deep breaths while my mom prattles away. "Why didn't you answer earlier, Kay? You haven't called. Are you alright?" she questions in rapid succession. Always assuming the worst.

"Sorry, Mom. I was busy. My neighbor is here fixing my air conditioner. I'm trying to finish some work and need to get changed to hang out with friends." I smile over my shoulder at Shane as I say the words. She doesn't need to know that they aren't *my* friends. His eyes crinkle on the edges as he breathes a little laugh.

"Isn't your neighbor a guy? Are you sure it's safe for him to be in your apartment? Don't you have maintenance for that? Are you meeting these people in public? You know you're not equipped to handle yourself in that city. Take your pepper spray." She rattles off before adding, "I didn't know you'd gotten a job, what work are you doing?"

Gritting my teeth to keep from being a total bitch in front of Shane, I struggle to keep my frustration leashed. "Mom, can you please calm down? Yes, my neighbor is a guy, and he's very nice. I'm a grown woman. I know how to be safe. And I was painting, my art *is* my job. I'm prepping for an exhibition at the gallery I told you about."

Angry tears prick behind my eyes as I explain for the millionth time that my choices are valid and quietly beg for respect from my family. The ones who should be thrilled for me and shouting from the rooftops instead of tearing me down and making me question my every move. My civility wears thin as I clench my jaw and add, "Sorry, this just isn't a great time. I have to go unless there's something you need."

"I don't know why I have to call you twenty times to get you to check in with your family, Kaycia. I just want to make sure you're okay." My mom is a queen at making me seem like the bad guy when all I'm trying to do is set boundaries and live my life.

"I'm doing fine. I'll keep you updated, Mom. I gotta go. Tell Dad hi." Dropping my phone into the chest pocket of my overalls, I turn my back to Shane and take a long sip of my wine, swallowing it along with my ugly emotions, while I try to school my face into something other than the mashup of negativity I'm feeling.

"Hey, you okay?"

With a yelp, I grip my wine glass, barely keeping it from spilling. In the last few breaths, Shane has moved to stand behind without making a sound.

"Sneaky thing," I mutter under my breath as I face him, earning a surprised laugh. His gaze is intent and searching as I sniffle, then erase my frustration with a shrug. "Yeah, I'm fine. Things with my family have been a little... strained since I moved. But that's not your problem. Are you sure it's okay if I come over?" I force myself to smile.

"I wouldn't have asked if I didn't want you there." His tone is gentle, matching the soft expression in his eyes as they dip to my lips.

Relieved, I reply, "Okay. Give me ten minutes or so to change and I'll be over?"

Shane runs his eyes over my overalls, reminding me once again that I didn't put a shirt on underneath. A look suspiciously like disappointment clouds his face momentarily before he clears his throat. "Sounds good. You can let yourself in. I promise I'll be wearing clothes this time." With a chuckle and wink, he lets himself out the front door while I blush like an idiot.

Chapter 5
Shane

Returning to my apartment when Kaycia was visibly upset is harder than I'd like to admit. I barely know the woman. Her family drama is none of my concern. But I understand strained family dynamics and missing home better than anyone, so the urge to comfort her shouldn't come as a surprise.

Raquel is helping herself to a beer from the fridge when I walk in. At the counter, Jamila artfully lays out cheese, meat, and fruit on one of my cutting boards. In addition to bartending, she moonlights with a catering company. I enjoy the benefits of her experience with delicious foods and risk getting my hand slapped when I snag a few bites while she opens another package.

"I thought we were ordering takeout?" I ask around the cheese and cracker I shoved in my mouth.

"Raquel was already bitching about being hungry, so I

brought this to keep her civil," Jamila replies, winking when Raquel makes a face. "Don't act like you aren't a brat when you're hungry."

"I'm never a brat," Raquel lies, nipping at Jamila's bare shoulder. Jamila smiles indulgently at Raquel, continuing to arrange the food.

"I'm not complaining," I add, snagging some pieces of dried fruit and taking the extra beer Raquel holds out to me. "I invited Kaycia over," I say, giving Raquel a warning look. "Be nice."

"Fuck yeah, you did!" Raquel bumps me with her shoulder. I hold my beer aloft so she can't hit it with the bottom of hers. She's notorious for causing messes and making it overflow to fuck with me. She narrows her eyes at being thwarted and adds, "And I'm *always* nice."

Jamila snorts a laugh, hiding it behind her hands with a whispered, "That's a damn lie." She unpacks the last of the food from her cloth bag as though she's said nothing, earning a glare from her partner.

"You know what I mean. Don't reveal anything you're not supposed to while she's here. I'll have to remind Max, if he shows up. Best behavior."

"I won't scare away your cute new girlfriend, Shane," Raquel assures me.

"She's not my girlfriend. She's just my neighbor."

"Riiiiight," Jamila pipes up, reaching for a beer from Raquel now that she's finished with her charcuterie construction. "Nothing more than the nice neighbor you mention in passing every single time we've seen you since she moved in." Her warm brown eyes sparkle with glee when I grimace in response.

"Regardless, she doesn't know the truth about me. I need you to keep it under wraps. I don't want her to be frightened. We both have to live here."

"Okay, *Dad*. Best behavior," Raquel promises with a sarcastic scowl. "You don't actually think I'm going to let it slip that shifters exist in front of a stranger, do you?"

"No," I admit, glancing around the apartment for anything that needs to be cleaned up before Kaycia arrives. "Just... behave yourself," I mutter, piling the empty containers in the trashcan under the counter and eying the few dirty dishes in the sink.

"Are you *nervous?*" Raquel asks, dark eyes sparkling with mischief.

"Let's go outside!" Jamila redirects. "It's a perfect evening. Grab the board." She nods for me to carry the tray while she gathers a handful of napkins and her drink. I catch a glimpse of Raquel grinning and sneaking a kiss when Jamila scoots past her. Jamila giggles when Raquel nips at her throat and they stand smiling at each other for a moment.

I look away quickly, sliding the door open to the balcony. The ease of their touch and the love in their eyes when they smile at each other tugs at my heart. Raquel may be a pest sometimes, but I envy the happiness she's found with Jamila. I hope to find something similar one day.

———

Ten minutes later, we lounge on the balcony waiting for Kaycia to arrive. A light tap at the door has me on my feet, striding quickly through the apartment to open it. This time, Kaycia waits patiently for me to answer, causing me to stifle a chuckle. When I open the door, the chuckle escapes fully. She stands holding a potted plant in one hand and a half-drank bottle of wine in the other, the stem of her wineglass dangling between her fingers.

"You need some greenery in this man cave," she explains with a shy smile when I raise my brows at the plant. "It's a pothos, you can't really kill it."

I'll admit, compared to the lush walls of greenery in her place my apartment *does* look a bit "bachelor pad", but it's comfortable and easy to clean. I may not win any decorating awards, but at least my mattress isn't on the floor and I have matching plates and some art on the walls, unlike some guys I know.

Kaycia bites her lip as she holds it out to me. Our fingers brush as I accept the gift, sending heat through my chest. All I can think about is how I want to be the one to bite that lip instead.

"Than—" I begin, before we're spotted.

"Oh, she's bringing in a plant! That's the first step!" Raquel crows through the sliding door from the balcony, intruding on the moment.

Fuck my life.

Kaycia's smile falters at the joke, as though she's

worried she's overstepped some invisible boundary, but the change in expression is so brief I wonder if I misread it. She quickly regains the smile that I can't get out of my mind. Brushing off Raquel's teasing, I cradle the ceramic pot and usher Kaycia into the kitchen.

"I figured seeing you in your towel earlier skipped us ahead a few steps, so you're stuck with the plant," she jokes, pulling the cork from her sweating bottle of wine and refilling her glass. She puts the rest of the bottle in the fridge door and beams a bright smile at me when she catches me arranging the plant on the kitchen counter.

"Thank you. Come on, let me introduce you." I grab my beer from the counter and lead the way through the loft to the open door where Raquel and Jamila sit on the balcony wearing their sunglasses and matching smiles.

"So, you're the neighbor. It's about time you joined the fun," Raquel greets Kaycia when she steps outside.

The golden hour light peeks over the skyline and paints the side of our building in a pretty glow, masking the ugliness of the city street below. The fading sun makes Kaycia's light blonde hair gleam as it limns her body, almost like a figure in one of her paintings. I catch myself staring for a moment too long until Jamila clears her throat with a knowing smirk over her beer bottle. Kaycia changed from her overalls into a cream-colored crocheted tank top and a loose pair of printed pants. Amusingly she still isn't wearing any shoes, so her polished toes peek from the hem.

"Raquel. Jamila. This is Kaycia," I announce, pointing to each of them in turn, then sitting in the farthest chair so

Kaycia can sit next to the other women instead of forcing her to sit by me.

"Nice to meet you both," Kaycia replies, extending her hand to shake theirs with a broad smile. "You look familiar," she says to Jamila, studying her.

"Oh? Let's compare notes." Jamila brightens and gestures for Kaycia to sit. "Where could we have crossed paths?"

As she takes the open seat next to Raquel, settling into the thick cushion, I catch Kaycia's eyes drifting to me, running from my hand holding my beer, and all the way to my feet before they return to my face. When she catches me watching her, she looks away with a shy smile, forcing my lips to quirk up in response. From my seat across the balcony, I can admire the blood rushing to Kacyia's cheeks when she sneaks another look at me, knowing full well I'm still watching her.

Biting her lip once, she turns to the other women. They begin to talk quietly, Kaycia's attention now wholly focused on Jamila while I remain enthralled by having her on my balcony until Kaycia exclaims, "Red Lark! Yes, that's it!" The sudden outburst snaps me back to reality and Raquel snickers at my uncharacteristic lack of composure.

"Oh, yeah! I've done a lot of bartending for their receptions. What a coincidence!" Jamila answers.

I lean back, crossing my ankle over my knee, and relax into the chair to enjoy the sunset, still stealing glances at Kaycia. Raquel continues to snack, listening to Jamila and

Kaycia while sipping her beer and making faces at me. Everything seems like it's smooth sailing as Jamila starts to ask about Kaycia's current project. Just as Kaycia parts her lips to answer, the shriek of a peregrine falcon interrupts their casual conversation.

MAR
GA
NA
2023

Chapter 6
Kaycia

"Holy shit! What the fuck?" I exclaim, jumping up as a freaking *falcon* lands on the balcony rail. The movement is so sudden that I slosh wine, sending the pale liquid all over my lap and the cushion beneath me.

"Shoo! Go away!" Jamila waves her hands at the bird, which cocks its head and stares at her for a moment before it looks at each of us seated on the balcony, then takes to the air with another shrill cry.

What a wild afternoon already: I've seen my hot neighbor in a towel, randomly gifted him a plant like a weirdo, met his two friends—who happen to be beautiful women—and now a bird of prey has landed on the balcony and screamed at us.

Raquel muffles a laugh, transforming it into more of a cough when Jamila gives her a pointed look. Raquel dips her chin and her glossy dark hair drops over her forehead to hide whatever gleeful expression shines in her brown eyes while Jamila hands me a napkin to blot at the wine on my chair.

"What the hell was that? I've heard of falcons nesting on buildings in cities before, but never seen one so close! Does it live here?" I ask, looking curiously between Raquel and Shane, who has hopped to his feet and moved toward the door. I quickly add, "I'm sorry about the spill."

"Don't worry about it." He holds his phone in one hand as though he received a text. "Max is almost here. Be back in a few," he mutters, avoiding my question and closing the sliding door behind him. I can't help but track his movements through the tinted glass now that I know exactly what's under his plain black tee and jeans.

"So, Kaycia, tell me about yourself," Jamila says, pulling my attention from my lustful musings just as Shane grabs a backpack and heads toward the front door. I puff out a little breath and refocus, feeling silly at the heat in my cheeks, and other places, from watching Shane.

"Let's see..." I take a deep drink of my remaining wine, ignoring the pit in my stomach leftover from my mom's call. "I'm from just outside Summerville. I grew up there and went to school there and finally escaped by moving here." I'm trying to decant my entire life story for them, serving the innocuous details while leaving the more personal aspects of myself behind, but I find there isn't a lot to tell. "I studied art in college. But I ended up working in a miserable financial firm as an assistant from the time I graduated until late last year. Then I decided to finally say 'fuck it'. I sold almost everything and moved here to focus on my art."

Good Kaycia. Simple and to the point without over-sharing. I take another small sip of my wine. There's not much left now between my clumsiness and need for fortification.

"Well, as a native to the city, welcome! That's amazing that you have work displayed at Red Lark. I love when I get to bartend for their events. What kinds of things do you create?" Jamila asks, probing for more details. Her deep brown skin creases at the corners of her eyes when she gives a genuine smile and encourages me to continue to speak.

"I paint. Mostly oils, sometimes acrylic. I do both figures and landscapes, but I love to combine the two. We're nature, too, after all." I feel comforted by Jamila and continue, "I've been working on a collection since I moved here to prep for an exhibition. I need to finish the last few and it will be ready to go. My inspiration has been a little lacking lately, so some have been sitting longer than I expected."

"Don't let her be modest. Her work is beautiful." Shane's voice surprises me at my back. He's leaning against the frame of the slider, still holding his half-empty beer and smiling at me. "I got to see some of it earlier."

I swallow my grin and finish the last of my glass, but my cheeks heat at the praise and I know it's not from the alcohol or the low-hanging sun. "Thank you."

"Who is *this?*" Another male voice carries from the

kitchen before the man I assume is Max walks out the door with a beer in his hand. He's shorter than Shane, a bit broader and more muscular, wearing a tight-fitting band tee, faded jeans, and a pair of worn sneakers. His shoulder-length, light-brown waves paired with manicured facial hair exude effortless cool. I picture him in front of a camera with a model draped on his arm, or on stage strumming a guitar with groupies vying for his attention. His smile is as bright and welcoming as Jamila's and he snags a chair to sit on her other side while raising his brows in question at me.

"This is Kaycia. My neighbor," Shane answers, stepping back onto the balcony to sit in his corner spot, watching over the group with his sharp gaze.

"Where have *you* been hiding, lovely?" Max's grey-green eyes glitter with amusement as his slow drawl caresses each word. "Shane, why haven't you brought her around more often?"

"Because I knew you'd say shit like that, Max," Shane grinds through his teeth, surprising me at how *not* friendly he sounds. I cock my head to the side as I watch him take a deep breath and finish the rest of his beer. He scans all of us, then retreats to the kitchen for another. It's as if he can't sit still like he's nervous or anxious or... *something*.

"So, now that I've talked incessantly about myself," I say with a small laugh, hoping to lighten the mood, "tell me about yourselves."

As I finish my question, Shane reappears on the patio with a new beer for himself, as well as fresh ones for Raquel and Jamila balanced in one palm, and my bottle of wine in the other. He tops off my glass with a sideways smile and places the almost drained bottle on the low table in front of us.

"Me first!" Raquel grins, taking a deep swig of her beer. "I moved here when I was sixteen after I was emancipated from my asshole parents. I waited tables, did odd jobs, and lived wherever I could until I could afford to go to trade school. Now I work on bikes at Shane's shop and live with this babe." She leans over and places a light kiss behind Jamila's ear, both their smiles softening when they look at one another.

"And, like I said, I'm a local," Jamila adds. "I'm a part-time catering assistant, part-time bartender, and all-the-time writer of poetry, short stories, songs, what have you. And yes, I can't seem to get Quel to leave so I'm stuck with her."

She wrinkles her nose in mock disgust, and sticks her tongue out at Raquel, who returns the look and answers, "You love me and would miss me so much if I ever left."

"You two make me sick with your happiness," Max teases with a laugh. "Max Acheson. I do freelance design and sing in a band." *I knew it!* He holds his beer aloft as if he's toasting me from across the balcony. "You'll have to come see me play sometime. Force Shane to leave his den and have a good time."

Shane's jaw flutters. I wonder if he's always this prickly around Max, or if it's just the idea of taking me out that makes him annoyed. Shane's been polite, but I realize I barely know him. I start to worry again that he's only invited me over as a charity case, the idea beginning to erode my confidence.

"And you?" I push Shane to answer, trying to ignore my self-doubt.

"Well, you already know my name and that I own a bike shop. I'm from Woodbine Hollow, it's a small town in the mountains a few days drive west of here. But I've lived in Argent for the past five years. There's not much more to know."

When he says his last sentence tension suddenly seems to hum between his friends, as if a thread connecting them has been tightened. But they each mask the unease, settling quickly and making me wonder if I need to slow down on the wine. My senses seem to be going haywire tonight.

"Let's order dinner," Shane changes the subject abruptly.

The takeout from the deli down the block arrives within thirty minutes, and it doesn't take long before we are all gathered around the island in the kitchen to eat, perched on stools or sitting on the granite countertops themselves.

"What kind of music do you play, Max? Do you and Jamila ever write songs together?" I ask between bites of the overstuffed sandwich I now regret ordering. There is absolutely no way to look attractive when you have sandwich fixings dripping down your chin and escaping onto your lap every few minutes.

"Ha! As if he'd be so lucky!" Raquel jabs, receiving a

chip tossed in her direction from Max. She snags it midair and pops it in her mouth with an impertinent smile.

"Different styles for sure, but we sometimes bounce ideas off each other," Jamila adds. "Max's band plays at the bar I work at pretty regularly, though. They've got a more folk rock/indie country vibe than I usually write."

"I could never do her poetry justice," Max admits. "She's extremely talented."

"The man *does* have some sense after all," Raquel murmurs in mock surprise.

Jamila smiles in thanks at his compliment and inclines her head. "Maybe one day we'll write a hit song together."

"How is it that you've attracted a whole host of artists as friends? Are you hiding secret notebooks of poems or watercolors somewhere?" I ask, looking toward Shane before pointedly sweeping my gaze around his masculine loft. It's meticulously clean, which I find charming for a bachelor. He does have a shelf of books, a few pieces of art on the walls, and a couple of coffee table books laid on the table in front of his leather sofa with photos of motorcycles and nature on their covers, offering a glimpse of his interests.

"I can't seem to shed these misfits, but I'm not an artist myself," he answers, his lips lifting into a sideways smirk as his eyes travel over his friends. "I just get to reap the benefits of their creativity."

"Ha! What benefits? You never come out with us!" Raquel challenges.

"That's not true."

"It's a little true," Max adds.

"Max—" Shane warns.

"Prove it then," Raquel interrupts. "Come to Max's show at Lucy's next weekend. Bring Kaycia. Jamila's working so we'll all be there. I don't want to stand around alone."

The tension between the trio seems to build while Jamila looks between everyone, then catches my eye and offers a wink.

Chapter 7
Shane

Max and Raquel know why I don't spend much time in the bars or out on the town. Even if it's been years since I've run into any trouble, I try to keep a low profile and a bar is exactly the kind of place that's hard to do. I've told them I'd love to gallivant with them if I could—well, maybe *love* is too strong of a word—but for whatever reason they're both determined to force me into this.

I catch Kaycia's curious gaze on me as I chew the inside of my cheek. I don't want her to assume *she's* the reason for my hesitation. She probably already thinks I'm a moody jerk after Max tried flying onto the balcony earlier and then proceeded to flirt with her. I have to remind myself he had no way of knowing I'd finally invite her to join us after months of talking about her.

"What do you think? You wanna grab dinner and spend the evening at a dive bar listening to this asshole next weekend?" I ask her, looking up as I rub my palm across the nape of my neck to mask my nerves.

I've been trying to keep from staring at Kaycia while she eats, but I can't help but run my eyes over her perched on my countertop next to the stove. It'd be simple to walk up to her, step between her knees, and breathe her in. Press against her curves. Taste her lips.

It's been a long time since I've had a woman in my apartment who isn't Raquel or Jamila. Even longer since there's been anyone I've wanted to get to know more closely on a personal level. No one has made me willing to risk spilling my past to them. Now this woman has me as nervous as an inexperienced pup asking a girl on his first date. I can't decide if it was a mistake for me to invite her over with everyone here, or better so I don't end up making a fool out of myself by trying to kiss her.

She considers my question, raking her blue eyes over me as she dramatically takes another bite of her sandwich. As she chews, her lips twitch into a smile. Then she takes a slow sip of her wine, keeping me on tenterhooks until she finally answers with a shrug of her shoulder. "I think that would be fun." I can't help the smile that crosses my face.

"I expect free drinks, J," I joke, but my chest warms knowing I get to take Kaycia out, that she thinks going out with me would be fun.

"I'll see what I can do," Jamila answers, grinning at Kaycia and bumping Raquel with her hip in delight.

With plans for next weekend settled, and everyone finished with their food, we return to the balcony to have another drink while the city lights illuminate the night. I toss Raquel a lighter for the citronella candles on the table. Raquel and Jamila sit farther from the door, and Max leans against the railing with the breeze in his hair. They all arranged themselves on purpose, forcing Kaycia and me to sit close together near the sliding glass door. Whether she notices or not she doesn't remark, taking a seat on one of the remaining cushioned chairs. When I sit in the chair next to her, my knee brushes the side of her thigh and sends a jolt through me, speeding my heart up a little when she doesn't make a move to shift away. If anything, she leans closer, her glass of wine dangling from her paint-stained fingers.

"How long has it been since you've seen real stars?" she whispers.

"Earlier this afternoon," I reply softly, thinking of the painting in her apartment with the gold leaf constellations across the inky sky. She huffs a laugh, her cheeks flushed from the wine, the heat, or maybe—hopefully—the connection between us. "It's been a while since I've gotten out of the city. The sunsets almost make it worth it when they're as pretty as the one today." I catch myself leaning toward her when Max interrupts.

"So, Kaycia, I missed it earlier, what kind of art do you make?" he asks, breaking whatever spell wove between us as Kaycia looks up and I bristle.

"I paint. Figures, the sky, landscapes. I like to experiment by combining them," she explains, her eyes bright when she speaks about her work.

"Like... naked ladies in the grass?" Max jokes.

Kaycia rolls her eyes and laughs a little, but continues to explain, "More like naked ladies made of starlight and wildflowers." Her gaze flicks to mine briefly. "Or handsome men made of sunset daydreams."

"Have you always painted?" I ask.

"Yes, almost my whole life. I majored in art in college even though my parents hated it. They said I was wasting my degree. There wasn't much I could do with it back home though, until I'd finally had enough and moved. My parents are still giving me shit about it. That's why the call earlier was so tense," she explains.

"Ah," I reply, thinking of the call with her mother. "They don't approve of your move?"

"They don't approve of any of it. The giving up my dependable paycheck, the moving to a city I've never lived in before, living like, in their words, 'a starving artist in some bohemian fantasy'. They keep pressuring me to come home because they think the world is chaotic and unstable. They don't think I can survive on my own. It's like they forget I'm fucking twenty-six years old." Kaycia pauses, her fingers gripping her wine glass tightly as she takes a breath.

Passion fuels her voice when she continues, "But they don't get it. When the world is chaotic and feels miserable, that's precisely when art matters. What if my art can inspire someone to keep going? What if it brightens someone's day whenever they walk past it? Isn't that more important than stability in some bullshit town you've never left?"

Everyone watches her when she stops, quiet while she exhales and blinks a few times. Her jaw is tense and she holds her head high, as though she's used to having to defend herself on this topic. When her eyes cut to mine, as though she expects a challenge, I'm struck with just how deep I'm in it already for this woman. I offer a half smile and tilt my bottle toward her in agreement, gently tapping it against her glass.

"Fuck 'em," Raquel says. "To living a bohemian fantasy." She holds her beer up and everyone joins in, clinking bottles and glasses together in solidarity.

"I'm sorry," Kaycia says after the toast with a nervous chuckle. "I get frustrated, and I let the wine talk for me."

"No. If you can't share your feelings with your friends, who can you share them with?" Jamila soothes. "And you're right. Art is always important, but especially in times of strife and struggle. It shows that we aren't alone. At least that's what I think."

"Wholeheartedly," Max adds, raising his beer in a salute.

"Well, I'm glad to have found someone to rant to. Hopefully, I'll be invited back. How did I get so lucky to have such a great neighbor?" Kaycia asks, leaning over to bump my shoulder with hers. She lingers for a moment, our eyes catching before hers flick to my lips. They part under her gaze, and I take a moment to inhale her scent. For a moment, I forget there are three other people on my balcony—two of whom can scent just as well as I can.

"On that note," Max interrupts, again, clearing his

throat. His voice refocuses our attention and reminds us we aren't alone. "I've got to head home. Quel, J, you coming?"

Raquel and Jamila stand, collecting the leftover bottles to throw away while I sit back from Kaycia.

"It was so nice to meet you, Kaycia!" Jamila smiles with a little wave, her hands full of empties. "Can't wait for next weekend."

Kaycia stands to help tidy up, too, and we all end up in the kitchen giving half hugs and saying goodbye. I pull Max to the side while Raquel and Jamila gather their things. "What the fuck, man?"

"You should be thanking me. Now you have a date with the girl you're obviously obsessed with since you wouldn't grow a pair and ask her out on your own." Max cocks his head to the side, so like the falcon he shifts into. He smiles and cuffs me on the shoulder.

"Bring my shit back next time." I avoid admitting that he's right, instead nodding to the clothes he's wearing. The clothes I keep in a backpack for quick changes, like the one he made on the landing after realizing an unexpected guest would have witnessed him shifting on the balcony.

"Will do. Now make sure you kiss her goodnight, you asshole." He gives a playful punch to my ribs then pats me on the back before heading to the door. "Let's go, ladies! Kaycia, nice to meet you."

"Goodnight!" Kaycia replies, waving as they all file out, leaving the two of us alone in my kitchen.

Chapter 8
Kaycia

I watch Shane's back as the front door closes. The tension in his broad shoulders relaxes when the latch clicks and he turns toward me. He rubs a hand across the back of his neck, an endearing, nervous gesture I've noticed him make several times tonight, as he raises his eyes from the tile to meet mine. His dark blond hair is longer on top, the sides buzzed close, so some falls across his forehead as he gives a sideways smile.

"Hope they weren't too much for you to deal with in one evening," he murmurs, stepping closer to where I lean against his kitchen island.

"They were wonderful," I say with a relaxed smile. I don't have to exaggerate. It *was* wonderful to meet people like me, people I could imagine inviting to coffee on Sunday mornings, exploring museums alongside, or spontaneously splitting a bottle of wine with on the weekend. "Thank you again, Shane."

"For?"

"Fixing my A/C, inviting me over, making me feel welcome," I reply with a sad little smile. "Today was one of those days where I was considering giving up. When the A/C went out and maintenance wouldn't answer, I really started questioning all my choices. I'm not sure I would have been able to block out my mom's nagging if you hadn't come over to help me. So, thank you."

"I'm glad I could help." His reply is husky and pitched low.

He's moved even closer now so that I can smell whatever deliciously masculine scent he wears, citrus and sandalwood maybe. His eyes don't drift from where they've landed on my lips, just like earlier on the balcony. The attraction between us is undeniable, it's been almost palpable all evening and now there's no one to interrupt. As he moves closer my breath hitches, and my heart patters in my chest. He's at least a head taller than me, so when he places one hand on either side of my hips, braced against the granite countertop, he looks down at me.

"I would hate for you to have a reason to move away when I'm finally getting to know you."

"I don't think you have to worry," I whisper, my breasts brushing against his chest when I take a deep breath. "I think I've got plenty of reason to stay right where I am."

Shane huffs a little laugh before angling my chin up with one hand, running the pad of his thumb over my cheekbone. His touch sends electricity zinging through my body. "Kaycia?"

"Yes?" My voice is so quiet I can barely hear it over the blood pounding in my ears. I desperately want him to kiss me, to press my body against him.

"May I kiss you?"

"Yes," I breathe, barely above a whisper. Any nervousness is obliterated by anticipation and desire.

As the word leaves my lips, Shane is already there, his mouth warm and searching as his lips tease mine. He nips at my lower lip, then sucks it into his mouth causing me to gasp and press myself against the hard planes of his body. The low growl in his throat in response makes my core go molten and I wrap my arms around him, one hand cradling the back of his head and gripping his soft hair while the other cups his cheek. His kisses are needy as he runs his hands over my back, holding me close as we explore one another. My body goes taut and loose at the same time under his touch, my breasts heavy with need and my core aching for more. But as our embrace grows more passionate, I feel him pull back, forcing me to open my eyes and meet his breathless stare. Shane's eyes are alight, the pupils blown black as he watches me. His lips are swollen from our kisses and a twinge of possessiveness and pleasure rushes through me knowing I've made him look so undone.

"I should say goodnight," he whispers, gently pressing his forehead against mine as he takes a ragged breath.

"Oh," I reply, dropping my gaze. "Okay, sure."

"Hey," Shane says, tilting my chin back up so I'm forced to look at him. "I want you," he murmurs, pressing the evidence of how his body has responded to me against my hip.

When I arch against him, he groans, "Gods, I want you. But you've had a rough day, you said it yourself. I don't want to take advantage of that." He runs his eyes over me, then his hands, gripping my hips as he runs his nose against my neck and steals all my good sense. With a final ragged inhale, he chuckles and offers a wry smile, pushing himself away from me. "Okay, so maybe I very much *want* to take advantage of it. But I won't."

I catch myself returning the expression with my own grin, a little giggle escaping my lips.

"Maybe you'll just have to take advantage of me after a real date then, huh?"

"Maybe so. I seem to recall you agreed to one next weekend," he returns, his expression turning wicked. It makes me want to do equally wicked things to him.

"I did. Well, in that case, goodnight, Shane. I'll see you around."

"Yes, yes you will."

———

Shane escorted me out the door of his place and watched, leaning against the frame, as I unlocked my own door. Heat flooded my cheeks with my last smile, seeing him looking as undone as I felt. He waited until I was safely inside before I heard his door shut, as if something would happen to me in the five steps between our apartments.

My head feels light as I flop down on my bed, and I know it isn't from the wine I drank. It's been years since I've been truly interested in anyone romantically. Everyone I grew up with either moved away or got married, narrowing my relationship prospects to nil once I broke up with my college boyfriend. Only first dates and disappointments have followed in his footsteps.

Since moving to the city, I've been so preoccupied with building my portfolio and getting to know my way around that I haven't even considered my love life. I've noticed Shane before, he's been the love interest in more than one lurid dream since I moved in. But I never considered he might have noticed me, too.

Until now.

Bless Max's big mouth—I get the feeling if he hadn't pressed the issue, Shane wouldn't have asked me to the show next weekend. Not because he didn't want to, the tension between us is definitely not one-sided, but according to his friends' teasing, he doesn't go out much.

Something we have in common, then.

I rub my fingertips against my lips, thinking about the kiss we shared in his kitchen, the passion and need in his touch, and I can't fight the smile that comes unbidden to my face or the quiet laugh that escapes my kiss-swollen mouth. I wish I hadn't said anything about having a rough day. Maybe if I'd been more guarded, I'd still be next door making out with him, preferably naked.

But no. It's better this way.

Plus, he proved he's a decent guy by backing off, even if I'd gladly have let him take things further.

Shit, I've already got it bad.

And I can't wait for next weekend.

I strip off my tank top and pants, thankful for the cool air that blows through the vents, and pull on an oversized tee. I know I *should* go to bed, but I'm too stimulated from the good company and the excellent kiss to even think about lying down. Instead, I pour a glass of cucumber water from the pitcher in the fridge and push the small window near my paints open. A few clicks on my phone has my speaker playing my favorite playlist before I place the new canvas on the easel.

I wasn't lying when I mentioned painting a handsome man at sunset.

No one needs to know I was only inspired today.

I grab one of the pencils from their jar and start a rough sketch—a side profile of a man with a sharp jawline, the rail of a balcony, the skyline of a city. All will eventually be rendered in sunset reds and pinks and oranges and golds. But, for now, it's a simple sketch to hold on to a memory of a night that just might mark a new beginning.

The start of a life where I'm understood and appreciated for who I am and what brings me passion. Where the rules are mine and mine alone.

Smiling, I step back to survey my work. It's been half an hour since I began, and fatigue is finally beginning to claw at me. Deciding to call it a night, I glance at the profile once more, then wear a smile the entire time I get ready for bed and curl up under the blankets. Laying in the dark of my loft I listen to the sounds of the city, too tired to get up to close the window, but too on edge to fall asleep. Shane's kisses awoke a fire in my belly that I can't ignore. Desire is coiled tight, reminding me how long it's been since I've had anyone touch me like that.

Actually, no one has ever touched me quite like that.

Like he'd devour me if I'd let him. I'm certain I would.

Remembering Shane's hands on me, and imagining what might have happened if I had gotten my way, I scoot to the side of my bed and open my drawer, pulling out my favorite toy.

Chapter 9
Shane

With everyone gone my apartment seems emptier than usual, the loneliness more stifling. I know holding back was the right choice, even if I regret Kaycia's absence now. I don't want to start something with her if it's going to just be a fling. Even if the attraction is mutual, I don't want to end up making a mistake and having to face her every day after a one-night stand. She's kind and funny, not to mention gorgeous. Her scent still lingers in my kitchen, honeysuckle and the faint hint of paint. Just thinking about her in my arms makes me groan. I wasn't lying when I told her I wanted her, but I'll wait until we have a date to get to know each other one-on-one before we take it any further.

The night has cooled off and a pleasant breeze blows from the riverside and down the tunnel of buildings. It snakes through my cracked sliding door and beckons me to return to the balcony for another beer. The melody of Kaycia's music drifts from her balcony. She must still have a window open. I close my eyes and imagine that I'm at my cabin, picturing Kaycia there beside me on the deck with the song on the radio and the wind in the trees.

Weary from the week, I finish my drink and stand to head inside when my ears focus on an unusual sound from Kaycia's. As if my wolf has attuned to her more than usual after our kiss. If I shifted, my ears would be pricked forward to listen. A low mechanical buzzing starts, accompanied by a breathy gasp, then a moan. My face heats. So does my belly.

Another moan follows soon after, and a sigh of pleasure drifts out on the breeze.

Oh, gods. I know exactly what she's doing.

I cannot be hearing this.

Now all I can think of is how I want to wring those sounds from her lips the next time we're together. I tell my feet to move. To go inside, close the door, and shove my head under a pillow to block out the sounds. But all forward motion is stalled when I hear her whisper my name.

Fuck. Is she imagining me while she touches herself?

Heat builds in my chest and my wolf preens with satisfaction. My cock doesn't give a shit that she'd probably think I'm a creep for standing here listening to her pleasure herself. Instead, it strains against my zipper when I hear her soft cry as she climaxes.

Breathing hard, I force myself into my apartment and turn on the shower. I tell myself I'll run the water on cold and think about sports, capital cities, or anything else, to calm my desires. But memories of Kaycia's soft body pressed against mine urging me for more, the electricity between us, and her mouth opening for my kiss take center stage. The sound of my name whispered while she came undone keeps my hand from turning the water to cold.

Under the hot spray of the shower, I wrap my familiar palm around my cock, wishing it was Kaycia's smooth grip instead. Her scent should have rinsed off under the spray, but I can't get it out of my mind as I bring myself to the edge, shuddering and biting back a groan as I come. I stand there panting, letting the water sluice over me with my forehead pressed to the slick tile wall, just like I pressed it to hers earlier.

This wasn't the way I expected things to go at all when I invited her over this afternoon.

It's going to be hard to wait all week to see her again.

———

The rest of the weekend passed in a blur. I went into the shop the morning after Kaycia and I kissed to take care of a few pieces of end-of-the-month bookkeeping and finish my work on one of the bikes for a regular customer to pick up on Monday. I haven't seen her since she slipped through her apartment door Friday evening. I know she's been home because I hear the low tones of her music here and there, but I've fought the urge to knock on her door each time I'm on the landing and to keep myself from wondering what else she's doing with only a wall between us.

Now, it's Wednesday, and I've listened to Raquel tease me about my crush for days. "You know you have to speak with her to make dinner plans, right?" Raquel digs at me while cleaning up her workspace and standing back to admire the newest modifications to her bike.

"I know that, Quel. Thank you. Despite what you think, I *have* gone on a date before." I plan on texting her after work, but that isn't soon enough for Raquel's taste.

"I just don't know why you sent her away! It's obvious that she's into you, and it's more than obvious you're into her. You practically snarled at Max for flirting with her."

She's not wrong. Even if I try to stave off my wolf's instinct to protect what I wish to claim as mine, it rises up beyond my control sometimes. Precisely why I keep to myself. Why I stay home instead of going to bars where drunk assholes do stupid shit that can get me in trouble.

"I sent her away because I'm not going to take advantage of my tipsy neighbor just because she's had a shitty day and I have a crush on her," I explain.

"Ah ha! You admit that you have a crush, then!" Raquel practically does a cheer routine at the admission.

Groaning, I scrub my hand over my eyes. "Yes, for fuck's sake, Quel. I have a fucking crush, okay? I'm like a damn pup, mooning after the girl next door. Is that what you want to hear?"

"Yes! Yes! That's exactly what I want to hear, you grumpy asshole!" Raquel is gleeful, her shiny black ponytail flicking behind her as she bounces around. "Jamila and I want you to be happy, you jerk. You're *lonely*. Just because you aren't part of a pack doesn't—"

"Stop."

"What?" She pauses, brow furrowing as her joy fades to seriousness.

"Don't mention the pack."

"I just think it's time you stop beating yourself up, it's been almost ten years and—"

"Quel, *enough*. I don't want to talk about it." My hands clench into fists without me even realizing it as I grind out the words.

Raquel doesn't mean any harm, but my past belongs buried in the woods near Woodbine Hollow where I left it. Taking a deep breath, I roll my neck and shake out the tension, ignoring the ache of yearning for my family that knots there. "I'm sorry. I just don't need a reminder of why I keep to myself. What I'm risking taking a human woman on a date. If anything, it should make me reconsider it, no matter how I may feel about her."

"Don't you dare. Don't even think about canceling on her. I saw the way you were looking at one another. This might be your chance, Shane." Raquel speaks softly now, approaching me with caution before placing a tan, tattooed hand on my forearm. "Don't fuck it up already. Remember,

Max and I will be there. We might not be wolves, but we both know to be on alert for you, okay? We have your back. Just promise you'll bring her."

"I know. And you're right, I do like her." Looking up at the ceiling, I let out a deep breath. "Don't worry, we'll be there as long as she doesn't cancel on me."

"Oh, I don't think she will. Not after you left her hanging." Raquel is teasing again, giving me a light punch to my shoulder as she skips away to examine her bike. "I'll lock up tonight, why don't you go on home?"

"Sounds good. See you tomorrow, Quel."

———

I realized when I got outside the shop and started to text, that I didn't have Kaycia's number, forcing me to interrupt her evening in person to confirm the weekend's plans. It only takes three little knocks before I hear soft footfalls on the wood flooring within, then the flap of the peephole as she looks to see who's waiting. When Kaycia opens the door, I fight to keep my jaw from dropping. I haven't seen her since Friday night, and I hadn't realized how much I was craving the sight of her. Her long blonde waves are braided in one long plait down her back and all she's wearing is an oversized shirt with... *something* underneath. It's hard to tell without staring whether they're tight-fitting shorts or underwear, but I swallow the desire that surges through me and force myself to look at her face. Nowhere else.

"Hi, stranger!" she says, stepping out of the way and waving me through the threshold. Her apartment smells like paint and candles, and *her*—a sweet floral scent that I'll probably never get out of my head. "Just getting home from work?"

She closes the door behind me and leads the way through the little foyer and into the open studio that mirrors mine. Walking behind her, I can't help but sneak a glance as her toned legs peek from under the hem of the shirt, the barest hint of black shorts showing.

"Yeah, I wanted to check in with you about the plans on Friday, but"—I hold up my phone—"I don't have your number. So, here I am."

"What's yours?" She snags her own phone off the counter, swiping the screen and looking at me expectantly. "I'll text you mine."

Smiling, I rattle off the digits and wait as she smirks, typing quickly, then looks up at me fluttering her lashes, biting her lip.

A moment later my notifications buzz with a text from a string of digits waiting to be programmed.

555-567-8901

Can't wait to pick up on Saturday where we left off on Friday night. ;)

I grin, wishing we could pick up where we left off right now.

"Something funny?" Kaycia asks, eyes wide with innocence.

"No," I answer with a feigned look of nonchalance. "I'm just waiting for your text. I think this one might have been from someone else."

She laughs, approaching to give me a half-hearted smack to the shoulder. "*Jerk.*" Her laugh turns into a little gasp of surprise when I snag her wrist before she can pull it back, moving quicker than she expected, and pulling her closer to me. Faster than a human would have.

Shit.

My grip is loose and gentle on her wrist as I stroke my thumb over the pulse point on the underside. I can feel her heart rate increase and can smell her scent change to one of arousal as I hold on. She could move back easily if she wanted to, but she doesn't. She leans closer, her pulse thrumming under my fingers, her cheeks flushing a pretty pink as she swallows and looks up into my face. I can't help but press a light kiss to the underside of her wrist, stepping even closer so our chests brush against one another.

Leaning forward, I whisper against the shell of her ear, "I'm looking forward to Saturday, too," pleased when I see goosebumps rise on her arms. "I thought we could grab dinner first. Would you prefer to walk or ride?"

"Your motorcycle?" she steps back, eyes wide as though she's startled by the offer.

"Or we can call for a car?"

"I've... never ridden a motorcycle. I'm not sure I'm up for that just yet."

"Well, sounds like I'll have to make sure you'll want a second date then, won't I? Don't worry, I promise I'll go slow." Her cheeks flare with heat and her scent changes just enough to know she likes me being this close. I can't seem to pull away, to let go of her soft wrist, but I force myself to unwrap my fingers and step back. She chuckles, tucking a stray strand of hair behind her ear.

"You'll have to impress me to get me on that thing." She winks, cheeks blazing even redder when she murmurs under her breath, "And maybe I don't want you to go slow."

If she only knew how much effort it's taking me to not pull her into my arms and kiss her until she begs me for more, she wouldn't have added that. I inhale sharply and blink my eyes closed, hoping they remain a plain—human—hazel.

"Want to see what I've been up to?" she asks, snapping my attention back to the present and turning toward her easel overlooking the balcony and the city beyond. The tension between us doesn't quite dissipate, but it's not as thick with the added space between us. Not as urgent.

My eyes are drawn to the painting I noticed before, the twinkling stars filling my nights while real ones don't. She's added the figure of a lithe woman outlined amongst them in white. Her face isn't visible, but she looks like she's made of moonlight amongst the golden starbursts.

A new canvas is on the easel, smeared with the colors of the sunset, just like the evening we sat on the balcony together. The paint is still wet. Bright. Vivid. The scent is pungent to my overly sensitive nose, a scent I'm beginning to associate with her as much as the floral of her perfume.

"These are beautiful," I tell her, not taking my eyes off the paintings. "Are they for the exhibition?"

"Hopefully," she sighs. "I'm tying them all together by the sky. Sunset, midnight, dawn. You, uh, you might have inspired this one." She gestures to the half-finished one on the easel.

"Oh, did I?" My heart flutters a little in my chest, pleased that she's been thinking of me. When I glance over, a pretty blush stains her cheeks.

"Yeah, the whole sunset daydreams thing I said the other day. I see you out on your balcony watching the sunsets, watching the full moon. I—" she stops, twisting her hands in her shirt as though she's embarrassed.

"What?" I press, turning to look at her fully.

"I never wanted to bother you when I saw you out there, you always look so far away. So lonely. Like you miss someone."

The happy flutter in my heart transforms into nervousness at her observation. I never realized I was so lost in thought or that she ever noticed me.

"I just miss home sometimes." It's not a lie. It's not the entire truth either, but I'm not ready to discuss my past with her yet.

"Yeah. I get that," she murmurs, looking at her fingers nervously.

"Hey—" I step forward, tugging her hand away from her hem and holding it in mine to draw her attention back from wherever it's drifted. "Let's not go down that path just yet. Tell me about this one?" I point at a smaller painting that's propped against another wall, hoping to change the subject and keep her mind from wandering to less pleasant places.

She brightens, pushing back a stray strand of hair before launching into the inspiration for the piece, captivating me as dusk overtakes the world outside.

Chapter 10
Kaycia

My heart will not stop pounding like I'm some silly teenager who has never been on a date before. It's *finally* Saturday night and I've had my outfit picked out for days. I even sent pictures to Meg for approval, giddy over the prospect of a night out. I've already showered, put on a little makeup, lotioned and perfumed and spruced myself, and I have... two hours until I can expect Shane.

I go ahead and slip into the red floral sundress I've been excited to wear since I picked it up at a resale place the first weekend I moved to the city. I told myself it would be perfect for weekends on the town and yet, up until now, I haven't actually had any of those. I love the print and how pretty it makes me feel. I add my extra broken-in vintage cowboy boots with silver bracelets and earrings. After waffling with the idea, I swipe on red lipstick to complete the look. It's bolder than I would usually choose, but I throw caution to the wind for the occasion. I leave my hair loose. It's longer than it's ever been, hanging nearly to my waist in pale, messy waves.

Stepping back from the mirror I can't contain the smile that spreads across my face. I look great and feel confident. For the first time, I truly feel like *me*.

The woman looking back at me reflects who I am inside and out. A little messy, a little worn, a little wild-hearted. Not some perfect image someone created for me to emulate. The real me.

I wonder if people back home would recognize her.

I'm not just excited about a date with a hot guy that I feel a connection to—although I *am* excited for that—I'm excited to go out with the first group of people I've connected with in a long time. People who met me on my terms, as my authentic self, and didn't critique me.

The light tap at the door that I've come to recognize as Shane echoes through my apartment an hour after I'm ready. When I swing the door wide, I find him standing on the landing in dark jeans, motorcycle boots, a tee, and an open faded denim overshirt with the sleeves cuffed to show his forearms. His shirt hides the tattoo I know covers his right shoulder, but reveals the shiny, puckered scar that mars the inside of his left forearm. I wonder what kind of injury would leave such a brutal mark, and what it would feel like to run my fingertips over it. He wears a hammered cuff bracelet, and several rings on his elegant, but scarred fingers—a hazard of working with your hands I suppose. Shane clutches an elaborate wildflower bouquet I recognize as the work of the boutique florist around the corner.

When his eyes run over me, I can't help but feel a rush of pleasure at his black pupils and the hunger in his gaze. It's clear by that look that I'm not the only one pleased with what they see on the other side of the threshold. I almost give in to the urge to press my thighs together under his scrutiny.

"These are for you," Shane says, extending the bouquet. "Since you said you miss wildflowers."

"You remembered." I flush with pleasure. "Thank you!"

Taking the flowers, I put them in a vase of water before we leave and arrange it on my entry table to greet me when I return. Shane is standing with the door open, devouring me with his hungry eyes when I turn toward him and step closer.

"You look gorgeous, Kaycia," he breathes, his voice catching before he swallows to clear his throat. "Red suits you."

"You don't look too bad yourself. Are you sure you don't moonlight as a model?" I ask, stepping from my apartment and locking the door.

"Ha! Do you think Raquel would ever let me live that down? It would have been the first thing she would have told you last weekend."

"You two are close," I observe as I shove my keys in my little crossbody bag and head down the stairs at his side. My sidelong glances catch him looking at me twice from the corner of his eye. The second time I catch him, he smiles, and I match his expression before I grab his hand

and entwine our fingers to walk down the sidewalk toward the dinner spot.

"We are. I met her shortly after I moved here," he answers. "She's like a little sister. And Jamila is a sweetheart. As a packaged deal you couldn't ask for better friends."

My stomach flips and flutters when he runs his thumb over the back of my hand. Feeling like a horny teenager, I desire nothing more than to push him against one of the brick facades of the shops that line our street and kiss him senseless. But I resist the urge, instead nestling closer to him. As we walk, my bare shoulder comfortably brushes against the soft denim of his overshirt.

"So, what's for dinner?" I question, letting him lead me through the blocks of our neighborhood.

"A little place I thought you'd like. It reminds me of you."

"Oh, places remind you of me, huh? I'm flattered." I make sure I sound like I'm joking, but in reality, I'm gleeful. Logically, I feel silly. I barely know this man. But so far, I'm liking what he's shown me of himself, and it makes me happy to know he might think of me as often as I think of him.

"You'll see why in just a minute." He rubs his thumb against my hand again, tracing little circles and sending tingles over my skin, my stomach flipping with each gentle caress.

Soon enough, we approach an alleyway, brick buildings standing high on each side. "A dark alley, hmm? Maybe I shouldn't have been so flattered."

"Come on," Shane murmurs with a wry smile, pulling me along behind him into the alley.

I pause as soon as we walk through, my mouth popping open on a little gasp. The alley is actually a walkway lined with potted gardenias, their sweet scent wrapping around me like a lover's embrace. Overhead are arches of vining flowers and greenery wrapped in fairy lights that illuminate the path to a hostess waiting to seat guests in the hidden restaurant beyond.

The sign above the door is carved with a stylized pair of antlers decorated with blooms outlining the name: The Wilde Hart.

"It's beautiful," I whisper before Shane tugs on my hand.

"I told you. It reminds me of you." His words are gentle, his smile and gaze soft, and I can't stop the surge of emotion that makes my eyes prickle with the threat of tears.

"Thank you."

"Now, come on. You can stare when we're seated." He chuckles as we walk through the archway. It's like we've been transported into some kind of fairy wonderland as we follow the young hostess through the tables to a little booth facing the entrance. The tables are each illuminated with jars of fairy lights to match those strung overhead and the entire space is airy and romantic with greenery and flowers for centerpieces.

"Do you want your usual?" Shane asks once we've slid into the booth, eyes traveling over the wine list.

"I have a usual?"

"Pinot grigio, right? That's what you're always drinking at home. Or do you want to look?" He holds the menu toward me. For a moment I study him, his sandy hair hanging artfully across his forehead before he runs a hand through it to push it back, eyes glittering in the low light of the restaurant.

"Oh! You noticed," I answer, my cheeks warming under his gaze.

"Of course I did. You like wine, plants, and art. And to be honest I'm shocked to see you with shoes on." His smile lights up his face as he nudges me with his toe under the table, making me laugh.

"Well, I can't very well walk around the city barefoot. Sorry to disappoint if you have a thing for feet."

"I have a thing for *you*, Kaycia Durand." Shane's voice is soft as he cuts his eyes from the menu to meet mine.

"Well, the feelings may be mutual, Shane McKinley," I reply. "And yes, pinot grigio is fine, that and champagne are my favorites."

The waitress arrives shortly after, ending our small confessions as she takes our drink order—a bottle of pinot grigio to share.

"I didn't realize you drank wine, too," I note when she's dropped off our water glasses.

"I enjoy it from time to time. It'll be refreshing on a

warm evening. So, how're things going? Any news on the exhibition since we last spoke?"

Chapter 11
Shane

I can't stop staring as Kaycia tells me about the plans for her upcoming exhibition and describes the gallery where it's to be held. Listening to her talk about her art is hypnotic. I got lost in our conversation a couple of nights ago watching her flit around the apartment pointing out the inspiration and features. I'm curious to see the ones she tells me about that are already at the gallery. She lights up from within as she lays out her plans for the exhibition and explains what she's struggling with to complete the pieces she showed me the other night.

The waitress pours the cool white wine, but I barely notice her as Kaycia sips a taste, then nods her approval. When the waitress leaves, she smiles and holds out her glass for a toast.

"To new friends in new cities," she toasts.

"To hopefully more than friends, and serendipitous escape attempts by rogue canvases," I retort.

"I'll drink to that." Her eyes are sparkling in the dim light, staring over her wine glass as she takes a sip, watching me do the same. She's gorgeous tonight, her long hair hanging loose around her bare shoulders and over the tiny straps of her floral dress.

What is it about sundresses that makes me go nuts? Is there some spell cast whenever a woman slips one on that immediately makes me imagine taking it back off?

Shaking my head, I take another sip of wine and watch her skim the menu. She's wearing more makeup than I've seen on her before, her eyes more defined, her lips as red as her dress. She's beautiful when she's covered in paint, barefooted in overalls, but tonight I can't stop staring. She's fucking stunning.

Shit, I've got it bad.

I scrub my hand over the nape of my neck as I flick my eyes between my own menu and her face. I catch her doing the same and we smile when we catch each other.

"See something you'd like?" the waitress asks, suddenly back in my periphery. She's waited on me before when I've eaten at the bar alone. She seems amused that I have a date tonight.

"I definitely do," I answer, eyes not leaving Kaycia's. The flush across her cheeks and chest makes my stomach twist, not unpleasantly.

The waitress stifles a small laugh, patiently waiting to see if I'll order.

"Same," Kaycia answers in a breathy voice. Clearing her throat, she orders and I follow suit. The waitress winks at me when I hand her the menus, shaking her head as she walks away to place the order.

Two glasses of wine and half a plate of truffle and parmesan fries down and the conversation has turned from flirting and innuendos to more personal topics. It's been so long since I've been on a date where I actually care about the outcome, or that isn't just about getting laid, that I've let down my guard a bit, dangerous as it may be.

"How did you get into motorcycles?" Kaycia asks.

"My dad rides. He gave me a dirt bike when I was a kid and taught me how to do the repairs on it. I fell in love with them. It was a natural move to make it a career," I answer. "You can't beat the freedom of the open road with the wind on your cheeks." I involuntarily close my eyes, thinking of running through the woods as my wolf. Motorcycles are the closest thing I can get to that feeling in this form.

"You don't worry about crashing?"

I chuckle. "It takes a lot to hurt me. Don't you worry." She doesn't know how quickly a shifter can heal. Laying down my bike isn't as serious for me as it would be for a human.

"Speaking of," she says, taking a sip of wine, then gesturing toward my left arm. "What happened there?"

I rub my palm over the scar, unable to tell her the truth of the cause. "An accident when I was a kid. I didn't get stitches like I should have, which is why it scarred like this."

"Hmm..." she hums. "Does it hurt?"

Not physically, I think, but reply, "Not anymore." Kaycia reaches across the table and gently strokes the scarred indentation with her first two fingers, sending a shiver over me. Pulling her hand back, she changes the subject, continuing to tread a bit close to my past for comfort. "Do you have siblings?"

"I did. I mean, I do. A brother and sister, both younger. But I don't really have a relationship with my family anymore." I hope the vague answer will encourage her to change the subject.

"None of them? I'm sorry, that must be hard," she answers, a sad smile taking the place of her earlier joy. "I don't know about siblings though, I'm an only child."

"Tell me about your family." I take the out and turn the conversation away from me. "You told me things are a bit strained?"

"Yeah"—she grimaces and takes another sip—"they mean well. But they're so focused on security and being practical that I think they've forgotten what it's like to dream. Don't get me wrong. I'm not naive, I know money is a necessary evil and being safe and secure are important. But when you're so focused on that, I think you miss out on opportunities to really live. To explore what might be a better fit. Does that make sense? Ugh, I'm rambling, aren't I?"

"It makes sense. And I like your rambling."

Kaycia chuckles, toying with the edge of her plate with a wistful look. "It's been hard. I don't think it's in my nature to disobey. I've always played by the rules and did what was expected."

"So, what you're telling me is that you're a good girl?" I let my lips quirk up as she blushes and squirms in her seat. When she bites her lower lip, I have to stifle a groan.

"Moving here was the most rebellious thing I've ever done. I wish I could say I never looked back, but when things are hard, or lonely, or I feel homesick, I sometimes think they were right. But things are looking up." She raises her eyes to meet mine.

"Oh?" I press with a grin.

"Yeah, I mean, I've sold a few pieces, I've found a gallery and I have this exhibition on the horizon, and—" She pauses, a wicked smile twinkling in her eyes. "My hot neighbor asked me out."

"And how do you see that going?"

"Well, he seems really nice despite his bad boy looks, even if he's a little reticent. But if it doesn't work out all his friends are pretty hot, too."

"Oh, I see how it is! You're using me to get to my hot friends. Waitress, check please!" I tease as she giggles, but when we both stop laughing the little thread of tension stretched between us goes taut, pulling from my gut as I study her face. When she licks her lower lip and pulls it between her teeth my breath hitches, and I have to adjust myself discretely under the table.

"I hope it goes well," Kaycia murmurs, her foot sliding up my calf.

"Me, too," I answer, a hunger surging through me that I know won't be sated at dinner.

After our meals and a shared cheesecake slice for dessert—one that Kaycia took full advantage of licking from her fork to my combined delight and misery—we walk back out the sweet-scented green archway and onto the sidewalk, heading to the bar. It's nearly nine o'clock. Max's band will be on in about half an hour, so we stroll hand in hand without rushing. It's nice to have someone to just be with. Kaycia seems content to hold my hand and walk, at ease with the silence.

"Have you been to this bookstore yet?" I ask, passing the window of the little used bookshop where the store cat hisses at me through the glass.

"No, but he doesn't seem to be a fan of yours." She laughs, looking through the window at the stacks. "We'll have to come check it out sometime. I'll protect you from the guard kitty."

I huff a little laugh, then gesture across the street to the roll-up door of the garage. "There's my place." The sign overhead that marks my shop—SM Moto Works—is softly illuminated.

"Oh! It really is close to the galleries, isn't it? I don't usually come down this street. I never realized."

"Thought I was just using a line on you?"

"Well... maybe? I'm still new here, you can't expect me to know where everything is," she confesses, bumping my arm with her bare shoulder.

"It's fine. You'll have to stop in one day. You can ride

home with me." I nudge her in return. I'll get her on the back of my bike sooner or later. She trembles a little, and I can't tell if it's in jest or real fear of riding on a motorcycle —the night's too warm for her to actually be cold.

"We'll see. Oh! Is this where we're going?"

We are a few doors down from the little bar where Jamila serves drinks and Max is playing tonight. The neon sign announcing *Lovely Lucy's* with the outline of a vintage cowgirl adorns the front, beckoning people to the light. A line trails down the street a few couples deep, but I usher Kaycia toward the door guy. I know Rodrigo, both from Jamila and working on his classic chopper. I never wait in line.

"Wait," Kaycia murmurs, pulling me to a stop under the awning of the neighboring building.

In the shadow of the storefront, I can easily see her with my sharp wolf vision, but with her human eyesight, it must seem much darker. She glances up at me through her lashes, pulling me closer by the front of my tee until her back is pressed against the door and I'm almost flush against her.

"I wanted to thank you for a lovely dinner before we're with everyone."

Instinctively, my hands go to her waist, pulling her hips tight to mine.

"Oh yeah?" I whisper, running my nose against her jawline so she shivers as she grinds against me. There's no questioning the cause this time.

"Yeah." She exhales her answer and then our mouths

collide. She's sweet like cheesecake and wine, and her fingers are tangled in my shirt holding me tight to her as she gasps against my lips. It's all I can do to keep from lifting her up or running my hands under the hem of her dress.

"Why are we going to this show tonight?" I murmur against her lips, drawing a little breathy giggle from her.

"For you to support your friends. For me to *make* friends. To dance! Don't worry, we have all night," she answers, giggling again as I groan and press my forehead to hers. The tension eases slightly, and we step apart, straightening ourselves. She wipes at my lips with her thumb to remove any lipstick that might have marked me. Her lips look perfect, albeit swollen from our kisses. I nip at the pad of her thumb, earning a satisfying little yelp and flirtatious giggle.

I wrap my arm around her, squeezing her hip, and pull her from the shadows. "All right, let's go."

Chapter 12
Kaycia

Dragging my eyes from Shane as we approach the open door of the bar, all I can think is, *He's right. Why* are *we going to this show?*

I'm a little tipsy, but it's only served to make me more assertive than I would usually be. Dinner was fun, even if he shied away from some of the more personal questions I asked. That kiss was more than fun. I have to keep myself from touching my lips thinking about the heat between us as I watch him clap hands with the bouncer and pull him into one of those back-patting hugs men do.

He's so damn attractive in a devil-may-care kind of way, confident and quiet, sweet but protective. He even made sure he was walking on the outside of the sidewalk as he guided me along the streets, on alert for things lurking in the dark. Blinking away my musings, I let him guide me through the door into the neon glow of the bar with a broad palm against my lower back.

It's one of those newly-remodeled-to-look-dirty, trendy kind of dive bars and reminds me of some of the haunts I used to go to with Meg for cheap drinks when we were in college and wanted to avoid the frat boy crowd. Old neon beer signs hang on the walls, the clack of billiards echoes over music, and a small stage sits at the back. Tall tables line the left side, a hallway disappears beyond with a jukebox and antique cigarette dispenser crowding the opening, and on the right is the bar. Jamila waves when she spots us, her smile genuine and wide. She looks gorgeous. Her dark brown skin is luminous in the glow of the neon signs, and she has her curvy figure on display in a tight white tank top and jeans. A bar rag hangs from her back pocket, swinging when she turns to grab two longnecks from the cooler. A shimmering gold headband that coordinates with her jewelry rests in her short, natural coils and catches the light as she moves.

As we wave and head over, I track where she's carrying the longnecks—Raquel and Max are already at the far end of the bar, two other musicians with them. My mood is already high, but seeing our new friends and having Shane's palm on my lower back nearly makes me giddy with excitement for the much needed night out.

"You two *finally* made it!" Raquel calls, standing to hug both of us tightly. She's wearing what I'm learning is her usual: black tee, black jeans, black boots. Tonight, her long dark hair is in a single braid down her back. Max is the perfect blend of trendy and disheveled in a vintage tee and ripped jeans.

"They're not even on stage yet. We had to have dinner," Shane grumbles, wrapping an arm around my shoulders. I tuck myself against him, beaming at everyone.

"Damn, Shane. Who's this?" one of the new guys asks, looking me up and down. I swear Shane *growls* in irritation at the attention.

"This is Kaycia. Kaycia, this is Ryan and Jet." Shane points out the two men in turn, but his voice isn't friendly. His body language isn't either.

Max smacks the one named Jet on the shoulder and he holds his hands up. "Ah, no offense. I didn't know she was your girl, man."

"She's not," Raquel offers with a gleeful grin and a wink before whispering loudly behind her hand to me, "at least not yet." Shane gives her a sharp look, but I just laugh, brushing off her teasing, and turn toward the bar to look at the drink options lined up on the top shelf. It's nice to be out. To have people to joke with.

"What do you want to drink?" Jamila calls over the music from the jukebox.

"Two light beers," I answer, slipping from Shane's grasp to lean on the bar. "That's okay with you, yeah?" I ask him over my shoulder, catching his eyes scanning down my back before he nods. I can't fight the grin on my face when I turn back to Jamila. I'm not saying I *like* possessive assholes, but I could get used to Shane looking at me like I'm a second dessert.

There's still time before the band is scheduled to play, so I settle onto the bar stool next to Max. Shane stands at my back, his side against the bar so we both face our companions. He keeps one arm around me, fingers toying with his beer bottle, while his other hand explores my back. His fingers drift between the strands of my hair, sometimes caressing the bare skin of my shoulders and upper back. It's warm in the bar, but I maintain goosebumps from his casual touch, my belly coiled tight and warm in response.

We make small talk for another ten minutes or so, but I don't really hear anything over my rapid heartbeat as I focus on Shane's covert caresses. As showtime nears, the room begins to fill and Jamila gets busier with customers. Max and his bandmates head to the stage where their gear is set up and waiting, leaving me with Shane and Raquel while Jamila pops tops and pours liquor alongside another female bartender.

"Where did you go for dinner?" Raquel asks, glancing between me and Shane. He's stepped away now, angling himself so he can scan the room and still talk to us. His beer casually dangles from his fingers, but his gaze is focused as though he's looking for someone or something to jump out and bite us.

"This cute place called The Wilde Hart."

"Oh, shit. Shane, you really worked the romance angle tonight, didn't you? That place is so pretty!" Raquel and I laugh while Shane shrugs and takes a swig of beer like it was no big deal.

"They have good food," he insists.

When I glance up at him again though, his eyes are soft and he gives me a little half-smile.

The noise of the bar quiets as the band plugs in. People turn in their seats and shift where they stand at the edges of the bar to listen. The middle of the floor opens for dancing and a few people wait eagerly for the music to begin. The jukebox played a mix of genres, so I don't know what to expect when Max begins to play. I hang back with Shane before committing to dancing.

The first song has a flirty country vibe and several women, and a few of the men, openly make advances toward Max from the dance floor—just like I imagined when we first met. He's a natural flirt, clearly enjoying the attention with a broad grin plastered across his face. The second song is folksy, and I catch myself swaying to the tune as I lean into Shane's side. His scent envelops me and I close my eyes to soak in his proximity. By the third song, they've slowed down further, beginning a tune with lyrics that are sad and romantic at the same time.

"Come on," Shane whispers in my ear, brushing my hair from my shoulder to plant a light kiss on my neck. "Let's dance."

Shivering from his kiss, I nod and leave my half-empty beer on the counter next to Raquel, letting him lead me through the crowd and onto the floor where a few other couples also dance. When he pulls me close, hands on my lower back, I immediately wrap my arms around his neck, pressing my cheek against his chest where I can hear his heart thundering over the beat of the song. We sway together, bodies pressed close under the neon lights as the song nearly drowns me with emotion. I pull back far enough to look up at Shane, to find him gazing down at me, too. For a moment, tension fizzes between us, seeming to tug me closer to him. Then we're kissing again, just like in the shadows out front. The other couples disappear, the crowd, the band, and it's just us and this moment.

I don't know if it's the beer, the atmosphere, my aching desire, or everything rolled into one that gives me the courage, but I pull back and whisper, "Where's the restroom?"

Shane's brow furrows as he cocks his head. "Oh, it's down the hall. I think the women's is on the right?"

"Show me." I tug him along behind me, past the band where Max gives him a curious glance before starting his next verse, and down the dim hallway.

Still confused, Shane points to the door marked with a painted cowgirl. Despite the crowd, it's still too early in the night for a line and shockingly there's no one inside when I push open the door. I'm still gripping his hand in mine and pull him in behind me.

"Kaycia, what—" Shane's shock is interrupted by my lips as I press him against the door and kiss him.

Any protests he might have die as his touch becomes urgent, his kisses deeper, nipping at my lower lip, my throat, the sensitive place where my neck meets my shoulder. He slips the thin strap of my dress down and kisses the curve of my shoulder, dragging his lips to the top of my breast, as I run my fingers through his hair and lean my head back to give him access to my heated skin. When his lips return to mine his kisses grow more desperate, like he fears I'll disappear. We both suck in ragged gasps when we break apart.

Shane's hands skate over the floral fabric of my dress, then slide under the flowy skirt and over my skin, lotioned earlier in the hope he'd do exactly that. I grind against him as he grips my ass, seeking the friction of his evident arousal pressing against the fly of his jeans.

"Fuck, Kaycia," he murmurs against my neck, his fingers drifting around until they slide over the lace of my panties. I whimper and arch into his touch, wanting him to stroke me again. "Your panties are soaked." A little thrill runs over me at his words; the verbal acknowledgment of how badly I want him. Want *this*.

"Shane, I want you," I whisper. I reach behind him and turn the master lock on the bathroom door, looking up into his eyes. They've gone almost completely black in the dim room and I fight the urge to pull at his clothes. His gaze is no longer sweet like it was earlier in the night, it's gone hungry with his need, like I'm truly prey waiting to be taken for a meal, and a deep rumble in his chest sends goosebumps over me.

"Gods, Kaycia, you have no idea how badly I want you, too," he breathes against my ear, running his hand up my side, palming my breast through the thin cotton of my dress, and then stroking my hardened nipple with his thumb. His other hand still explores under my skirt, slipping under the lace of my thong and sliding over the slick heat of my core. I moan as he teases my entrance, circling my clit and then sliding through my center before finally inserting his fingers into me.

"But you're going to have to wait." He slides those clever fingers in a little farther, then teases me slowly before pulling them from under my skirt.

"What?" I pant, confused and aching as he inspects the slick arousal on his two fingers. I don't know if I'm going to come or combust when he parts his lips and slides them into his mouth, savoring the taste like he dipped his fingers in a jar of honey before he removes them from his mouth and slides them between my own parted lips.

"I've waited months to ask you out," he whispers against my ear. "I'm not going to fuck you against the dirty wall of a dive bar bathroom. I want to see that pretty little sundress on my apartment floor."

My knees go weak at his words, at the taste of my arousal on his fingers in my mouth. Before I know what's happened, he pulls his hand back, reaching under my skirt once again. The sharp sound of lace tearing is barely audible over the music in the bathroom. Then, I'm bare under my skirt and my shredded lacy thong is in his hand.

His eyes are still dark and desirous as he grins at me. "This way I know you're ready for me when we get back home."

He shoves my panties in his pocket, leans down to

plant a rough, claiming kiss on my mouth, and then turns me toward the door with a squeeze to my ass cheek. I catch sight of my flushed expression in the full-length mirror as we walk by.

I barely recognize the wild couple in the reflection, but I like their style.

Chapter 13
Shane

I have no idea what came over me in the bathroom, but now I'm guiding Kaycia back through the crowd with a raging erection, her panties in my pocket, and blood pounding in my ears louder than Max's singing or Raquel's attempts to get my attention. I wave at both of them, so focused on Kaycia and the fact that she's soaking wet for me right now, and escape out the front door into the warm night air before anyone can stop us.

It takes three times longer than it should to get back to our apartment building. Now, the walk is punctuated by pauses to kiss and explore one another, earning more than one gleeful honk from cars that pass by.

Kaycia pulls me into the darkened doorway of a coworking space around the corner from our building, pulling my lower lip into her mouth while she slides her slim fingers along my zipper. I grip her hips and grind into her palm, moaning and stealing her breath with a kiss. I have to summon all the control I can muster, both as a man and a wolf, to not unzip and take her against the door when my hand slips under her dress and feels the smooth skin of her bare ass, especially when she whispers an offer to let me do just that.

Groaning, I tug her out into the streetlights and toward our building. Finally, we stumble up the three flights of stairs to our landing.

"My place or yours?" I ask between kisses. Kaycia's blue eyes are hooded and her cheeks are flushed under the overhead lighting.

"Yours," she answers breathlessly. "You *did* say you wanted to see my dress on *your* floor."

Fuck, this woman is going to kill me.

I manage to get my keys out and the door flung open, staggering into the apartment where only the lamps on the bedside tables and the glow from the city outside the back windows illuminate the loft. She follows me inside, pushing my overshirt off and to the floor, then tugging at my belt. I have to remind myself that, even though my fingers itch to rip the thin straps, I can't give in to the urge if I want to see her in this dress again.

"Do you have protection?" she whispers against my mouth as we move toward the bed.

"Yeah, of course," I answer.

"Give me just a minute?" She heads across the room toward the bathroom, leaving me staring at her with my pants half open and my tee shirt rucked up. All I can offer is a nod as I catch my breath.

By the time the water turns off I've adjusted the lighting and turned music on low.

"Hey," Kaycia whispers from the doorway of the bathroom.

"Hey," I reply. "You good?"

"Definitely."

She's kicked out of her boots and socks and pads across the floor toward me where I lean against the arm of my sofa. Pushing off the couch, I meet her halfway between the living and sleeping spaces and slide my hands around her waist, letting them rest on her hips. My abs flex of their own accord when Kaycia runs her index finger across the top of my boxer briefs and the rush of butterflies in my stomach makes my heart pound. Running her hands upward she pushes my tee up and tugs it off when I obediently hold my arms overhead. She explores my chest with her palms, kissing where her fingers have traced. Shuddering and sighing, I run my fingers through her hair, tangling them in the silky strands and gripping gently before tilting her chin up to claim her mouth with mine.

What begins gentle soon returns to the urgency from the bar, tongues and teeth clashing, and I remind myself that I need to keep my wilder urges under control. Tugging on her hair, I tilt her head up to look at me and run my thumb over her lower lip, admiring the fullness and how fucking beautiful she is.

"You're sure you want this?" I ask.

If she wants to stop, or if she's changed her mind after

the bar, I don't want to push her. We can still call it a night and not cross this line.

"Yes," she responds, reaching down to slip her hand under the waistband of my underwear and wrapping her fingers around me.

I groan against her mouth as she starts to work me, kissing me and pulling me with her until her ass hits the back of the sofa. I lift her hips so she's seated on the low back, unable to control the movement of my hips as I match her pace, but I step back and grab her wrist to pull her hand free.

"Dress on the floor, remember? Take it off or I just may rip it off you."

She looks shy for a split second, making me worry that I've been too forceful, but then she unzips the side and slips the dress off her shoulders, letting it fall in a red puddle on the floor. She wasn't wearing a bra, it was evident when I brushed against her nipples earlier, but seeing them in the shadows of the low light, absolutely perfect, makes me need to taste them, to taste every inch of her.

Kaycia responds instantly when I graze her taut nipple with my teeth, kneeling between her open thighs. She arches into my touch with a breathy gasp as my hands and mouth explore her body, running open-mouthed kisses up her inner thigh until I reach the heat of her pussy.

"Fuck, Kaycia," I murmur, running my fingers through the wetness I find as she moans and bucks her hips. "You're still so fucking wet for me."

She must like what I say because she writhes under my touch, so I add my mouth to my fingers, tasting and teasing. Her little whimpers turn into moans as she grips my hair and grinds against my mouth, chasing her pleasure while I ache to take my own.

"Oh gods," she cries, her fingers clutching my hair to hold me where she wants me. Her thighs tense and her breathing turns ragged as she comes. Shuddering, she releases me and grabs at my shoulder to draw me back up to her mouth. I surge to meet her lips, standing and cupping her face as I step between her legs.

"You taste so fucking good," I whisper against her mouth between kisses.

"Gods, that mouth," she murmurs, then adds, "I need you," while she holds me closer with her legs wrapped around my hips.

It's almost my undoing.

"Come here," I order, pulling her from the couch.

Chapter 14
Kaycia

I'm standing naked in Shane's living room, still trembling from whatever magic he just worked with his mouth, when he pulls me toward his bed.

I follow without question. Something about Shane makes me want to abandon all propriety that might make me have second thoughts. I would have been happy for him to have me against the bathroom wall or in a brick alleyway with the way he makes me feel. The way my heart stutters when I catch him looking at me from the corner of his eye. The way my skin heats from the barest graze of his fingers. Now I'm on fire, aching for him to keep kissing me, to taste and touch him in the same way.

He spins me when we get to his bed, lifting me under my thighs and laying me on my back on the soft, dark linen comforter where I scoot up onto the plush pillows. "It's not fair," I murmur while he still stands by the edge of the bed, his pants unzipped and hanging off his hips. My eyes run over the planes of his muscles; the deep vee cut at his hips that draws my attention lower.

"What?" he looks confused for a moment, his confidence wavering as his brows knit.

"That you look like *that*. That you're real," I tease, pursing my lips in false frustration, "and that you're still wearing clothes." The tension leaves his face and he gives a wry smile in return.

"I think we make a fine pair, baby girl. You're fucking gorgeous," he answers, before he sheds his pants and underwear, revealing how much he wants me. His movements are slow and sensual, almost animalistic, as he prowls toward me in the low light. I swear his eyes glow as he takes me in lying naked on his sheets. My heart thunders and heat spreads from my chest and between my thighs.

"Shane, please. Don't make me wait any longer."

Shane runs his hands over me, tracing my curves with fingers and lips as though he's worshipping me, memorizing the planes of my body, and I can't help but rock my hips to meet him. He groans into my hair as he slides his hard length against me, slippery with my arousal.

"Fuck, Kaycia. I knew you'd be ready for me." He moves to my side, reaching into the nightstand drawer to grab a condom. In one quick motion, he tears open the foil packet, rolling it on before he covers me again, propped on one hand to look into my eyes. "You're sure?"

"Yes," I answer, arching again and demanding the delicious friction of his body.

Shane lets out a breathy chuckle. "Eager aren't we?"

"Gods, yes."

When he slides into me, I gasp, digging my nails into his shoulders as he groans into my neck. His movements are slow and sensual as he rocks his hips, like he's savoring every second. Pleasure coils low in my belly as his speed increases, one hand gripping my hip as he thrusts.

"Kiss me," I whisper, pulling his mouth to mine, tasting myself on him as we move together. My focus fades as my muscles coil, tightening with my release until I can only pant incoherently against his lips as I come around him. "Oh, gods."

"Oh, *fuck*," he gasps, sliding his hand from my hip to loop under my thigh, pulling my leg up so he pushes even deeper into me. After a few moments, he shudders, my name on his lips as he moans with his climax. Stilling, he draws my lips to his, kissing me deeply. For a quiet moment, he catches his breath, running one hand over my hair while he stays balanced on his other elbow, eyes roaming over my face as I smile up at his gentleness. Pressing a kiss to my forehead he pulls out of me and rolls away, disposing of the condom before he pulls me against him. When I shift to look at him, the soft light of his bedside lamp highlights the flush on his cheeks and the light stubble peppering his jaw.

"Are you blushing?" I joke, smiling as I run my fingers over his cheek.

"Highly likely," Shane answers with a shy smile. He

steals a soft kiss, then whispers, "I hope you weren't planning to sneak next door now."

"Do you want me to?"

"No." His expression shifts as if he's nervous. "I'm not ready to let you slip away yet."

"I don't want to."

"Never," he replies, leaning over and kissing me gently. I reach up with both arms to wrap them around his shoulders as he shifts his body to hover above me, resting on his elbows. He looks down, eyes devouring the sight of my naked body beneath his. "Gods, you're beautiful."

"Now, *I'm* blushing," I whisper. "But I also have to pee." I giggle, kissing him once more before he rolls away with a groan as I throw off the sheet and parade through the apartment toward the bathroom wearing nothing but a satisfied grin.

The sun brightens the living area of Shane's apartment the next morning, waking me earlier than I expected. I'm in a pair of his boxer briefs and a ratty band tee that smells like his laundry detergent while he's bare-chested next to me, sleeping soundly on his stomach. Not wanting to wake him, I slip from the sheets and gather my things. I've never slept with a neighbor before. I've rarely even stayed the night with some of the guys I've regularly dated. I'm not sure of the protocol here, but I'd rather make him breakfast in a familiar kitchen, so I sneak out the front door and into my own apartment.

After I drop my stuff on my bed, I send Shane a text.

> Good morning, sleepy head! Come over for breakfast when you're decent (or naked, I'll be happy either way). ;)

Starting the coffee machine, I turn my music on low and send a text to Meg in reply to her late-night check-in message letting her know the date went exceptionally well. I grin as I hit "send". She has no idea how juicy the story I have for her is. I brush my teeth, pull my hair into a messy bun, and then head to the balcony with a cup of coffee to watch the city wake up and wait for Shane to do the same.

Chapter 15
Shane

Stretching in the morning sunlight I roll toward the side of the bed where Kaycia slept last night. The scent of her perfume lingers along with the smell of sex, but she's nowhere to be seen. Listening, I can make out the sound of music playing softly through the shared wall and my chest tightens with apprehension, realizing that she already left. I hope I didn't come on too strong last night. I practically begged her to stay with me.

My phone isn't on the nightstand where it usually charges, and after digging around in my discarded clothes, I find it in my jeans pocket. Kaycia's name at the top of the notifications melts the worry away. The flirty text to come over for breakfast is a good sign.

The rest of the messages aren't.

My smile drops a little when I see the other texts, beginning last night after we left the bar and continuing through this morning, both from Max and Raquel. I send a response to Kaycia first.

> You little tease, you should have woken me up. I'll be over in a few.

Then I parse through the messages from Max and Quel.

MAX

> Did you two fuck in the BATHROOM? Hot damn, buddy!

RAQUEL

> I hope you two had fun, but we need to talk.

MAX

> Did you catch a whiff of the guy Quel was worried about? Or were you too distracted by your girl?

RAQUEL

> Seriously, Shane. You need to call me. There was a guy I'm worried about at the bar.

RAQUEL

> Are you still asleep? Call me.

MAX

> Hey man, call me or Quel when you get out from between your girl's legs.

RAQUEL

> CALL. ME.

My heart hammers as I read through the messages. The last one is from just fifteen minutes ago. I hit the call button next to Raquel's name and she answers on the first ring.

"For fuck's sake, Shane. Did you finally come up for air?" Raquel greets me.

"Good morning to you, too. What the hell is going on?" I ask, pulling a tee off a hanger in my wardrobe.

"Look, I'm glad you and Kaycia hit it off. I could smell the sex wafting off you from the bar. But Max and I both zeroed in on a stranger last night. He was a wolf, Shane. Didn't you smell him?"

"What?" I pause, dropping my tee where I stand. "What are you talking about?"

"These two guys were at a table on the other side of the bar. I got a couple of whiffs of a strange shifter while you and Kaycia were dancing, I think he came in after you were already out there, but he was *very* focused on the two of you. You seriously didn't notice him? Big guy, shaved head, older? He smelled like a wolf." Raquel's voice barely hides a hint of panic as she explains.

"No," I admit. "I didn't notice."

How could I? I was so overwhelmed by the scent of Kaycia on my hands, my lips, and then on getting out of the bar and back to the apartment to even think about an unknown shifter.

"He was with another guy I'd never seen. Jamila says they hadn't been in before either, but I know how you feel about other wolves. I was worried. Sorry for blowing up your phone. Hope I didn't ruin your morning sex."

"Ha!" I laugh, snagging my shirt from the floor. "She's already at home, no morning sex for me."

"Bummer. Are you *so* bad in bed that you scared her off already?"

"Fuck off, Quel," I joke.

"You too, buddy."

"Thanks for the heads up."

"Anytime. See ya tomorrow."

Ending the call, I pick up my shirt in a daze, letting it dangle from my fingers as I sort through my thoughts.

Fuck.

Two strangers. A strange wolf. I'm furious with myself for not being more vigilant. Hopefully, it's nothing and the guy's just passing through. It happens from time to time. The Cameron and Ross packs aren't the only wolves in the country, even if there aren't many packs in territories near the city. It could be a coincidence.

I'm not ready to explain my past or the shift to Kaycia. I like her—gods, do I like her—I don't want to scare her off. Rage begins in my chest, blurring my vision for a minute while I try to breathe through it. The tang of blood and fear coat my mouth as memories of the night that sparked my exile claw into the forefront of my mind. When I look down my shirt is shredded between my shaking hands.

"*Fuck!*" I snarl in the silence of my apartment, running my fingers through my hair and tossing the ruined shirt aside. I've got to get myself under control before I go next door.

And I *have* to go next door.

I can't let Kaycia think I'm just some asshole who fucked her last night and didn't come over the next morning. Even if *she's* the one who left at dawn.

Pulling on another tee and a pair of jeans, I shove my phone in my pocket and take a couple deep breaths before I head next door.

All the tension falls away when Kaycia opens her door, revealing her messy blonde bun and broad smile. The sight of her still wearing one of my tees and boxers makes my wolf tingle under my skin, pride and possession swelling in my chest at how beautiful she is.

How she wears my scent now.

How much I want to claim her again.

But now isn't the time.

I need to at least give her an idea of what she's getting involved with before we take this any further. Before I can speak, she's pulled me inside the door and is kissing me, her lips curling into a smile as she sinks against me and runs her hands through the short hair at my nape.

"Good morning," she whispers against my lips. I can't help but smile in return, even if I'm torn with worry. This is the first time in a long time I've wanted to share my past, my secrets, with someone who isn't a fellow shifter. I shiver a little at the thought of letting her in completely.

"Good morning, beautiful," I answer against her hair, memorizing her scent.

"What's wrong?" she asks suddenly, stepping back and studying my face. Her smile drops. "Oh shit, you regret it don't you?"

"*What?*" I take a step of my own, toward her though, not away. "What are you talking about?"

"I heard you on the phone through the wall. Not what you were saying exactly, but you didn't sound happy." Kaycia looks remorseful as she explains. I feel like a total asshole.

"No. Kaycia, fuck no. That phone call had nothing to do with what happened between us last night. Not directly, at least. Certainly nothing to do with *you*." I snag her hand and pull her close again, tilting her chin up to look at me. "I mean it. I need to talk to you though. About my past. Before this goes any further you need to know some things."

She looks wary, almost shrinking away from me, and guilt aches in my chest at ruining what should be a pleasant morning. But when she shrugs out of my embrace, she simply heads to the kitchen to grab a second mug, pouring me a cup of coffee and asking, "How do you take your coffee? We can't possibly have a serious discussion without some caffeine courage, right?"

Chapter 16
Kaycia

When I heard Shane through the wall, his frustration was palpable. Just the timbre of his voice told me he was upset without hearing the words he spoke. I immediately assumed it was about me and our night together.

Self-centered anxiety: not one of my best qualities.

Panic bubbled up when I opened the door and saw the tension on Shane's face. I was relieved when he kissed me back and held me close, even if he still wasn't as relaxed as he was last night. Now that he's said we need to talk about his past I begin to worry anew.

What do I really know about the "hot guy next door"? What is he hiding?

I pour coffee into the handmade mug and try to be as nonchalant as possible, even as his gaze lingers on me and makes me want to pull his shirt off and continue where we left off last night.

"Cream, or milk, whatever you have," Shane answers my question about how he takes his coffee, snapping me back to the present. I had planned on making us breakfast, but something tells me he needs to get this off his chest now, or else he might lose his nerve.

I'm not sure if that makes me more or less nervous about what he wants to tell me.

Handing him the mug, I wrap my fingers around my own and lean against my kitchen counter watching him. The restlessness in him is visible as his eyes scan my apartment, running a hand through his still sleep-tousled, honey-colored hair, his coffee clenched in the other.

"Do you want to sit on the balcony?" I ask, wondering if the fresh air might make him less jittery.

"Sure," he sighs, letting me lead the way into my little green oasis. "Kaycia," he begins once we sit down. "First of all, last night was—" He meets my eyes and smiles, making my chest ache and my stomach fill with butterflies. "It was fucking amazing. But I should have told you the truth before I let that happen."

Oh, gods. Is he married? Does he have a girlfriend? I start thinking of the worst possible scenarios, my stomach changing from the tickle of butterflies to the gnawing agony of dread.

"My past is rocky. It's why I moved to the city. Why I don't have a lot of friends. Why I don't go out much," Shane says, leaning his elbows on his knees while he cradles the cup between his hands, not looking at me. "When I was younger, I was involved in an accident. Two people died and I was blamed." He swallows and when he looks up his eyes are tight and glassy, like he's struggling to find the right words to share.

"In the end, I got off easy. The authorities chalked it up to being stupid teenagers and determined the death wasn't intentional, but nothing was ever the same. The other guy's family had it out for me, my family, and my friends. It was safer for my loved ones if I got out of town. But they never stopped looking for me to try to pay me back."

"I'm so sorry." It feels like such a pitiful sentiment for something that's distressing him so much, so many years later, but I don't know what else to say.

"It's been a decade since I left. At least six or seven years since I've run into anyone who knew me before," Shane says, sighing as he gives a sad smile. "Until maybe now."

"What do you mean?" Fear squeezes my throat, it seems unreasonable to be so worried about someone I barely know, but I can't bear the idea of something happening to him.

"Raquel and Max both texted me last night about a suspicious guy at the bar. I missed him. I wasn't as cautious as I usually am."

"Because of me," I murmur, guiltily.

"No, because *I* didn't pay attention. I should have explained better before we went out, but honestly, I have no idea if he's even a concern. This may just be years of being cautious making me paranoid." He reaches across the space between our chairs to grab my hand, intertwining our fingers and rubbing his thumb across the back of my hand. "I don't want to fuck this up, wherever it's going. But it wouldn't be fair to keep this from you. You deserve to know that I've got a past and that it could be dangerous to get close to me. To make you aware in case you don't want to get involved with me."

My stomach sinks. I know I should have warning bells going off and that I should tell him 'Thanks, but no thanks'. Instead, my heart aches at the idea of calling this off before it even has a chance to blossom. Exhaling my doubts, I reply, "Thank you for telling me. I appreciate knowing." I squeeze his hand and receive a tight smile in return. "We can't help our pasts, even if they haunt us sometimes. Did this guy do something after we left to worry the others?"

"No. It's just a feeling," he answers, more guarded than before, but then the tension ebbs as he adds, "I don't want you to be worried about it, Kaycia. I'm sure it will all blow over." He strokes his thumb across the back of my hand, then brings it to his lips to kiss my knuckles. "I think we had far more fun coming home than we would have if we'd stayed at the bar anyway," he whispers against my skin, then winks, tugging on my hand so that I'm pulled into his lap. "Good morning."

"Good morning," I whisper with a grin, my heart hammering as he nuzzles against my neck and pulls me close for a kiss, alleviating my worries and distracting me with my craving for him. "Want breakfast?"

Shane slides his hand up my bare thigh, smiling against my mouth. "I want anything you're offering, beautiful."

Chapter 17
Shane

Kaycia handled my story—well, my abbreviated story—better than I expected her to. The memory of watching Ethan's death and the subsequent retaliatory killing of Logan Ross is a dull ache. The loss of my best friend, then being torn from my family and my pack in one ruinous evening, and the fear and loneliness I've felt in the years since, is something I don't dwell on often anymore.

I wouldn't survive if I did.

I wish I could tell her more, tell her about my wolf form, about Raquel and Max's other forms, and the joy of running free with them at my cabin. I hope to, but not yet.

Humans don't always take the news of the supernatural well. It's why we keep to ourselves, our packs, it's safer to stay hidden.

When Raquel fell for Jamila, it took her more than six months before she finally confessed everything to her, and that was difficult enough *without* having a dangerous past looming over her. How am I supposed to explain that not only am I a wolf, but that it wasn't just some childhood prank gone wrong that forced me to flee? That it was a bullshit threat against my best friend by the cocky son and heir of a rival alpha that started everything. A challenge we all ended up paying for—them with their lives, me with my standing in the pack. And maybe my soul.

Holding Kaycia against me as the sun shines over the skyline I force the memories back down, inhaling her scent and memorizing her skin with my fingertips while she kisses me and offers to make me breakfast. Of course, as soon as I let myself hope for a future with someone besides a platonic raccoon or falcon, my demons would resurface. Instead of focusing on the worst-case scenario, I turn my attention to Kaycia's lips, drowning in her eager kiss.

When our coffees have gone cold and my stomach growls too loudly to ignore, Kaycia finally peels herself out of my embrace to head back into her apartment. I stay on the balcony for a few more moments, reveling in the greenery surrounding me. It reminds me of the woods and almost blocks out the city. The scent of bacon pulls me into the kitchen where Kaycia scrambles eggs and makes toast to the tune of the bacon crackling and the low music she seems to always have playing.

"Need any help?" I ask, leaning on the counter and watching her, still pleased she's wearing my clothes so I can admire her bare legs.

"You can cut some fruit if you want. But I've got the rest," she replies.

After slicing strawberries and adding them to a bowl with blueberries and blackberries, I wander around the space she's separated as her studio. Paintings in various stages of completion rest against any available surface. The one of the sunset still sits on the easel, with more hues layered on to give it more texture and depth. She's outlined a masculine profile against the oranges and pinks. Her portraits aren't detailed, you can fill in the blanks of the subject's expression and features, but this one is decidedly familiar. I fight a grin as I call over my shoulder, "Hey, does this mean *I'm* your muse now?"

"What? Oh!" Kaycia laughs, a pretty blush spreading across her cheeks. "You caught me. I guess after last night I don't have to be shy about my crush anymore."

"Mmm... tell me more about this crush," I tease, stalking back across the room to cage her in with her back against the countertop, my arms circling her hips.

"Oh, just that my neighbor is super hot and I'd hoped to have an excuse to paint him. Or talk to him. Or get into his pants," she replies, tugging me closer by my belt loops.

Leaning closer, I nip at her ear and whisper, "I don't think he'd have any objections to any of the above. But first, let's eat."

One leisurely breakfast—and a not-so-leisurely encore of last night—later, Kaycia untangled herself from me and hopped in the shower. We agreed to get together Wednesday evening for dinner and that I would help her take some of her finished pieces to the gallery over the weekend. She was incandescent with happiness when I told her I could borrow Max's truck to transport them instead of having to carry them by hand or on public transit. It's worth the price of the whiskey I'll owe him just to see her that happy.

Back in my apartment, I realize that for the first time in a long time, I feel content. Hopeful even.

Despite the shadow of the unknown shifter at the bar, the restless tension that always coils through me and makes it harder to keep my wolf contained has relaxed after this weekend. I knew it had been a while since I'd been with a woman, meaningless hookups included, but something feels different with Kaycia. There's an ease with her. I want to know her—what she likes, what she doesn't; her dreams and desires; and how I can be a part of them. The urge to protect and please her is equal to the physical desire I feel when I'm near her.

I smile and shake my head at the thought of her having a crush on me for the past few months, especially knowing she's watched me in secret as much as I did her. I wonder if we would have still been circling and stealing glances had she not bumped me on the stairs that day, or if fate would have still nudged us together somehow.

"Okay, buddy, spill the details!" Raquel demands with a knowing grin when she walks through the roll-up door on Monday, removing her helmet and shaking out her ponytail. "Did you spend all weekend in bed? Did you tell her everything? Was it sickeningly romantic?"

"Calm down, nosy," I reply from where I crouch beside the bike I'm working on. "I'm a gentleman."

"Bull-fucking-shit. Gentlemen don't smell like pussy when they walk out of the bathroom with their girlfriend." She crosses her arms over her chest with a pointed look before bursting into laughter at what I assume is my shocked expression.

At my continued silence, she gasps, "Oh, shit. Don't tell me she called it off once you talked to her." Quel's glee fades for a moment as she considers the possibility things *didn't* go well. "Seriously, what happened, Shane?"

"It went fine. I just explained that I have a rough past and that you spotted someone that may or may not be involved. I don't want to scare her for no reason, we need to be cautious and keep a lower profile. Maybe they were just passing through. It's possible they don't know me and were just curious about another wolf."

"That sounds awfully optimistic for the Shane McKinley I know." Raquel gives me a sideways glance. "Did you tell her about... *us?*"

"No. I didn't tell her that we can shift. Not yet. It took you months before you told Jamila."

"Yeah, but that was different. *I* don't have anyone out sniffing around to drag me back home for retribution," she mutters, snagging a file folder from the wall rack. She turns quickly to face me again at the sound of metal hitting the floor when I drop my wrench and growl low in my throat.

"Stop pushing, Quel. I'll tell her, okay? I just... I couldn't tell her that I turn into a fucking wolf and that my lack of control killed someone. That was a long time ago. I'm not like that anymore and I don't want her to think I am. Just... let me handle it on my terms. Let me finally have something good for just a little while." My teeth ache at how hard I'm clenching my jaw, the heat of angry tears building behind my eyes and burning in my nose.

I'm not going to fucking cry over this bullshit. That night has haunted me for years—I'm over it. I'm not letting my past ruin the potential for a good thing that's presented itself to me now. Not anymore. "Now, get to work."

Raquel holds her hands up in defeat, even if her flattened lips and flared nostrils tell me she's not remotely ready to drop the topic. But she does. She stays shockingly quiet for the rest of the morning and through lunch as well, earbuds securely in place while she works, only taking them out to ask about one of the bikes a new customer brought in late in the day.

When I'm finished for the afternoon, I tap her on the shoulder to get her attention. "I'm heading out. We good?"

"Yeah, we're good. Watch your back okay, Shane? I mean it."

"Yeah, I know. 'Night."

"'Night," she answers quietly. I can feel her dark eyes on my back as I get on my bike and fasten my helmet. I can deny it all I want, but I know she's right and I dread having to tell Kaycia the whole truth.

Chapter 18
Kaycia

"So, are you going to ride on his bike or just him?" Meg teases me over the phone. The sound of cartoons blares in the background, but I'm so happy to be chatting with my best friend that I don't even care that she can only half listen to me talk about my weekend.

"Stop!" I laugh, pretending to be shocked. "And I already did the latter, soooo..."

"*What?* And you didn't *start* with that part? You slept with the hot neighbor on a first date?" she squeals. "I'm scandalized. Tell me everything!"

So, I do. I tell her about hanging with his friends, our date, the bar, the night we spent together, *and* the next morning, leaving out the part where he tore my panties off and his cryptic confession about his past. I don't want to ruin the illusion of a perfect date just yet, and, fine, I don't want to think about the sadness and tension that conversation brought out in Shane. Furthermore, what did happen to my panties?

"Kaycia? Are you there?" Meg asks as I get lost in my own thoughts.

"Yeah! Sorry, what?" I answer, feeling the heat in my cheeks at the memory of Shane's hands on me. It's Monday morning and I've been lounging in my pajamas with my coffee, daydreaming about how to finish the piece on the easel, and about my whirlwind weekend.

"Are you seeing him again?"

"I mean, he's my neighbor. I'll probably see him all the time," I answer with a grin.

"Smart ass. You know what I mean. Are you going out again? Or was it just kind of a one-time fling situation?" The baby starts crying in the background and I know I only have a short time left on this call before she has to get back to mom life.

"Yeah, we're set to go out again Wednesday and then he's going to help me out at the gallery to get my stuff taken over."

"That's great! I hope it works out. I'm so happy for you, friend. It's like everything is falling into place. I'm so proud of you. You're doing the damn thing, Kaycia! Just like I knew you would. I wish I could fly out for the show, but you know how it is," Meg says wistfully. "Money and childcare and life are just not working out this time."

"I know. Thank you. You're the only one from home who's proud, I think. And don't worry about it, I wish you could come, but I get it. I miss you, though. You'll have to plan a visit soon."

"I miss you, too," she replies before her toddler's voice screeches over the television, "I gotta go. Text me later, okay? Keep me posted on how this week goes."

"Will do! Talk soon!"

"Bye!"

And then I'm alone with my thoughts again in my empty apartment. But this time, instead of feeling a twinge of homesickness at the loss of Meg's comforting voice, I feel excited to get to work, to keep building whatever I've started here. It finally feels like I'm figuring everything out.

By the end of the afternoon, I have all the finished paintings that are ready for the gallery wrapped carefully for transport. A few that I'm on the fence about, or that need final adjustments remain propped against the walls. It will be so much easier to move them all at once in a truck rather than try to carry them one at a time, and hopefully, the show will result in sales so they don't have to be trucked back.

When I checked my bank account this morning it became painfully obvious I need to make a few sales soon, or else I'll be on a job hunt within the next month or two. The savings I cashed out from my retirement has most of my rent covered for a year, but my other bills and necessities are taxing my remaining savings. The reality of living in the city is starting to set in, even if I've convinced my parents and everyone else otherwise.

The rumble of a motorcycle outside has my heart

speeding in my chest, happily distracting me from my financial straits, but I resist the urge to run out onto the balcony to watch Shane slipping his helmet off. I manage to stay inside and not look like a desperate teenager scoping out her crush when I hear his steps on the stairs. A part of me wishes he'd knock on my door, but I know that's silly. We've barely started dating, even if we did end up in bed together, and we already have plans Wednesday. He wouldn't immediately stop by—he already has a life outside of me.

Just because my personal life is woefully lacking doesn't mean his is, too.

Shane's door closes and I can hear the low hum of his television a few minutes later over the quiet beat of my music. I pick up my brush to start working on the half-finished painting on my easel, but I can't focus, resigning myself to the mundane task of making a grocery list instead.

As I'm adding to my list my phone buzzes, the text interrupting my entry and making me grin like an idiot.

SHANE

How was your day, beautiful?

Productive. Yours?

SHANE

Distracted. :) What are you up to?

I snap a picture of my open fridge and send it with the message:

Making a grocery list. Very exciting.

SHANE

Wanna go to the store on the corner? I'll walk you?

I immediately want to say yes, but can't decide if I should be playing harder to get. Then again, we've already slept together. Twice. I don't think I did a good job playing that game in the first place.

Sure. Come over in ten?

SHANE

Done.

When I open the door, Shane's leaning against the railing of the landing. His hair is damp from a shower and his tee clings to his long lines making me want to rake my fingers over the lean muscles beneath. Instead of his usual boots and jeans, he's wearing cuffed, cotton pants and sneakers, more casual than rugged, but something about him still gives off the don't-fuck-with-me vibe he sported at the bar this weekend—until he flashes a grin.

"Hey," he says, pushing off the railing and pulling me into a quick embrace.

"Hey, yourself," I answer returning the hug and pulling my door closed. "Nice shoes." Looking down, Shane laughs at the fact we wear the same style of sneakers.

"You have good taste," he quips.

"Yeah, I do." With a laugh I grab his hand, our fingers naturally folding together as we head down the stairs and to the corner store.

The store at the end of the block is well stocked with basics, so I fill my hand basket quickly, allowing Shane to take it for me as it gets heavier. He's quiet this evening, his eyes searching the store when we walked in, traveling over the other shoppers with a stern expression. I catch the muscle of his jaw fluttering a few times, but when he sees me staring, he softens and smiles.

"Everything okay?" I whisper, finally unable to ignore his restlessness.

"Yeah, still just a little tense after this weekend."

"How could you be tense after..." I tease, winking at him before adding a carton of coffee creamer to the basket. But Shane doesn't laugh. "Oh. The stranger," I mutter.

Shane doesn't seem to be listening, though. His grip on the handle of the basket turns white and he hands it off to me quickly.

"Kaycia, take this. I'll be right back," he whispers.

Without further explanation, his long strides eat up the small aisle of the shop as a broad-shouldered, bald man enters the front door. I peek over the top of the shelf, watching as Shane seems to transform into a more frightening version of the man I know. As though he's eager to accept the challenge, the stranger's eyes glitter, and an ugly smile cuts across his weathered face.

"Well, well..." the man begins, but Shane blows past him, bumping his shoulder roughly as he pushes through the door. The man looks around, his eyes lingering briefly on me before he turns and stands on the sidewalk with Shane. The hair on the back of my neck lifts in response to the scrutiny, making me want to cower in the back of the store.

Instead, I sneak around to the next aisle for a better view out front. *What the fuck is going on?* I wonder, my hands trembling as I watch the two men speak through the window. I act casual, browsing the pasta and sauces, even if my eyes are focused outside, observing Shane's expression harden and wishing I could hear what they're saying.

Chapter 19
Shane

"Pretty girl you got there, McKinley," the stranger prods at my back when we stand on the sidewalk.

I'm struggling to keep my anger leashed.

It's early evening and the sidewalks are full of pedestrians; I don't want to attract more attention than we already do. Not to mention the fact that Kaycia is likely watching through the tinted glass of the store. The last thing she needs to see is me lose control. Stupid fucking idea to walk her down here, but I wasn't sure if something exactly like this might happen and I couldn't risk her being approached alone.

"Who are you?" I ask the unknown shifter. He fits the description of the guy Raquel described. His scent is all wolf.

"Just a friend of the Ross pack. You've been off the map a while, McKinley. Imagine my surprise when I scented you at some dive this weekend with a falcon, a raccoon, and a pretty human all over you."

The name of my family's neighboring pack sends ice down my spine. I've kept a low profile for years, why is this happening now? How did they find me? But the mention of Kaycia boils away the fear. The threat in his voice is implied, making my urge to protect her seethe.

"Leave her out of this," I snarl through my teeth. "I paid for what happened. The scales are even." The stranger's eyes flick down to the deep scar on my forearm. It's a constant reminder of exactly how I paid. An ugly smile spreads across his face.

"We'll see about that. You've been away a long time. Leadership has changed. The new alpha will be interested to know you're playing house in the big city—"

Before he can finish his sentence, my hand is around his throat, squeezing as I shove his back against the glass of the storefront. Rage surges through my veins as I whisper through my teeth. "Leave her the fuck alone, do you understand? You heard what happened when I lost control before. I'm warning you; you don't want to know what I can do now that I *have* control. *Do you understand?*"

I slam his back against the glass again, causing the pedestrians to gasp and step away, muttering and giving us a wide berth. The owner of the grocery comes outside with threats on his lips and a phone in his hand.

"Shane, what are you doing? Stop!" Kaycia's voice cuts through the haze of fury and I cringe at my loss of control, releasing the stranger.

"That's right. Good pup. Listen to your girl," the shifter condescends with a chuckle. My skin crawls as he takes a deep inhale. To anyone else he's catching his breath, but I know he's catching her scent.

Our scent.

Because it *is* ours now, from our embrace, our hand-holding, everything.

"I'm serious. I paid my dues, leave us the fuck alone."

"Duly noted," he says, sneering at Kaycia before turning and walking away down the street.

Watching him retreat, I wait until he rounds the corner before grabbing Kaycia's hand and tugging her in the opposite direction toward our building, leaving her basket of groceries abandoned in the store. I should slow down. Kaycia's practically scurrying at my side to keep up as I try to steady my breathing and arrange my thoughts, but I want to put as much distance between her and the other wolf as I can. She remains painfully quiet for the duration of our walk and I avoid making eye contact with her. I'm embarrassed that she saw me lose my temper, but it doesn't negate the fact that I'd do whatever I must to protect her. Even if it drives her away.

"Shane? Is everything okay?" Kaycia asks when we reach our front stoop.

"No," I finally answer. "I'm sorry."

"Who was that?" She sounds scared. She probably looks scared, too. But I can't muster up the courage to look at her. This is all my fault.

"I don't know," I reply, pulling my keys from my pocket. "But he knew me."

"Is it about what you told me? The people who are still mad about your past?"

"Something like that." I stick my key in the lock, still not able to face her.

"Nope," Kaycia says as her small hand tugs at the fabric of my shirt. "You are not getting out of this that easily." When I don't reply, she grabs my bicep with a tight grip, forcing me to turn toward her. "You don't get to be sweet and romantic one minute, almost strangling a guy in the street the next, and then pretending it didn't happen without talking to me, okay? If you're one of those moody bad boys I'm going to need you to tell me now, because I do *not* have time for emotional whiplash."

Sighing, I finally look down at her. A laugh bubbles up involuntarily at the stubborn expression on her pretty face.

"Tell me what's up because I'm kind of pissed I won't have enough coffee creamer in the morning." Her hands are on her hips as she purses her lips at me and I finally do chuckle. She looks as though she might actually stomp her foot with frustration.

"I *am* sorry, Kaycia. He knows the people I told you about. He was the one at the bar Saturday night and recognized me. I'm worried he's reported my location to them, and when he mentioned you, I lost my cool." I can't help myself from affectionately running my thumb across her cheekbone, the need to touch and soothe her overriding the knowledge that she's irritated with me. "I'm sorry about ruining your grocery trip, but no one is going to threaten my girl or my friends."

"Which am I?"

"What?"

"Am I your girl, or your friend?" Her expression softens a bit and some of the tension falls away as she cocks her head with a wry smile.

"I mean, I've certainly never done the things we did this weekend with Quel, J, or Max, so I guess that puts you firmly in the first category," I reply, running the same thumb over her pouty lower lip. "If I didn't just scare you away."

"You were definitely scary, but—gods I hate to admit this—it may have made you even hotter." She quickly adds, looking up at the ceiling as if she's embarrassed, "Don't you dare let that go to your head."

A little chuckle escapes me, but it dies on my lips when she asks, "Am I in danger though? Was that just posturing or is that guy seriously someone I need to be worried about?"

A tremor travels over her and I realize how much she's been hiding her emotions on the walk home. Her scent has shifted, bitter fear tainting her usual sweetness. She's scared. I pull her tight, opening my door and pulling her inside.

"Look, I hope nothing comes of it," I begin once she's sitting on the couch. "But I heard your mom mention pepper spray on the phone the other day. Carry it with you and keep your eyes open. Let me know if you notice anyone suspicious."

"Okay," she whispers, curling her legs under her.

"Let's do dinner in on Wednesday, okay? I'll have everything ready; you bring the wine. I can help you with the gallery stuff you needed over the weekend. I have some work I have to get done at the shop this week, but if you're willing, I can take you somewhere next weekend. Get out of town for a little bit and see if things settle?"

"Deal," she replies, lighting up a bit at the prospect.

Chapter 20
Kaycia

I returned to the grocery store the next morning without incident. The owner wasn't there, just one of the part-time clerks, so no one mentioned the drama from the previous evening. I wasn't lying when I told Shane watching him manhandle the strange, older man was hot, but I failed to mention the fear that shot through me at the sight of him so angry. Or how nervous I am now that I know someone is watching him. And maybe me. It's almost shameful to admit how sad I felt watching him look so dejected as he opened his apartment door, as though he expected me to just let him walk away and disappear without stopping him.

Maybe I should have let him go, but a knot formed in my stomach at the idea of that being it between us. I spent last night lying awake and wondering if I should call things off, that tangle of sadness tightening as I tossed and turned. I don't want to. It's early in our relationship, but I really like Shane, and he's done nothing but be kind and gentle to me. But the sensible part of me that kept me in my hometown for years past the expiration—working a stable job and being the good girl everyone always expected me to be —was busy making a pros and cons list of why this whole situation is a bad idea.

Was he in a gang of some sort? The mob? Why is he so closed off about it all? Was it really an accident or did he murder someone? Potential reasons, each worse than the next, popped up one after the other until I finally took a melatonin and forced myself to sleep. The same musings pirouette in my head as I walk back home, scanning the streets for anyone who might be watching me, pepper spray clasped tightly between my fingers.

When I near our building the cry of a falcon grabs my attention, pulling my gaze from the main stoop to the railing of Shane's balcony. Sure enough, a peregrine falcon is perched on the wrought iron staring down at me. I don't know if it's the same bird that we saw the night we all hung out, but I laugh a little at the keen little thing. The bird cocks its head to the side and I get the distinct feeling that it's watching me. Giving it a little wave, then feeling silly that I'm waving at a wild animal, I open the main door and head up to my apartment.

Groceries unloaded, I step out onto the balcony to find the falcon still perched on Shane's railing, head tilted toward me. "Hi, you," I whisper, not wanting to scare it off. I snap a quick photo on my phone, sending it to Shane with the message:

> Does this bird live here? It seems content. :)

SHANE

You aren't running around in your underwear for him, are you?

> LOL – jealous of a bird now? Should I worry about you being a possessive jerk?

SHANE

I mean, have you seen what you look like? I'm jealous of everyone. ;)

SHANE

Everything all right this morning?

> All good. Grabbed my groceries. Have a good day!

SHANE

Good. You too.

I smile a little at him asking if I'm giving a bird a show, then settle in to work — first, making a list of everything I need to take to the gallery, then daydreaming about the weekend away Shane promised.

———

Packing the paintings into Max's truck the following weekend is a relief. They lay flat, protected by cardboard and bubble wrap. What would have taken me several trips over multiple days is handled in one, and Shane expertly navigates the busy city streets on the way to the Red Lark. He backs into the loading area of the building with ease, one hand on the wheel and one on the back of my seat as he looks behind us. My stomach flutters when he casually brushes his fingers against my hair, making me want to climb over the console into his lap, but we have work to do.

Red Lark Gallery is one of the smaller venues on the block, but I'm still grateful to Kelly for taking a chance on an unknown. It's still surreal to see my art hanging on the walls and to know I'll be taking up an entire portion for the upcoming exhibition. I cried tears of joy the day she called to congratulate me on selling my first two pieces and that I should bring a couple more in to replace them. It was my first sale in the city and paid my bills that month. That sale proved that I hadn't made a mistake with this move, and Kelly's moral support has kept me afloat on days I doubt myself.

Now, it's like a waking dream. Shane and I carrying in pieces for my first solo exhibition. It's hard to believe in six and a half months I've already gotten this far, not only professionally, but personally as well. When I meet Shane's eyes over the canvas he's lifting from the truck bed, I can't help but grin. Something special is happening here, however things work out.

"Kaycia, these are lovely," Kelly remarks, strolling past the paintings I have propped against the walls while I plan out where they should hang. Her high heels click on the concrete floor with each step. She's polished head to toe in a black sheath dress with her dark hair smoothed into an elegant chignon. Her jewelry glitters as she gestures to the pieces. "What are you thinking for the layout?"

"Well," I start, remembering the speech I've rehearsed. "It's a progression of the sky, so I'm deciding if I want it to begin at dawn, dusk, or midnight."

"Sunset," Shane murmurs, staring at one of the paintings that's already hung. The colors are similar to those I've used on the painting still in progress, the sunset scene with his image, but this one centers on the outline of a woman sitting in a field dotted with flowers, elbows on her knees as she stares at the sinking sun.

"Pardon?" Kelly asks, not catching his soft words. She appraises him as she speaks, looking at him like he's one of the pieces of art I've come to display.

Clearing his throat, he says louder, nodding toward the painting, "Sunset. It's the best time to daydream. That's where you should start." He may be answering her question, but his eyes bore into mine as he speaks.

"Sunset Daydreams," I reply. "I think that's the name of the show."

"I love it!" Kelly says with a smile, clapping her hands together and checking her smart watch. Scrolling through the message she looks back up long enough to say, "Arrange it how you like and I'll have Anna and the techs make sure everything is hung accordingly. How many more do you have? I believe we discussed ten?"

"Yes, I have two more to finish and we should be there. Lots of ideas to work with."

"Wonderful, I'll leave you and your boyfriend to it."

"Oh, he's not my—"

"Thanks, you have a beautiful gallery. Hopefully, I'll see you again at the show," Shane interrupts with a sideways look, reaching out to shake her hand.

"Thank you!" she replies, then whispers to me with a wink, "Inspiration indeed."

Shane chuckles as she saunters off to speak with a couple at the front of the gallery, her clicking heels fading away with her, then pulls me close for a kiss. "Sorry, I just liked the sound of me being your boyfriend."

"I didn't want you to feel uncomfortable, we haven't defined anything. We barely started dating."

"I told you, you're my girl. I'm not looking at anyone else," Shane whispers against the shell of my ear. He presses a kiss to the skin below before adding, "But I'll let you tell me when you're ready for a label," before returning to his task of gathering the discarded cardboard and bubble wrap, leaving me standing in front of the progression of the sky with butterflies in my stomach.

Chapter 21
Shane

Kaycia insists on buying a case of beer for Max to thank him for letting us borrow his truck. She has no idea that I already gave him a bottle of whiskey for keeping watch over our building most of the week in his falcon form. He's confirmed that the stranger from the store hasn't come back. No news is good news, allowing me to let my guard down over the past few days.

"Wanna grab dinner before we go home?" I ask, swinging my arm over her shoulder as we step off the steps from Max's condo.

"Sure! I also want you to tell me about this secret getaway you promised me," she replies with a sharp poke to my ribs.

"You have to pack light," I answer cryptically.

"What do you mean?"

"You have to travel light if you're going to ride with me."

"On your bike?" Kaycia's eyes widen and her steps halt. "Shane, I dunno."

I pull her closer. "It's just a little over an hour away from the city as long as traffic is light over the bridge. I promise I'll keep you safe." Running my thumb over her cheek, she trembles and lets out a shaky breath. When her lips part I can't help but lean down and kiss her. She has no idea how true my words are. The more time I spend with her, the more my desire to protect her increases.

I'd never do anything to harm her or risk her safety.

Except allow her to get closer to me.

It's selfish, but I can't seem to make myself push her away like I know I should. Being with me, especially since the incident at the store, puts her at risk. But I can't deny how much I like her company, and how much I want to spend time with her. To get to know her more deeply.

So, selfish it is.

When she opens her lips to me, I hold her more firmly, tilting her head back to taste her. I wish we were closer to home so I could carry her back to my apartment, but we're across town, so that will have to wait. When we break apart, she smiles up at me, tugging her lip between her teeth as though she's thinking.

"I trust you," she finally agrees. "I can pack light."

Dinner is a casual affair, pizza and beer at one of Max's favorite sports bars down the block, followed by ice cream closer to home. In the fading light, Kaycia's blonde hair catches the streetlights as they blink on. I listen to her talk about her ideas for the blank canvases she has waiting in her apartment. She still doesn't know where exactly I'm taking her next weekend, and a part of me regrets not borrowing Max's truck so she can bring her supplies to my cabin. The skies there are exactly what she's craving, but I can't very well pack a large canvas on the back of my bike.

Tension coils in my muscles the closer we get to home, my instincts ratcheting up with each block we walk as I try to unobtrusively scent the air for the shifter that confronted me in the market. I gently pull Kaycia closer to my side where she tucks against me, just in case. Luckily, all I smell is her shampoo and the sharp tang of her arousal. I have to fight the low rumble of pleasure that threatens to escape my chest, smiling at the knowledge that she wants me. I meant what I told her earlier, I'm not looking at anyone else while Kaycia's interested, but I'm not going to press her into anything more serious than she's ready for. She's trying to build a life and career here; she doesn't need my bullshit on her plate, even if I want to be a part of that life.

My wolf is partially to blame for getting attached so quickly and making me fall hard and fast. I could easily explain my attachment away with my animal side, coupled with the long span of loneliness I've felt separated from my pack and my family. But I can't hold my wolf completely accountable for the intensity of my emotions. Kaycia is bright and sweet and talented, not to mention beautiful. She makes me want to go out and introduce her to the city and build memories of our own together. Raquel and Max have taken the edge off my isolation, offering friendship close enough to be family, but it's not the same. I realize how much I've longed for a true companion now that I've found Kaycia.

"What are you doing tomorrow?" I ask while she digs her keys out of her bag on our shared landing, inserting them and turning the lock but not opening the door yet.

"Probably finishing a small piece, then I don't know," she replies toying with her keys as she glances back at me. "You?"

"Oh, I didn't realize doing me was an option for you to pencil in on your agenda," I reply, taking advantage of the opener she gave me.

"Psssh... you're awful!" she scolds, turning toward me with a laugh. It fades quickly as her breath hitches and she looks between my eyes and lips.

"You like it," I whisper, stepping closer so she's pressed against the wood of her door.

"I do."

The air is charged, like lightning waits to strike between us. That electricity spirals higher when I run my fingers through the hair at her temple, then farther back, pulling lightly so she gasps as she tilts her lips toward me. Her scent threatens to set me off, and I fight the urge to pull her hair harder, to slam her against the door and claim her in the hallway, regardless of who might pop out from the lower floors. I win the internal battle and simply brush my lips against hers, giving her the option to take more from me if she wants.

My girl doesn't let me down, opening to me with a sigh

as she curls her fingers in the fabric of my t-shirt, pulling me closer as I explore her mouth, nipping at her lower lip so she whimpers.

"Come inside," Kaycia murmurs against my mouth.

"Excuse me?" I widen my eyes in feigned shock, turning her words into another innuendo.

"My apartment, Shane," she scoffs. "Come inside with me. Stay with me tonight."

"You don't have to tell me twice," I answer, reaching behind her to turn the knob before scooping her up and carrying her into the soft light of her apartment.

Chapter 22
Kaycia

"Are you sure you aren't moving too fast, Kay?" Meg asks when we catch up with one another on Monday afternoon.

"I like him, Meg." I hope she can't hear my irritation through the phone when I answer. "And I have no idea if it's fast or not. The last serious boyfriend I had was in college. Thankfully, Shane is nothing like the guys I used to go out with."

"No, he's mysterious with a shady past," she says sarcastically, followed by a pointed silence.

Sighing, I change the subject, regretting that I filled her in on the creepy guy and subsequent conflict at the grocery store. Instead, I ask about her kids and her husband, getting caught up with the gossip from the town we grew up in, but when we say our goodbyes, I realize how different I feel about all of it now. How different my friend and I are these days.

I'm so glad she's happy, even if she confesses to me that daily monotony is exhausting for her. But our lives have been steadily diverging for a while and it's sometimes hard to relate, even if we will both always be there to confide in.

For the first time in weeks, I realize the tug of homesickness has faded since I've begun spending time outside of my apartment—whether with Shane, or the rest of his friends—and, while I feel slightly guilty about it, I'm also relieved. It's not just the connection with Shane either. It's the feeling of finally fitting in without altering myself or being compared to who I was years ago. Meg and I will always be friends, but I'm figuring out it's okay to grow and change. She will always remember me as the girl I was in Summerville and remind me of my roots, but that girl has morphed into someone different she's going to have to get to know.

Shane and I met up with Raquel and Jamila at their place last night for drinks and a movie, where Shane and I spent the time whispering and stealing kisses while Raquel tossed popcorn at us and Jamila fussed that she'd be vacuuming up the lost kernels for weeks. Watching them together in their home was amusing—they act like an adorable old couple. Shane's helping Max and his former roommate move some boxes from Max's place today, so he and I made plans to meet for dinner tomorrow night after he's finished at work.

I have a couple of pieces that I should work on, but my eyes can't stay off the sunset-toned portrait of Shane. I've been adding to it for days and I hope to have it finished in time for the show. Since the gallery is closed Mondays through Wednesdays, I plan on going by tomorrow to take a few measurements that I missed in the bustle of the weekend to figure out which remaining pieces I should focus on and to finalize the ideal layout and how everything should flow.

My phone buzzes before I get settled in to work, my mom calling to check in. It's been a week since we've spoken, mostly conversing through texts since I've been spending more time out. I sent her several photos of the gallery, but her responses weren't as excited as I'd hoped. I don't know why I still let it get to me, but it does.

"Hi, Mom," I answer, trying to keep my voice bright. "How's it going?"

"Hi, Kaycia. Same as usual here. How are you?"

"Great, actually. I'm getting really excited for the exhibition. What did you think of the pictures I sent?"

"It looks good. You know I don't know much about all this art stuff. I just hope you aren't wasting your time." Her words feel like a lead weight dropped into the center of a still pond, producing ripples of anger, doubt, and sadness that wash over me. "Who was the guy in the background of the one?"

I hadn't realized I'd sent one of the ones with Shane in it. Putting my mom on speakerphone, I open my photos and scroll through them. Sure enough, Shane is in profile, standing off to the side with his head tilted thoughtfully as he examines one of the pieces in the gallery. Seeing him against the clean white walls of Red Lark, a place I think of as my domain, brings a smile to my lips and dulls the irritation that's building.

"That's my neighbor, Shane. He helped me get some paintings taken over to set up."

"Well, I can see why you've been spending so much time with him. He's *very* cute."

"I'm so glad the attractiveness of my neighbor is what you've decided to fixate on," I snap, my jaw tight with annoyance. "Not how hard I've been working. Not what my art looks like. Not that I have a solo exhibition scheduled. But that I've attracted a good-looking guy."

"Why are you being so short with me? You're always so sensitive," my mom retorts.

"I'm not being sensitive!" The words rush from me in a single breath, and I can't hold the rest back now that they've escaped. "My feelings are hurt, Mom. You and Dad are supposed to be my biggest fans and you can't even be bothered to get excited for this opportunity. You've been against me moving and doing this from the beginning, but good things are happening for me anyway. Can't you see that? If you want me to call you more, and include you in my life, then maybe you should make me actually want to!"

The tears fall now, ones that I've held in for months because I've convinced myself it's not worth crying over. Certain that my parents will understand once I sell a painting, or once I'm displayed at a gallery, or once I have an exhibition of my own. But I realize now that they may *never* understand or support the life I've chosen. Disappointment settles over me like a fog.

"It's okay if you don't 'know much about art stuff'. I've never asked you to be an art expert. I just want my parents to be proud of me." I sniffle and my voice breaks on a small sob. "I have to go. I love you but I need to go."

"Well, I'm sorry you feel that way, Kaycia. You know we love you." My mom sounds indignant, but I no longer care. At least I've told her how I feel, even if it's in a far more emotional manner than I intended.

"Bye, Mom."

Still holding my phone, I press the heels of my hands against my eyes, hoping to stop the tears that run down my cheeks, but they can't be dammed. Something about finally voicing my feelings and letting them fall is cathartic even if my hands are shaking in the aftermath. A few minutes later, when they finally run dry, my chest is lighter and my resolve is stronger than ever.

Just like I am.

It took strength to admit what I wanted in life and to make the changes I needed to stay true to that dream. It took bravery to leave everything I knew to recreate myself.

I don't plan on giving in now.

Dialing one of the newly programmed numbers on my phone, I wait until Jamila answers. Anxiety spools as it rings, hoping I'm not being needy. My only other close contact in the city is Kelly, but I don't want to burden her with my personal life. Our relationship is friendly, but professional. I don't want to blur those lines too much.

"Hey, Kaycia, what's up?" Jamila's voice is warm when she picks up.

"Hi, Jamila! Are you busy today?"

"Nope, just lounging around thinking about writing but not actually doing it. Quel is covering the shop for Shane so I'm on my own. What's up?"

"I was wondering if you wanted to go grab a coffee or something. Just hang out for a girls' day? I need to get out of the apartment."

"That sounds great! Let me text you a place."

The bookstore Jamila texted me is across town, so I take the subway and arrive a few minutes late, getting turned around once before I spot it. It's a neat mix of bookstore and bar that serves coffee, tea, and alcoholic options.

Jamila stands from one of the little tables on the left side of the entrance, slipping from the stool with grace before embracing me in a tight squeeze.

"Hey! You made it!" she greets me, gesturing to the stool across from her.

"Yeah! Sorry, I had to wait on the subway and may have made a wrong turn or two once I got back above ground." I give a sheepish smile and Jamila chuckles.

"It happens, girl. I'm off today and tonight, so I was just wasting time at home. Thanks for the call. It saved me from having to fold the laundry that was staring me down." She nods toward the menu above the bar. "Want a drink?"

We both grab drinks, a tea for Jamila, and a latte for

me, then settle back in at our seats in easy companionship. The bookstore stretches beyond the bar and deep into the building, with shelves and shelves of colorful spines stacked to the ceiling covering all genres.

"This is a cool place," I say, taking a sip of my coffee.

"Isn't it? I hang out here a lot when I'm writing and want a change of scenery. They have a cute patio out back, too, and I've done readings a few times in the evenings." Jamila watches me with curiosity, her dark eyes studying me as though she knows I didn't just want a chill girls' day.

"That's awesome! You mentioned you're a writer. Are you published? Or is it more of a hobby you do for yourself?" I avoid her inquiring expression, not quite ready to spill my neuroses.

"I've had works featured in a few anthologies. Short stories and poems. And I sold a song once, but nothing major yet. I studied creative writing in college, and my parents keep asking why I haven't gone back for my next degree yet, but I'm happy where I am for the moment." She smiles, so calm and unbothered by my questions, so confident in her choices. "I like how flexible my catering and bartending gigs are. I can work on my writing and do what I want. I mean, you get it."

"Yeah. But I mean, you said your parents *don't* get it? Do they give you a hard time?"

"Well, they do and they don't. My parents are hyper-focused on academics. My mother is a professor and my dad is an attorney, so the fact that I only have an undergrad degree and haven't done anything further is confusing to them." Jamila smiles when she talks about her parents, making me assume they have a good relationship. "They're the first in line to buy anything I'm published in, but they're also constantly asking when I'll go back to school so I can do something besides catering gigs. It's a struggle sometimes."

"I get that," I reply, sipping more of my coffee. My heated conversation with my mom replays in my mind, wondering what it must be like for your family to be excited about your art like Jamila's. "Mine are definitely in the 'don't get it' camp."

I chew the inside of my cheek and tap my forefinger on the side of my mug to keep the frustrated tears from falling. I may be sad about my parents, but I'm not going to add pathetic to the list of adjectives that describe me in Jamila's mind.

"Kaycia? Are you okay?" Jamila asks gently.

"Not really," I finally admit with a self-deprecating chuckle and deep exhale. "I had a rough call with my mom earlier. I mentioned before that she and my dad aren't happy about me moving here or about my art, and they make sure they let me know every time they touch base. It just really got to me today. I'm so tired of pretending it doesn't hurt when I speak with them." I sigh again, keeping the irritating tears tickling the back of my eyes at bay.

"Ah, gods, that's rough. I'm sorry. But listen, some people just don't get it. No matter how well you do, they won't understand. And that's okay! It's *your* life, right? You can't please everyone."

Jamila reaches across and places her palm on mine, giving it a little squeeze of encouragement. "Shane told us your art is really good. And how excited are you about having your first solo show? You're doing things, Kaycia. Be proud of yourself. And let us all be proud with you, okay? Your parents will either come around or they won't. That's their problem. Don't let that fuck with your head."

"Yeah," I sniffle, embarrassed at the tears that have finally welled in my eyes at her kindness. I dash them away with a laugh. "Yeah, okay. Thank you. Really."

"Shane really likes you, and Raquel and I think you're a sweetheart. We have your back if you need us."

"Thanks for meeting with me on such short notice. And for being so nice. I don't know a lot of people in the city and I was worried I was bothering you."

"It's never a bother! That's what friends are for. I'm sure I'll need to bitch about something one day and you're going to be first on my list. Now"—Jamila drinks the last of her tea, the ice cubes clinking against the empty glass as she places it on the tabletop—"let's go look at the books, forget our parents' expectations, and get to know each other better."

I down the remainder of my latte and grin before following her past the bar and into the rows of books in a much lighter mood than I was when I left my apartment.

Chapter 23
Shane

"Well, we're screwed now," Raquel says solemnly, walking through the bay door as she removes her helmet.

"What do you mean?" I ask, sitting on a rolling stool to sip my fresh cup of coffee.

"Our girlfriends hung out yesterday, all our secrets will be out in the open soon."

"We don't have any secrets, Quel. You never keep *anything* to yourself," I reply, then catch her helmet one-handed as she throws it at me in response. "What the fuck! I almost spilled my coffee. As long as Jamila doesn't talk about us shifting—which I know she won't—we'll be fine."

I knew Kaycia and Jamila hung out yesterday. Kaycia told me when she snuggled up against me on the couch after I got home from Max's. I could tell she was in a mood; her scent was different and she wasn't as playful as usual, but when she told me she was fine I didn't press her. She apologized for texting me when she heard I was home, afraid she was bothering me. As if I could be bothered by spending time with her. It tugged at my heart to know she thought she might be a burden.

She always says little things like that: "I don't want to impose", "I don't want to be a bother". Making it seems like she isn't worthy of my time or taking up space.

"And she's still not my girlfriend," I add, laughing when Raquel rolls her eyes dramatically and tosses her hands in the air.

"Gods, what are you? Twelve? And please don't call her your mate. I can't stand that wolf shit," she teases, making a face to show her disgust with wolf traditions.

"I don't want to force her into anything."

"Trust me. I've seen you two together. She wants you just as much as you want her." Her expression shifts to somber when she asks quietly, "How long 'til you tell her the whole truth? You've been spending a lot of time together, Shane. It seems like it's getting serious quick. With that wolf hanging around you really should tell her. If not for your relationship, for her own safety."

"I know. I was thinking about when we go away to the cabin. It would be easier there."

"Do you need our help?" I understand what she means —do I want her and Jamila to come to prove that I'm not crazy? Or that *Kaycia* hasn't suddenly started seeing things when she finds out the guy she's been sleeping with turns into a wolf.

"I'll let you know. Thanks, Quel."

The day is quiet as I lose myself in my uneasiness over confessing my true nature to Kaycia. I recognize that I need to tell her soon before something slips. But I don't know what I'll do if it scares her away. I've become more attached to her than I anticipated, and the idea that she would walk away from what we've only begun to build makes my chest tighten painfully. The fear that I would go back to seeing her in the hall, or passing her on the stairs, without being able to reach out for her causes my chest to constrict painfully. I'm not sure I can stand losing someone this important to me again.

As though she knows I've been thinking of her, a text comes through from Kaycia with a photo of one idea for wall layouts for the gallery, then one of an updated website design. She told me she was meeting with Kelly this morning, and then was going to work on updating her website to prepare to open an online shop for prints since it would be quiet in the closed gallery office and the lighting is good for taking photos. I wish I could join her.

KAYCIA

What do you think?

I think it looks great. I like the progression. How's it going?

KAYCIA

Fine. I think I figured out the website stuff for now. I should be finished in a little bit.

KAYCIA

Don't freak out…But there was this guy hanging out front of the building when the delivery guy left earlier. He gave me the creeps.

Her text makes my nostrils flare and my knuckles whiten around the phone in my hand.

What do you mean?

KAYCIA

I don't know. He's just been hanging around on the sidewalk. I noticed him when my lunch was dropped off, but didn't think much about it until I saw he was still there a few minutes ago. The front door is locked, but Kelly left hours ago.

Instead of texting back, I dial her number.

"Hey, you didn't have to call. It's probably nothing, but since you said I should be cautious I wanted to mention it. I have my pepper spray," Kaycia says before I say anything. Her voice is tight, like she's trying to hide how nervous she feels.

"Describe him." I put the phone on speaker and wave Raquel over to listen. "Raquel's listening, too."

"Oh, hey, Quel. He's probably mid-thirties? Dark hair, scruffy look?"

"Is he tall? Long hair or short?" Raquel asks, meeting my eyes.

"Umm…he's shorter than Shane, but not short. Short

hair. I'm just kind of worried about leaving by myself if he's still out there since no one else is here and I have to walk to the subway." Kaycia's voice has a little quiver to it now, confirming my instinct that she's more worried about the guy than she wants to let on.

"Stay inside. I'll be there in a few minutes," I tell her.

"Shane, you don't have to do that. I don't want to bother you and I'm a big girl."

"Stay inside," I command, then hang up and look over at Raquel.

"It's him. The human that was with the wolf at the bar. I'm almost certain," Raquel confirms, locking eyes with me. "I'll come with you." She goes to the top of one of the toolboxes and pulls out a small pistol, tucking it at her lower back before pulling on her jacket and snagging her helmet.

I roll down and lock the bay door, securing the shop before exiting onto the sidewalk in a rush. Raquel revs her engine a time or two waiting for me. Her bike is a sports model that's made for speed compared to my vintage cruiser, the engine humming at a higher pitch than the deep rumble of mine. I swing my leg over my bike, kick it into gear, and take off behind her heading toward the gallery.

Rage builds in my chest the closer we get, my senses homing in on whether any shifters are in the vicinity. But I only smell Raquel's familiar scent as she rides in the lane with me. She turns off a block over, circling to come around the other direction to back me up, or to get Kaycia away if I need her to.

I've run out of time to tell the whole truth.

I thought I would have until this weekend to continue in the blissful bubble we've created, but it's becoming clear that my past isn't going to fade away this time.

Two buildings away from the gallery, I spot the man leaning against the brick of the neighboring shop. I'm not sure what he's been told about me, but the smirk across his face tells me it isn't enough to make him aware of what danger is coming for him.

Chapter 24
Kaycia

The familiar rumble of Shane's motorcycle outside makes the tension in my chest loosen, even if my anxiety over what he might do to the man outside, or what the man might do to him, skyrockets. I felt weak and silly when he said he was coming to get me, but I won't deny I was relieved, too. I hope my worry is unwarranted and the guy leaves so we can laugh about me being paranoid and just go home. But after what happened at the market and Shane's warnings, I can't believe it's a coincidence that the stranger is hanging around while I'm here alone.

I grab my backpack from where I had tossed it against the wall. At least I was able to focus enough so my paintings are laid out for the tech to hang and my new website is just a couple of clicks away from being active. I reach the front of the building in time to see Shane drive his bike up to the sidewalk in front of where the man leans against the shop next door. My eyes widen at the ferocity in Shane's expression. He's overtaken by a wildness that's more animal than human as he reaches down to detach one of the footrests of his bike. In a fluid motion, he sharply snaps his elbow and the detached piece extends into a tele-scoping baton.

I should be frightened of him like this, the violence promised by his grip on the metal, the flex of muscles in his arms, as he prowls toward the man with his lips curled back in a snarl.

But I'm not.

I feel safe knowing he's here for me. Because I needed him to be.

I can't hear the man speak until I push open the front door, pressing against the plate glass that travels the entire length of the gallery front while the automatic lock clicks shut behind me.

"—your little bitch," the man is saying. My anger flares knowing he's talking about *me*.

"I told your friend to stay away. And he sends *you*? I hope they're paying you well." Shane barely sounds like himself, his voice gravelly with rage.

The stranger starts to reach behind him, and I begin to shout to warn Shane that he might have a weapon, but Shane is quicker. With an inhuman growl, he swings the baton with more speed than I would think possible. The crack when it meets the man's hip makes my stomach churn, and his grunt of pain makes me involuntarily recoil, pressing against the glass as if I could melt back into the safety of the gallery's white walls.

"Good to know they were right, though," the stranger grunts through the pain. "That you'll protect her even when you should stand down to avoid attention. Haven't changed a bit have you, McKinley?" A groan escapes the man who protects his injured side with a forearm. "You gonna die over a piece of ass like your buddy did?"

Shane brings the baton across his arm with another vicious swing, the crunch of bone and the man's wail of pain as he sinks to the sidewalk tells me it's broken. Shane's breaths come fast as he stands over the man.

He snaps his attention to me suddenly, as though he forgot I was there. His wild eyes meet mine as he grits through his teeth, "Put on the helmet and get on the bike, Kaycia."

I stand frozen, watching while he pulls a hidden pistol from the man's waistband. It startles me to see him tuck it into his own in one smooth motion. Luckily, the neighboring store owner has only just noticed the commotion, opening the door with a worried expression. But she missed the fight. And the gun.

"Do I need to call the police?" she asks me.

"No," I answer quickly, my voice shaking. "This man was waiting outside the building for me. I'm okay though. My boyfriend made it before he could do anything."

"I think I should still call someone," she says, looking over at Shane and the broken man rolling around holding his arm. He's inching away from the gallery, dragging himself along the dirty concrete, but still hasn't gotten to his feet.

"He won't be touching anyone else," Shane says, suddenly at my side, making the shop owner step back. "Kaycia, *please*. Get on the bike."

I still hesitate, trembling at the thought of riding on the motorcycle and the violence Shane just dealt to the stranger. But despite my better judgment, I don't argue. I don't want to walk home alone with the risk of someone else following me, and we can't leave Shane's bike here. Following him to the motorcycle, Shane hands me a helmet, then gets on, motioning me to get on the seat behind him.

"Where's *your* helmet?" I ask when he starts the bike. It roars to life, vibrating and rumbling like a creature woken from hibernation.

"Don't worry about me. We need to go home and pack, our trip is starting earlier than expected," he shouts over the rumble of the engine.

"*What?*"

Turning to face me over his shoulder, Shane's eyes are desperate and pained, searching my face like a man lost at sea seeking a rescue that might pass him by. "Kaycia, please trust me. If you want to come back early, I understand, but I need you to come with me tonight. To explain everything. Raquel and Jamila are coming, too. We'll keep you safe."

"I know you will," I reply, my head spinning. "I trust you."

Wrapping my arms around his waist, I lean against him, feeling the heat of his skin through his shirt and the pounding of his heart, almost as rapid as my own. He guides us back off the sidewalk with sure footed steps on either side of the bike. Patting my hands once to reassure me, he pulls into traffic and heads toward our apartment. Passing the next block, a black sport bike zooms from an alley and pulls up alongside us. The rider has a long, dark braid and wears all black. A raccoon sticker waves from the back of their helmet. Shane makes a thumbs up motion and the other driver responds with a salute, riding with us another few blocks until they turn off on another side street and disappear into the late afternoon traffic.

Chapter 25
Shane

I wait for Kaycia to pack her backpack for our trip, even though in my heart I anticipate that it isn't necessary. She'll chuck it into Max's truck for the ride back home once I tell her everything. I'm nauseous at the thought that this is the end. That she's going to run screaming from me and my life. But I've always known I would have to tell her, and with her being in the crosshairs of what I suspect is the Ross pack's vendetta, it's essential she knows everything.

"Wear jeans," I call toward her bathroom where she's rustling around with toothbrushes and cosmetics. "And boots."

"Shane?" Kaycia steps from the bathroom to look at me. "Should I be scared?" My heart stumbles at the tremor in her tone, the fear I see in her eyes when I look up at her from the chair in her living space.

"Not of me," I reply, even though that may not be totally true.

I would never hurt her. But being with me could.

It only takes her twenty minutes to have her bag packed and to change into jeans, a tee, and the same worn boots she wore the night we went to see Max play. Slinging her backpack over her shoulder she grips my hand in hers, pulling me close. "Hey," she whispers, studying my face. "Are you okay?"

"I will be. Let's just get on the road," I answer, sighing and running a hand through my hair in frustration over the afternoon and everything that's snowballing. "I should be asking you that. You're the one stuck in the middle of this shit."

"Shane, I'm fine. Hey, look at me."

Before I can turn away, she palms my cheek, standing on her toes to brush a kiss against my mouth. Her touch breaks my resolve. I wrap my arms around her, holding her against me as I slant my mouth against hers and groan as our breath mingles. I feel like I'm clinging to her for all I'm worth, memorizing her scent, her taste, the way her curves feel under my hands.

Just in case this is the last time I get to do this.

"We need to go. Raquel, Jamila, and Max are all meeting us there."

"All three? Why?" Kaycia steps back in surprise.

"It will all make sense when we get there. I promise. And if you don't want to stay you can ride back with them."

Her brow furrows and her eyes shimmer with hurt, as though I've told her I don't want her to stay. In reality, I expect that after I tell her the guy next door that she's shared a bed with turns into a wolf, is a murderer, and is being hunted by a rival pack she will run back to the safety of the city. Possibly even to another apartment. Or worse, back to Summerville. I don't want to put this on her and then have her feel like she's trapped with a monster all weekend.

"Turn around," I instruct. She does what I ask with only a raised brow. Running my fingers through her long wavy hair, I separate it into thirds and quickly braid it back, pulling a hair tie from her counter where several are collected with other odds and ends in a bowl. "There, now your helmet will fit better."

On the landing, I unlock my apartment and grab a jacket and spare helmet from the coat closet before re-locking the door. I hold the jacket out to her, hopeful that she'll like it and that it fits.

"What's this?" Kaycia asks, taking the jacket from me and handing me her backpack while she slides her arms into the sleeves. "Confident, huh?"

"Wishful thinking," I answer. I bought it for her in anticipation of our upcoming trip, hoping she would be willing to ride with me. Luckily, it arrived early.

She runs her fingers over the padded portions, a little smile tilting the edge of her lips when I reach forward and fasten the zipper. My hands linger at her waist a moment longer than necessary, afraid of her slipping away.

"Thank you," she says as I hand her backpack to her. "You don't have a bag?"

"No. I keep things there for when I visit. Travel light remember?"

"Shane. Where are we going?"

"My vacation cabin."

She breathes a deep exhale when we step back into the warm evening air and approach my motorcycle waiting at the curb.

"Why am I so fucking nervous?" she murmurs.

I can't tell if it's meant for me or just to herself, but I reply, "Because you've been taught to be cautious. And because today was intense." She sputters a sarcastic laugh and gives me a sideways smile. "I promise I'll keep you safe."

I hand her the spare helmet and she slides it over her hair before I adjust the chin strap. I tap her chin affectionately, then rub the pad of my thumb across her lip before putting my own helmet on and mount my bike.

"All right," I say to her. She stands nervously to the side watching me. Without the urgency of fleeing the gallery she has time to think about what she's doing. "Let me go over the basics now that we have a minute. Climb on behind me like before."

She puts her palms on my shoulders and swings her leg over, sliding forward against my back. I turn to look over my shoulder to give her a run down on what she needs to know. "Try to relax. You can put your hands on my hips or around my waist. Tap twice if you need to tell me something or to stop. Lean with me on curves and turns—

looking over my shoulder while we turn can help keep you with me. I'll tap your leg if you need to hang on, okay?"

I can scent her anxiety and guilt floods me that she's so nervous. With a brave smile she nods. My heart stumbles when her arms wrap around me, and all I can do is hope this goes smoother than I think it's going to. I place my palm on top of where both her hands touch on my chest, squeezing once before separating them and placing them on my hips, then start the engine and head out of the city.

Chapter 26
Kaycia

The breeze is cooler the farther north we drive from the crowded streets of the city, but this deep into summer it's not the cooling relief I crave. I ignore the sticky sweat between my boobs and at my lower back from the thick leather of the jacket Shane gave me. It has reinforced and padded sections, and while there are vents built-in, it's still warm. My heart swells a bit at the thought that he bought it for me in hopes I'd be exactly where I am now—behind him on his motorcycle, riding down the road into the sunset. Under different circumstances, I could see the appeal of it and I could focus more on the beauty of the fields that begin to appear about forty-five minutes into our ride, or the golden hour glow lighting our way. Instead, my nervousness refuses to dissipate. We can't talk on the way like we could if we were driving in a car, so I'm stuck playing out every worst-case scenario on repeat the farther we get from the familiarity of our apartment building and the shining glass and steel of Argent.

When we stop at a flashing red light in the middle of nowhere Shane turns to shout, "Do you need a break? There's a gas station a little up the road."

"No, let's just get there."

He gives a little nod and we continue on, farther into the heavily wooded foothills of the mountains looming in the distance. About half an hour later we pass a sign for Snow Fern Tarn, slowing once the trees are tall on both sides of the two-lane road, cocooning us with their branches. A gravel driveway waits on the left, the rocks crunching under the wheels as we wind through the trees to a clearing. Pulling up next to Max's truck and the sport bike we saw earlier, Shane cuts the engine and pats my hand gently. Relief fills me at the break from the ride, but Shane's head is dipped as though in sadness or defeat.

"Here we are," Shane announces softly. He holds my hand while I climb off the bike onto shaky legs, unclipping my helmet for me, and then taking my backpack so I can remove my jacket. My legs are as wobbly as a fawn while I stretch from the long ride. When he dismounts, Shane removes his own helmet, running his fingers through his sweat-dampened hair and placing both helmets on the bike. With a sideways look and deep sigh, he slides his hand in mine to lead me around the truck.

"Oh!" I gasp once we round the truck and the house comes into view. "It's beautiful."

An A-frame cabin sits in the center of the clearing with

a wooden deck off the front wall of windows. Yellow light shines from within, allowing me to make out a small, cozy interior. Raquel, Jamila, and Max are arrayed in chairs on the deck, waiting with serious expressions that don't fit with the relaxing surroundings.

"Thanks," he replies. His voice is oddly hollow and my heart sinks. "Let me show you inside real quick so you can freshen up if you want."

"No." I pause, pulling his hand so he stops short. "Shane, I'm freaking out. I need to know what's going on. Now."

Shane just nods, his lips a flat line of tension as he pulls me toward the deck. "Come on."

Max stands as we approach. He's wearing his usual ensemble of a slim-fitting tee, torn jeans, and boots. His shoulder-length hair is tied back, but instead of his typical flirtatious smile, he looks serious when his eyes travel between Shane and me. "We doing this?" he asks Shane with a raised brow.

"Max, they just got here. Give him a minute," Jamila scolds. "Kaycia, come sit with me, okay?" She pats the empty spot on the cushioned bench next to her.

I pass Raquel on my way to sit with Jamila on the little outdoor sofa. Raquel gives a tight smile, then saunters over to stand with Max. Shane looks uncertain, running his hand through his hair several times, leaving it messy and on end, and twisting one of the rings he wears around his finger until Raquel places her hand on his shoulder.

"You want to show her first? Or tell her the story?" Raquel asks.

"Show her," Jamila offers. "It's what worked best for me." She smiles at me before adding, "Don't worry, Kaycia. It will all make sense in a minute."

I offer a nervous laugh. "Are you about to show me where a body is buried?" I joke, but my heart is hammering in my chest and sweat coats my hands. When Raquel and Max start taking off their shirts my nervousness swiftly turns to confusion. "Wait, what are you doing? Are you in some kind of sex club or something?"

Max laughs. "They wish!"

"Shut up, Max," Raquel snipes standing in her sports bra and jeans. "Come on, Shane."

Looking into my eyes for a moment, Shane reaches behind his head and pulls his shirt off, then they all kick out of their shoes and jeans to stand in the low light in their underwear.

"I still don't understand," I whisper to Jamila.

"Just wait."

"Okay, I'm ready," Shane says with a swallow, exhaling deeply before his body twists.

"Avert your eyes if you're shy, Kaycia," Max jokes, stripping out of his boxer briefs while Raquel pulls off her bra.

"What—" My question dies on my lips, replaced by a shriek. My surprise over their sudden nakedness morphs into shock as all three begin to shudder and change, shifting from the human forms I'm used to into something entirely different. Blinking rapidly, I jolt backward, but Jamila grabs my hand and holds me in place as questions fall from my lips. "Am I losing my mind? Did he give me drugs? Did we crash the motorcycle? Am I dead? Or high? Or both?"

"No, give them just a minute." Her voice is calm, almost amused, but she holds my hand tight, offering support while I spiral. "They won't hurt you. You'll see."

After another minute, I sit with my free hand over my mouth and my eyes wide. I'm speechless. I can't believe what has replaced my friends, or what my eyes witnessed that my brain can't quite work out.

A wolf, a raccoon, and a falcon all stand in their places.

The raccoon makes a sound that reminds me of a cross between a whimper and purr as it scurries over to us and jumps up on Jamila's lap. Even though I'm still wildly confused I can't help but reach out toward the little beast who harmlessly rubs her head on the palm of my hand.

"Raquel?" I ask, looking between the animal and Jamila. "Can she talk?"

"No. She's finally quiet," Jamila teases, causing Raquel to hiss at her.

"So, *you're* the falcon that flew onto the balcony to spy on me?" I ask the bird of prey.

The falcon flaps his wings in response, then launches from where he's perched on the back of the chair, screeching and circling in the air overhead.

"And Shane?" My voice trembles as I finally turn to the wolf sitting across the deck.

He's huge. I've never seen a wolf in real life. I always assumed they were the size of a big dog, but I was very wrong. "Is that you?" The wolf whimpers in response, ducking his head as though in submission. "Can I... pet you?"

Jamila laughs and Raquel purrs while Shane gives a little whine and trots over, tail wagging as though he's begging for me to run my hand over his furry head. He bumps my hands with his nose until I scratch behind his ears with what's likely an idiotic expression.

"How is it even possible?" I ask, looking between them all. I return my gaze to Shane's, marveling at the beautiful wolf. "Is this all you were worried about? Showing me this?" Shane whines again, this time sounding less like an excited pet and more like a tortured beast.

After another few pats, Shane prowls back over to where his clothes lay in a heap, transforms back into human form, and quickly dresses in silence. Raquel stays curled up on Jamila's lap, content to remain a raccoon, but Max follows Shane's actions, pulling on his clothes and grabbing a beer. Max offers me a drink, but when I decline, he turns his attention to the fire pit, focused on lighting the kindling and adding logs before offering an answer.

"No one really knows *how*. We just *are*," Max explains while Shane swallows nervously. "There aren't a lot of us and we keep it quiet from humans for the most part. You know how they can be with their prejudices and curiosity."

Max looks over at Shane, holding out a beer with a forced smile, but he shakes his head and warily focuses on me as if expecting me to freak out. I study him as he slowly approaches, like a beast stalking its prey even though he's fully human again. I search his face and body for any evidence of the supernatural that I should have caught on to, but how do you look for something you had no idea existed? His eyes flash gold when they meet mine, the only sign of being something more than human. Something I'd noticed before, but always assumed was a trick of the light. His ability to move so quickly and silently makes sense now, even if I had rationalized it away before.

"No. That's not what I was worried about, Kaycia. This is," Shane finally says, sitting across from me and holding out his deeply scarred forearm, twisting it so the firelight catches the shiny depression. "The full truth about what happened in my past."

I suck in a breath, leaning forward to listen. Although I'm unsure what he's going to tell me, I'm certain it can't be anything that will push me away. Can it?

If watching him turn into an animal didn't scare me off, what could?

"Do you want some privacy?" Jamila suggests, stroking her fingers over Raquel's back.

"You all know the story," Shane replies. "You can stay unless Kaycia wants you to leave."

"No, it's fine." Having Jamila next to me is comforting. I'm not afraid of Shane, but having another human nearby is reassuring, at least until I know what he's going to tell me.

"I didn't just leave my family for their safety. I was

exiled from my pack. Cut off from my family because of stupid choices I made when I was younger. I told you part of the story, but it's time you know everything." Shane rubs his palms over his face with a deep sigh, as though dreading what he's going to tell me. Before I can offer any words of encouragement he continues, "My best friend, Ethan Cameron, was the son of our pack leader. He and I were only a few months apart in age and grew up like brothers. When he was eighteen, and I was still seventeen, the son of a neighboring pack leader challenged Ethan. It was so fucking stupid looking back. All over a girl who Ethan was having a fling with. Logan Ross claimed she was his." Shane's jaw clenches, as though remembering his past hurts. "Those words mean something to wolves, so Ethan accepted the challenge, teenage pride outweighing sense. Of course, I was his second."

"Like a duel?" I ask, morbidly fascinated by the savage prospect.

"Yes, but with fists and fangs, not guns," Shane replies, cutting his eyes to me before returning them to the firelight in the low pit. "It was supposed to be to first blood. We had both been friends with Logan and his little brother, Colton, regardless of our packs having animosity in the past. Despite our childhood friendship, Logan fought dirty. He injured Ethan so badly that he couldn't defend himself anymore and couldn't heal fast enough to negate the damage. When Logan wouldn't let up, I couldn't control myself. Back then, when I was younger and was just learning about my abilities, it was nearly impossible to control my shift or my anger. I was irrational, and I lost it when I saw Ethan brutalized. Both Ethan and Logan died that night. Over fucking teenage jealousy."

"Oh Shane, that's terrible," I murmur. I scoot forward, reaching out to lay my hand on his arm while he hangs his head "But you were defending your friend."

"I killed someone Kaycia." His head snaps up suddenly, startling me at the intensity in his gaze. "An *important* someone at that. It was either our pack exile me or offer me or one of my family members for execution in exchange. My father pled for exile, even though it meant I would be on my own without any connection to them any longer. It's a punishment almost as painful as death for one of us, but I kept my life."

Tears threaten, burning behind my eyes as I witness the pain on Shane's face and hear the sorrow in his voice from the memory.

"They cut my pack mark from my forearm"—he rotates his arm, showing me the ugly scar I'd asked about on our first date— "and forced me to say goodbye to my mother and father, and my little brother and sister, that very night. Even though their alpha made the terms and our pack agreed to them, it didn't mean all of the Ross pack thought it was fair, or that they would abide by the rules. Logan's second was his younger brother, Colton. He had held Logan's head in his lap when he took his last breath and cursed me when I was dragged away.

"When his father found exile to be a fair punishment for me, seeing as both packs lost their heirs, Colton raged against the decision and swore he would find me. For years some of his allies and supporters always did. I lost them in the cities, though, and it's been a long time since anyone approached me."

"Except for us," Max interrupts, gesturing to Raquel, laying on her back and getting her furry belly rubbed by Jamila. "We dragged you out of your den, finally."

Shane nods toward Max with a sad smile. "I hadn't had friends for years. No one to call, no one to lean on. Not until these two"—he gestures toward his friends— "and Jamila." Glancing at me from the corner of his eye he adds, "And for these past weeks, you."

Standing from where he sits, Shane begins to pace. "But my selfishness has to end. It's clear that Colton knows where I am, and that he thinks you're a weakness. I can't have them after you. They can come for me, but I won't put you in danger anymore, Kaycia."

"I don't understand. Are you sending me away?" I'm frustrated that he thinks he can decide things for me, without even asking what I want. And I'm embarrassed now that everyone is still here listening to us. I don't want to sound desperate, but I don't want this to be over, either.

"I'm giving you the option now that you know the whole truth. This isn't what you signed up for when we started seeing one another, and I'm sorry I didn't tell you everything upfront. But it's hard to tell the girl you're falling for that you turn into a wolf *and* that you're a murderer."

"You're *not* a murderer. It was an accident," I insist.

Wait—did he just say the girl he's falling for?

"I killed him in cold blood, Kaycia. He deserved it, but I'm not innocent. You need to know that. I would do the same to protect any of you."

Sighing, Shane rests his elbows on the railing with his back to us to hide any emotions that might slip through. Over his shoulder he murmurs, "You can ride back in the truck with Max and Jamila. I understand if you want to go back to Argent to think it over." Then he walks down the three stairs and toward the back of the house, disappearing into the night.

"Just give him a minute," Max advises, his drawl like warm honey as he sits in Shane's vacated seat, closer to the rest of us. "He doesn't like talking about his past, and I think it's twisting him up that they found him just when he found you."

"Does he really think I'm going to leave?" I ask, looking between Max and Jamila. Raquel finally scurries to the edge of the deck and stretches back into her human form, slipping into her clothes and coming to squeeze in on Jamila's opposite side.

"Unfortunately, it would probably be the smartest thing if you did," Jamila says, picking at the cushion and earning a glare from Raquel. "Well, it would. These men are dangerous. *Shane* is dangerous." She pauses when Raquel and I make a similar sound of irritation. She sighs and adds, "But he's also one of our closest friends and would defend any of us until the death. He can be dangerous *and* a good man. I've learned that the laws of humans don't always apply to shifters."

"It's been so good to see him with you, Kaycia," Raquel adds. "And J is right, shifters abide by their own rules. But we'll respect whatever you want to do—as long as you promise to keep our secrets. We'll drive you back to the city and help you pack your apartment. Even help you find a new place if you want. It's all your call."

My mind swims with everything they're telling me. With the fact that my new friends are *shifters*. Something I didn't even think was real until tonight.

With the fact that Shane just said he could be falling for me, and the fact that I'm certain I've already fallen for him.

And the biggest issue—that his past may very well be putting both of us in danger.

"I changed my mind," I blurt, pulling everyone's attention to me. "I *do* need a drink."

Chapter 27
Shane

Walking away from Kaycia isn't the hardest thing I've had to do, but it's right up there with it. I didn't think I'd ever feel as broken as I did leaving my pack and family behind, but this misery is awfully close. I saw the indecision on her face once I'd finished speaking. I didn't want to make it harder on her by sitting there staring at her like a puppy she left on the side of the road when she walks away from this mess I've pulled her into.

The wind blows from the forest as I stare up at the sky, watching the stars I've missed so much blink into existence in the dark. The moon is nearly full again, but I'm empty inside. I usually find peace here, but tonight nothing will bring me comfort.

Closing my eyes against the burn of tears, I breathe in the scent of the forest and the clear pond behind the cabin. In the distance, Max's truck doors open, then slam shut. The engine roars to life and the gravel crunches under the tires as he backs out of the driveway. I listen to the truck all the way down the drive, knowing in a few more moments they will be on the road and heading toward the city.

Soft steps are barely audible behind me. I can't smell her scent with the way the wind blows, but I would have heard Quel's bike start and follow the rest if she'd left.

"She ride back with J and Max?" I ask over my shoulder when the footsteps stop behind me, keeping my attention focused on the twinkling sky.

I don't want Raquel to witness me break.

"I'm not leaving."

My heart stutters—nearly stops—at the sound of Kaycia's gentle voice. Raquel's bike starts, then revs once, twice, before gravel flies and she's down the driveway after the truck, leaving me with Kaycia.

"What are you doing, Kaycia?" I whisper, spinning to face her.

"Staying with you."

"I–" I don't have words. I want to argue with her and send her away, but Raquel and the others made it impossible for her to leave unless I take her. "I don't understand. I told you it's not safe."

"I don't care. I've spent my entire life playing it safe. I played it safe through college, through the years afterward in a job that stole my soul. I'm playing by *my* rules now, choosing my own path. And I choose you." Her eyes are glassy with unshed tears as she speaks, her voice trembling. With a little laugh and half-hearted shrug, she adds, "If I'm already wrapped up in this why wouldn't I stay where I want to be? If I'm going to be collateral damage for whatever revenge plot these people have out for you anyway, I might as well enjoy my time with you instead of running away to be miserable alone."

Two strides are all it takes before I have her in my arms, holding her close and kissing her. Her mouth, her cheeks, her throat. Breathing in the scent I thought I'd only have in memories.

"Are you sure?" I ask, offering her another opportunity to leave, to make the smarter decision.

"I'm sure. Now, kiss me under the stars again."

I oblige, cupping her cheeks and pulling her mouth to mine. When we break apart, I wrap my arm around her shoulder, tucking her in tight to my side while we stand in the silence of the woods. The breeze is pleasant and the sky is clear, putting the stars on full display. While it's much quieter than in the city, the insects and night dwellers are out, chirping and singing to one another.

"It's beautiful here," Kaycia whispers. "Thank you for sharing it with me. For sharing all of it, Shane."

"Let me show you the house. You can shower if you want, or we can sit by the fire?"

"Let's shower," she replies, turning her face so I can see her wicked smile and the gleam in her eyes. Taking that as an invitation I scoop her up, carrying her in my arms back to the cabin.

Without pausing to show her the living space, I march us straight to the small bathroom and put her on her feet so I can get the warm water running. When I turn back to face her, she steps forward pulling my shirt over my head and tugging at the button of my jeans. "You better not hog the hot water, McKinley," she jests.

While I remove my boots and jeans, she strips out of her clothes until she's only in her thong. My nostrils flare at the scent of her arousal, making my cock ache with want. "Gods, you're beautiful. You remember what happened to the last pair of lacy panties that got in my way," I taunt, prowling closer to her and pulling her against me. "Unless you want *these* torn off you, I suggest you strip and get in the shower."

"Mmm, is that a threat or a promise?" She grips me in her palm, stroking over my length until I groan, but then steps back and takes her panties off, sliding past me with a hairsbreadth between our bare skin, and stepping into the heat of the shower. "Now, get in here."

Chapter 28
Kaycia

When Shane begins to rub his soapy hands over me, I can't help but let a little moan escape. His palm skates between my breasts, down my belly, and stops just above the apex of my thighs before returning on its path upwards. I arch my back, pressing my ass into his hard length, encouraging him to explore. In response, he chuckles against my neck and denies me.

On a second pass, he cups my breast, nipping at the side of my neck as he teases me, then slides his hand down between my legs. His other arm wraps around me, holding me tight as he wraps his palm around my throat and tilts my head back. "You heard what I said earlier. Words mean things to wolves, Kaycia."

"Yes," I mumble, trying to focus on his rough whisper while he slides two fingers into me.

"You're mine, baby girl. I don't want anyone else. Is

that what you want, too?" He begins to press the heel of his palm against my clit so I can't help but writhe against him.

"Yes. I want you. Just you," I whimper, riding his fingers to ease the ache between my thighs.

"Then tell me."

"I'm yours, Shane." My muscles are coiled tight, my release so close I groan the words. "I'm yours, and you're mine.

"Mine." His voice is ragged as he holds me against him and nips at my throat, his fingers speeding up. "Now, come for me, Kaycia."

I shatter around him, crying out as I come while he grips my throat gently and holds me tight. My legs are weak and shaky as he slides his hand from between them, running his palm over my hot skin as the shower steams up the small space.

"That's my girl," Shane murmurs as he nuzzles my neck. When he turns me to face him, he slants his mouth over mine, gripping my ass and holding me against him for a moment before he turns the shower off. "Now, let's get out of here so I can fuck you properly."

With a breathless giggle, I step onto the fluffy bathmat and Shane wraps a thick towel around me, pulling a second one from the cabinet over the toilet to use on himself, but it's not long before we're standing in the dissipating steam, arms wrapped around one another as we kiss with towels in a forgotten heap on the floor. When Shane drags his fingers over me, he mutters, "*Fuck*, you're dripping for me," igniting my core once more. "Let me go grab a condom."

Snagging his arm, I pull him back and explain, "I have an IUD, and I haven't been with anyone in over a year besides you. I've tested negative for everything. If you've tested, you don't need one. I just wasn't going to tell you that if this was a one-night thing."

"Shifters are immune to human infections, plus it's been a while for me, too." His eyes are dark with his arousal, pupils blown in the dim, steamy room as he skims my naked body, running a thumb over my lower lip. "Turn around." Shane spins me so I face the mirror over the sink, my hands gripping either side of the basin. My eyes are wild in the reflection, my desire evident in my flushed cheeks and swollen lips. "Look," he murmurs, turning my head with a gentle grip, so I can see the full-length mirror mounted on the door of what I assume is a closet. "You wanted me to fuck you in the bathroom that first night. Is it because you wanted to watch?"

"Yes," I whisper, shocking myself that I'm admitting my desires out loud, and gasping as he grips himself to run the tip of his cock through my wetness.

"Tell me what you want." Shane's voice is gravelly behind me.

"I want to watch you fuck me. I want to be dripping with *you* after you finish."

"Fucking hell, I'll give you whatever you want, Kaycia," Shane replies. He slides his palm up my spine, then pushes me forward so I lean over the sink. "Hang on, baby girl." His voice is harsh with need as I watch the reflection of him gripping my hip and sliding into me with one rough stroke.

Our combined gasps echo in my ears as he slides his hand up my body, caressing the sides of my waist, then tangling in my hair while he uses the other to hold my hip. He isn't gentle, but I can tell he's still holding back. Watching his muscles tense while he takes me makes me want to come undone at the sight of our joining.

"Harder, Shane," I moan, bracing myself with a hand on the backsplash. I want him to let go completely, to show me who he truly is. "Please, don't hold back."

The hand he has in my hair slips free, circling my throat and pulling me upright while I grip the sink. His other hand snakes forward to rub my clit and the change in angle is delicious, forcing me to cry out with pleasure as he grows wilder with his thrusts. As I watch in the mirror his eyes glow golden as he claims me, nuzzling his face against my throat and breathing in my scent. I tumble over the edge again as I watch our reflection, a guttural moan falling from my lips. If it weren't for the way he's holding me tight against him, I fear my legs would give out.

"You're mine," Shane groans with a final thrust as he reaches his own climax. "Mine," he whispers into my hair, breaths ragged and wistful as he repeats the word to himself.

"And you're mine," I softly reply, placing my hand over his where it still gently circles my throat.

"You're so fucking beautiful, Kaycia." His words bring

a darker flush to my skin as he pulls out of me and lets me lean forward against the counter. Stroking his long fingers over my swollen core, he smirks at me in our reflection in the mirror. "Is this what you wanted?" he asks, bringing my attention to our combined release coating between my legs and inner thighs.

A little moan escapes me before I breathe, "Yes." Nothing Shane's done makes me doubt myself, but hesitation rises in my mind anyway. Meeting his eyes in the mirror in front of us I wonder aloud, "Is that weird?"

"No." He plants a kiss on my shoulder. "Nothing that brings you pleasure is weird to me. I told you; I'll give you whatever you want. And *this* is hot as fuck." He slides over me once more, grinning against my bare skin as his fingers scramble my thoughts and crush my self-doubt. "Whoever made you think otherwise is an idiot. Let's get cleaned up and go sit by the fire. I want to give you a break before round two."

I shiver with anticipation and catch my breath while he reaches for our towels.

We spend the rest of the evening, and deep into the night, sitting around the fire pit and pointing out the different stars while sipping our drinks—whiskey for him, wine for me—and burning marshmallows over the flames.

"So, now that everything is out in the open, tell me

about your family and where you're from," I prod after a particularly burnt marshmallow. "If you want," I amend when he looks pained at my request.

"I grew up in a cabin in the mountains. More remote than this, but the house was bigger. The pack surrounded us on the land in smaller ones. Each wolf territory is similar, the entire pack is like family, whether you share blood or not." His voice is strained, and his eyes are misty with remembrance.

"You miss having people around you, don't you?"

"There are people everywhere in the city. I'm never alone." His eyes flash gold with his sarcasm, reflecting the firelight.

"You know what I mean. *Your* people. People who know you. Not strangers on the street."

"It was hard, really hard, for a while. I happened to run into Raquel one day and we got to talking bikes. Her hackles were up immediately since she smelled that I was a predator, but she warmed up quick. Then she introduced me to Max, and later, Jamila. They're my pack now, I guess."

"And me."

"And you," he replies, reaching across the narrow gap between our chairs to take my hand. "I'm glad you hit me in the face with your canvas. It gave me the excuse I needed to talk to you."

"Ha!" I laugh. "You make it sound like I planned that."

"Oh, you didn't? What about the air conditioner?"

"I'm not that sneaky. It took you long enough though, I

don't know why you thought you needed an excuse. I'd been drooling over you since I moved in," I tease, feeling my cheeks heat.

"Oh, yeah? Just too old-fashioned to ask me out yourself?" Shane tugs on my hand, drawing me out of my seat and into his lap.

"Too shy, maybe? Too focused on my own shit and getting settled in the city. I'm sure I would have gotten up the nerve eventually." With a smile, I press a kiss to his forehead, then his cheek, then finally his lips.

"Your turn," he mutters against my mouth when I pull back slightly.

"My turn?"

"Tell me about where you're from, not just the overview you rattle off when everyone asks."

"Not much to tell."

Shane gives me a look that tells me he doesn't buy it.

"I mean it! I don't have a secret fanged and fluffy side, everything is pretty much out in the open already. Small-town girl, went to college close by, got a boring job, lived in a boring apartment in the suburbs, dated boring men. I did everything I was told I was supposed to do." Bitterness coats my words, even if a pang of homesickness weaves through my chest.

"Am I just another way to shed your boring past?"

"What?" I pull away sharply, but he laughs in response at what I assume is the shock on my face.

"I'm joking, Kaycia."

"Well, you're certainly *not* boring, in any sense of the

word." Relieved, I sink against him, resting my head on his shoulder as we stare at the charred wood and red and orange coals in the firepit.

"Did one of those boring men make you think you couldn't ask for what you wanted?"

"What do you mean?"

"Earlier, you asked me if I thought you were weird for telling me what turns you on." He nuzzles my throat, missing the deep blush that coats my cheeks at the memory.

"Oh. No. I mean, maybe? One of my exes never really wanted to try anything new. He expected me to worship him and that I would bow to him at the altar of matrimony and motherhood. He was sorely mistaken. I got sick of his shit and broke up with him. That was a long time ago."

I'm so thankful I didn't listen to my mother's encouragement to settle down. I would have been miserable.

"Good. You deserve to be the one who's worshipped and satisfied."

I blush, wondering if my cheeks can get any hotter than they are at this point. "I haven't been comfortable enough with other guys to tell them what I like."

The heat spreads to my belly when he runs his hand up my thigh and nips my throat. "I'm glad you're comfortable with me." When I huff a little laugh in response, he holds me close, turning my face so I have to look into his eyes. "I mean it, I'll give you whatever you want, Kaycia."

After a long kiss, he adds, "I'm glad you came to

Argent and ended up next door. Even if I'm sorry about the danger that being with me brings to your life."

"I am, too. I knew it was the right choice for me, even when it was hard. You're the right choice, too. I'm not going anywhere, Shane."

Relaxed, I press my forehead against Shane's for a moment, breathing him in while the fire burns low and the crickets and frogs sing us a symphony.

Chapter 29
Shane

"I'll be back in a little while—I need to run," I whisper to Kaycia. I'm not sure she's awake, wrapped in the sheets and cuddled under the quilt on my bed.

"Okay," she sighs, not opening her eyes.

"Stay inside, I'll lock it with the keypad." I kiss her forehead, receiving a smile and nod in response, before I leave her sated and dozing to slip out the front door of the cabin. I don't anticipate she'll wake until morning after the excitement of the night and our encore of the bathroom after we came in from the firepit.

Though the moon is almost full, the sharp urge to shift that tingled under my skin last month has dulled to a manageable craving. Even so, I can't wait to strip off my jeans and shift into my wolf. My senses are further heightened and Kaycia's scent clings to me, overpowering even the wildness of the woods and the still pond. Stretching, I howl once, even though I know no one will reply to my call, then trot into the tree line before breaking into a full run.

The freedom of the wilderness, and the warmth of knowing Kaycia accepts all of me, lifts my spirits more than they've been since before my exile. I spend a half hour racing through the trees before backtracking to rejoin Kaycia in the cabin.

We sleep late the next morning and I wake rested in a way I haven't in years. I'm not certain if it's because I was able to shift freely and run, or if it's the lightness in spirit I feel now that Kaycia knows my secret.

Despite the positive developments in our relationship, worry about the Ross pack's goons still vexes me, like an annoying song that you can't seem to get out of your head no matter how hard you try. But skinny-dipping in the pond, and showing Kaycia the sunset as the sky turns from blue to pink and orange to twilight over the forest, keeps the tension safely at bay.

"I wish I had my canvases and paints," she whispers, eyes wide as the colors fade and the stars begin to illuminate.

"We can bring them out sometime. Max doesn't use his truck often; we can pack it all up and bring it."

"I'd love that," she answers, snuggling against my side where we sit on the blanket by the pond. "Maybe I could start a new collection. It's too late to start anything new for the exhibition, but I can plan for next time."

"Thinking positively and planning for the next one, huh? Are your parents going to fly up to see this one? Will I get to meet them?" As soon as I ask, I regret it.

"Not likely." The excitement in her voice bleeds out and she toys with one of the blades of grass next to the blanket. "They don't seem to think an art show is worth getting on a plane. I even offered to buy the tickets for them, but they haven't answered me. My friend Meg wanted to come, but she has too much on her plate right now."

"Well, I'll be there. And so will Quel and Max and Jamila."

I squeeze her hand. I haven't met them, and I only have one side of the story, but irritation at Kaycia's family smolders in my chest. The desire to protect her, even from petty criticisms from her family, is deeply rooted in me already. Despite my epic fuck ups, I know my parents still love me and would be proud of the life I've built here, even if it's not the one they would have chosen for me. It hurts to know she doesn't think her parents feel the same, just because she made a change for her own happiness.

"Thank you. For all of this. Coming to save me, the cabin, the weekend. Trusting me with your secret."

"Thank you for not running off screaming into the forest." I chuckle, but it's half-hearted. A little part of me still worries she'll run once the romance of the cabin wears off.

Kaycia slides her fingers up my arm and across my chest, letting it drift up to my cheek so she can pull my attention fully toward her. "Nothing you can say or do will scare me away. I know I'm safe with you, Shane. Plus"— she shrugs nonchalantly, but smiles gleefully— "I've always wanted a pet. You're like having scary dog and scary boyfriend privileges all wrapped into one."

I open my mouth to give her shit, but before I can speak, she adds, "Shut up and kiss me." Smiling against my mouth she pulls me closer, laying back on the blanket. Kaycia guides me to follow until I'm propped above her on my elbows. Our gentle kisses grow urgent, and we make love under the moonlight.

———

"Ready to go back to reality?" I ask, washing the dishes from breakfast while Kaycia carefully folds her few belongings and places them in her backpack.

"No, but we must. My plants need water and I need to get some ideas sketched out. I was dumb to forget my sketchbook in the hustle to pack my bag." She's buoyant this morning, her blonde ponytail bouncing as she sweeps through to make sure she's grabbed everything.

"You were under duress. And, yes. The plants. Good for them that I have to earn a living or I just might keep you to myself out here."

Kaycia's chuckle drifts from the other end of the house. "Busy week?"

"I have three bikes to finish working on. Raquel said the parts are all in, and she wasn't happy about having to hold everything down alone unexpectedly for quite so long."

Raquel's texts have gotten snippier as the days pass. One of my long-time customers is anxious to have his bike back and she's already swamped.

With everything packed on the bike and the cabin locked up, Kaycia zips her jacket and I hand over her helmet. She looks over at the cabin longingly and sighs, "I miss it already," before sliding the helmet on.

I clip the strap of my own helmet and smile, waiting for her to slide behind me and get comfortable. "I know. I always feel that way. We'll come back soon. I promise."

I pat her thigh, earning a little squeeze from her in return before starting the engine. With the bike rumbling beneath us, I rest my palm over her hand where she has it covering my heart and wonder if she can feel how hard it beats with her nearby. If she can tell how full it feels since she walked up behind me by the pond. It's far too early for me to be making declarations of love, even if that's what I was doing by claiming her as "mine", but I can't deny what I feel for this brave human woman. I can only dream she feels the same.

I pull up to the curb in front of our apartment building a few hours later, after we stopped for lunch at a favorite café on the route back to the city. The concrete and civilization feel heavy compared to the freedom of the rural getaway. As soon as her head is free of the helmet, Kaycia

starts muttering about her plants and concepts for paintings, as though her mind is so full of ideas she can't parse
out what she should do first. My warm smile drops almost
immediately when the exterior door swings open and we
step onto the dingy tile of the main foyer. I silence her with
a quick grab of her forearm, pulling her back from the
stairwell.

"Hush."

"Excuse me?" Kaycia retorts, looking up at me in shock
which quickly turns to hurt. As though I'd dare speak to
her that way unless something was wrong.

"Something isn't right," I reply, loosening my grip and
stepping in front of her as I scent the air.

"What is it?" she whispers urgently, understanding
that I wasn't being a bossy asshole.

"I don't know. Follow behind me and run if I tell
you to."

"Shane... you're scaring me."

I glance over my shoulder at the tremble in her tone.

"I know," I answer grimly, breathing deeply to identify
the scent of an unknown wolf all over our building,
someone different than the one from the grocery store. My
phone begins to ping with text notifications a moment
later, but I silence it in my pocket with a flip of the switch,
too focused on keeping Kaycia safe as we begin to ascend
the stairs.

Nothing is amiss for the first two floors, aside from the
stranger's scent, but when we reach our shared third-story
landing, I suck in a startled breath at what awaits us.

Fuck.

"Kaycia, wait! Let me look—" But she's already pushed past me before I can finish speaking. Her door is splintered, the deadbolt is still extended from the lock of the door, but the frame is busted where it was forced open. Deep gouges from claws mar the exterior and, even from my vantage point in the hall, I can see that broken ceramic and dirt litter the floor.

"Oh no! No no no!" Kaycia's sobs echo through her destroyed apartment. I stand helpless in the doorway as she drops to her knees. Paintings—finished and in progress —are shredded, as are blank canvasses that were stored against the wall. The colorful remnants are strewn about like confetti from a cruel celebration. The handmade pots that held her beloved plants are crushed all through the studio, dirt spattered on the walls where they were thrown, and the greenery lies wilted where it landed.

In the center of the room, Kaycia cradles a single untouched canvas in her lap. The only one not torn into strips. The one of me watching the sunset on the neighboring balcony. My chest breaks open at the sight of her anguish and the tears streaking her cheeks.

All my fault.

"Why would someone do this?" she asks, hiccupping on her despair. "They didn't take anything, they just... ruined it all."

"Because of me. I let them know you're a way to get at me. I'm so sorry, Kaycia. This is what I worried would happen and now I've ruined everything for you."

"Fuck that," Kaycia snarls, wiping her face on the slick sleeve of her leather jacket which does nothing to dry her tears. Her sadness flipping to fury so quickly surprises me and has me unsure of whether to step nearer or not. I expected her to wail and tell me to leave, but I should have expected more from my girl. "And fuck them," she adds, standing and clutching the half-finished painting. "They can't have you and they can't use me to get you."

Before I know what she's doing, she's in my arms, clinging to me, gripping the back of my jacket in her fingers, and letting the canvas drop between us.

"Did they get yours, too?" she asks, sniffling and glancing around.

From this angle, her easel—or what's left of it—is in pieces, and oozing paint tubes are crushed to create a messy rainbow smear near the sliding door.

Anger boils in my chest at the undeserved destruction. They'll pay for this. I'll hunt them down and take care of it.

"Let's go see," is all I say.

With my jaw set, and my hand in hers, we walk back out to the landing, stepping over the dirt and broken ceramic as best we can. My door is marked with similar claw marks, but the lock must have been picked because the door is closed and the knob turns without effort. They wanted us drawn to Kaycia's first, knowing it would hurt her worse. Glasses and plates lay shattered on the floor, my linens are shredded, and my bookshelf is toppled, but the destruction doesn't hurt as much. I never had as much *me* in my apartment as Kaycia did. These are all things I can easily replace. They know the most important thing to me is *her*.

I made an error in threatening the shifter at the store and attacking the man sent to harass her. I made it too obvious that she was mine, even if she didn't know it yet.

I've placed a target on her back.

"Shane," Kaycia whispers. "Who's this?" She stands at my kitchen island, staring at a piece of shiny paper lying on the granite in front of her. When I reach her side, my heart tumbles.

The photo is old, but I remember the day vividly. I can almost feel the heat of lazy teenage summers again. We were still pups who had just begun to shift, excited about the potential for the future. Even if our packs historically had a rivalry, it mostly lived on through jest and jeers, like fans of opposing sports teams razzing one another. The bloody debts of our ancestors didn't matter to us. Animosity wasn't something we could imagine would ever fester.

Staring up at me from the counter, the print slightly out of focus, are Ethan, Logan, Colton, and me—lanky in our youth with wide grins and arms slung over each other's sunburned shoulders next to the pond we spent hours fishing and swimming in.

Vermillion oil paint from Kaycia's apartment slashes across Ethan and Logan's faces.

And mine.

Chapter 30
Kaycia

I pack a bag, gathering clean clothes, underwear, and other odds and ends that survived the break-in while Shane quietly sweeps up the disaster of my apartment. His silence is tangible. An unwelcome guest hovering amidst the chaos. The tremor of his muscles while he stared at the picture on his counter betrayed the calm front he was trying to hold together for me. The way he flexed his fingers into white-knuckled fists made me wonder if he would have shifted and added to the destruction if I wasn't present.

To say I'm upset is an understatement.

I'm devastated.

All the energy I've funneled into my paintings, my apartment, my life here. All the money I've spent on supplies and decorations to make this a home. All my soul poured into my art to ward off homesickness and fear. Torn into tatters.

But I'm also enraged.

Old me, the me who felt alone even amongst friends and family, who couldn't bear the idea of making a decision that wasn't influenced by someone else's idea of propriety, would have gone running for the hills, or at least the closest airport, by now.

To be used as a pawn to get to Shane is infuriating and I refuse to be frightened away from him over this. His past was a mistake, he paid his price, and I won't abandon him now. No matter how many times he insists we shouldn't be together for my safety. I refuse to play into the tactics of these monsters. This warfare on his heart.

Maybe a few years ago I would have played it safe, even if it broke both our hearts. But they picked the wrong woman to use as leverage, now.

Not this Kaycia.

I accepted Shane's reality this past weekend. All the messy, guilt-ridden, broken parts. Just like he accepts mine. I won't turn my back on him now. I'll make sure I know how to protect myself. I won't give them what they want or let him give them anything either.

"I'm ready," I croak, my voice hoarse from the tears I couldn't seem to stem. At first, they were from shock and fear, then sadness. But then they burned hot with my anger, cleansing me before leaving me empty and resolute.

Propping the broom against the wall, Shane dumps the overflowing dustpan in the trash before snagging his own backpack.

"I'll text maintenance and let them know they need to

repair this," he says as we pull the broken door closed, even if there's nothing for it to secure to anymore. Looking defeated, his head hangs as he adds, "I'm so sorry, Kaycia."

"Stop apologizing!" I snap, stopping him with a tug on his arm. "*You* didn't fuck up my apartment. They did."

"But your work—"

"I'm pissed about what they damaged, but at least the major pieces are already at the gallery. Their security is good. Unless they want video footage to go to the police they can't hurt it."

"No, they won't want that," he agrees, jaw tight and eyes downcast. "They just want me."

"Well, they can't have you." I possessively hold his face between my palms. My voice doesn't waver when I force him to look into my eyes. "You're *mine*, remember?"

The fire returns to his eyes when I say those words, gold glinting behind the misery as he straightens his spine. "I remember."

"Have you told Raquel and Max what happened?"

"Yeah, Quel called me and said there weren't any unusual scents at the shop, but they're both on alert. This happened hours ago, probably when it was still dark. No one comes up to this floor but us. I don't know if they were watching the apartment or what. I'm surprised no one reported the noise, but the second-floor neighbors leave early for work at the hospital, so maybe they're on shift. I'll take a different route out of town this time, just in case."

He's standing a few stairs down while I'm still on the landing, so our eyes are on the same level. Shane takes advantage of the proximity, pulling me close for a soft kiss. "Max said he can bring out whatever you need for work this week, just text him a list."

"Thanks," I answer, my chest squeezing with affection for the flirty falcon shifter. "I'll figure out what I need once we're back at the cabin. I'll check in with the gallery and let Kelly know I'm a little out of pocket."

"I think—" Shane sucks in a sharp breath mid-sentence as if he needs to fortify himself. "I think I need to call my parents. Something must have happened to cause things to suddenly escalate like this."

"We can figure it all out once we get settled. Together." With a sharp nod and a tense jaw, Shane agrees.

"Let's go, baby girl," he murmurs, gripping my hand while we hurry down the stairs to his waiting motorcycle.

He stops in the middle of the sidewalk, still and silent as he takes several deep inhales and scans the surroundings. I assume everything is clear when he waves toward the bike, taking my bag and tucking it in one side case, then stows his in the other. We both pull our helmets on and mount up, my arms clinging to him. It was less than an hour ago that we were like this, riding a high from a weekend well spent wrapped around one another. Now, we return in a much more somber mood.

On our first trip to the remote cabin, we took a shorter, direct route. This time, Shane insists on the longer way in case anyone follows. We ride across one of the metal bridges over the river that hugs half of the sparkling city of steel and glass. Each thud of the wheels over the bridge supports jolts me and I fight to keep from squeezing Shane too tight. I'd looked forward to a break from riding earlier, my body already sore from the trip, but I ignore the ache now, clinging on. If Shane minds, he doesn't show it, patting my hands once before resettling his on the handlebar. The little thrill of fear from our first ride has dissipated to a pleasant warmth in my chest, and I try to concentrate on the wind on my cheeks instead of the other emotions the day has brought. The unsettling welcome home ruined the glow of the weekend and it's easier to think about the physical world as we race to the cabin.

Once we clear the city completely, the roads pass through suburbs, and then turn more rural. The pastoral calmness is soothing, and I turn my mind to the list of supplies I need to compile for Max, focusing on the things within my control until Shane finds out more about the situation from his family.

Stretching my arms over my head is heavenly when we finally reach the cabin. I can't suppress a little groan of pleasure at the change in position. Our more circuitous route took about an hour longer than I expected, weaving through small towns and remote forests, and has my legs feeling like jelly. Happily, we didn't see any suspicious vehicles following behind us on the remote roads. I breathe a sigh of relief when Shane confirms no new scents linger anywhere along the perimeter of the cabin.

Was it really just this morning that we left this same place in the rose-colored haze of a newly minted relationship?

Shane's expression is guarded and tight. His jaw muscles tense and his lips flatten into a firm line bracketed with worry as he pulls out his cell phone with a heavy sigh. "I guess I need to get this over with. You can unpack inside, or go out by the pond. Whatever you want. Just stay where I can see or scent you, okay?"

His suggestion indicates he wants to call his family in private. I wrap my arms around him, kissing him deeply before ducking into the cabin to unpack and make some tea. I'm not sure what that conversation will reveal for us, or how it will impact Shane emotionally after everything that's been building these past few weeks. I hope the call is less tense than the recent ones with my own family, but I recognize that the strain and distance is much greater for Shane. Upon reflection, I decide tea may not be strong enough.

Chapter 31
Shane

My hands shake as I open my contacts and find the number I never thought I'd be calling again. I don't really need to search for it. I know the digits by heart. They're the ones I wrote my entire childhood for emergency contacts, permission slips, everything. But I haven't dialed it in a decade. My heart beats rapidly, a painful ache in my chest, and the rush of blood in my ears nearly masks the sound of the phone ringing through the speaker.

"Hello?" my mother's sweet voice answers, a tone of hope reaching me through the line. She wouldn't recognize my number. She hasn't known how to reach me since I was exiled.

"Hey, Mama," I reply, swallowing thickly against the tears that burn in the back of my eyes. The comforting sound of her voice soothes me even at this distance.

"*Shane?*" she whisper-shouts in surprise, making me wonder if someone else is home. She speaks softly after the initial surprise wears off. "Baby, is that you? What's happened?"

"Well, I was hoping you'd be able to tell me. Someone's been looking for me."

A door slams in the background and a woman starts chattering to my mother. I listen for a moment before recognizing my sister's voice. "Lana, hush," my mother scolds away from the phone, then says to me, "What do you mean looking for you? Where are you?"

"You know I can't tell you that. I just need to know if there's been any changes in the packs. Ross enforcers have been all over me these past weeks. They mentioned a new alpha," I explain. "I thought I was through with this shit. I don't know how they found me or why they're hunting again."

I sit in one of the chairs near the fire pit but stand again and start pacing between the house and the pond as we talk, unable to settle anywhere. It's been so long since I've spoken to my family and the sting of homesickness I thought had died years ago begins to throb in earnest, reminding me how badly I miss them.

"I wouldn't have called if it wasn't important. I know you can't get wrapped up in this."

"James Ross died. Three months ago. The mourning period is over and Colton has taken control without a challenge. It must be what's changed."

"Mama? Who are you talking to?" My sister's voice is closer than before and filled with concern. She's twenty-five now, and yet I still picture her as the scrappy teen she was when I was sent away. I've missed so much of their lives.

"Don't tell her," I snap. "I can't risk anyone finding out I called. But they've found me and they're threatening me and my girl. If they come around there, let me know. I wanted to warn you something was different."

"I understand. Are you okay?" My mother's tone is gentle, but her voice catches, spilling over with emotions she's held in. "We miss you so much."

The lump in my throat threatens to choke me and I wipe at my eyes before I answer her. "I'm doing well. Things had gotten *really* good lately. Until this shit began."

"I'm so glad to hear it. But I'm sorry they're giving you trouble again. Let me know if you need anything, regardless of the rules. I never should have let this happen in the first place."

As if she could have stopped it. My father is the second to the alpha of our pack, but neither he nor my mother could have changed the ruling, we all know it. A phantom pain in my forearm drags my eyes to the scar where my pack mark was carved from my skin as I remember that night. My father had to hold my small, fierce mother back as she screamed obscenities while they physically severed me from the pack.

"Sean isn't home, or I'd let you talk to him. Everything is shaken up right now with the new leadership. The rivalry had died while old man Ross was in charge, but with Colton taking over everything has become strained. Things are changing. It was already a bit tense at home since Aubrey's made the shift, so this is just an added layer of stress for your father."

"Aubrey made his shift already?" My little brother was almost ten when I left, of course he has. I can't imagine him as a man now. I feel guilty I'm not there to help teach him how to manage his wolf. "Damn, I've missed so much."

"I know. It isn't your fault." My mother soothes me even if her words are false.

It is all my fault. Because I couldn't control my temper.

"*Mama*," Lana pesters, "Is that who I think it is?"

"Lana, damn it. I said *go on*," my mother chides, then says, "Listen, I need to go, okay?"

"Yeah, I understand. You can reach me here if anything comes up. I love you." I swallow down my emotions and try to keep my voice from cracking.

"You too, baby. Goodbye." My mother's sadness is palpable through the line, and when she disconnects the call, I stand staring at the blank screen with only my hollow-eyed reflection looking back at me. I can't even clearly remember my parents' faces. I wonder if I'd know my brother and sister if I passed them on the street. Would they know *me?*

Slipping my phone into the pocket of my jeans I press the heels of my hands to my eyes and tilt my head back. The cool breeze off the pond and sounds of the woods surrounding the cabin soothe me, even if I can barely control the shaking that's taking over as I fight the urge to shift and run.

"Shane?" I spin, a startled snarl on my lips, to find

Kaycia holding two beer bottles. She steps back quickly before I blink away any of my wolf that might have shown.

"Your eyes," she whispers, cocking her head. She's not afraid, but she's wary nonetheless.

"Sorry. Gods, Kaycia I'm fucking sorry about all this." I blink a few times, hoping the gold in my eyes has faded back to their regular hazel before I approach her and take the proffered bottle.

"I can go grab you a whiskey if you need something stronger," she suggests with a nod at the beer, giving a little sideways smile. "Did you reach them? Are they okay? Are *you* okay?" she asks, pulling my free hand into hers and tugging me closer.

"I talked to my mom. We haven't spoken since I left home, but she told me the rival pack's alpha died. His remaining son took over and it seems whatever truce there was between me and their pack is null and void to him. Colton vowed he'd never forgive me for what I did. It explains why this is happening now."

"So, what do we do?" she asks.

"We?" I ask with a scoff, pulling my hand free from her gentle grip and taking another drink from my bottle. "*You* should be running away from me and working on your exhibit. I should be running too." I scrape my hand across the back of my neck, then drag it over my face where days of stubble are rough against my palm.

"I already told you. I'm not going anywhere unless you make me." Kaycia pulls my hand away again, cradling it between her soft ones.

"If I were a better man, I'd have Jamila or Max come get you and take you to a hotel."

"Shane..." she starts, gripping my hand tighter in hers as though I might slip away from her.

"But gods help me, I'm not a better man."

I pull her toward me, slanting my mouth across hers as she sighs and melts against me. The feel of her softness pressing against me, the scent and taste of her enveloping me, soothes the ragged ache of regret in my heart and fills in the cracks where it broke so many years ago. I can't bear to send her away, even if it's for her protection. I lost so much when I was forced to leave my family and my pack. I won't lose her because of my fatal mistake, too.

Chapter 32
Kaycia

Shane's kisses are urgent, bruising my mouth as he tilts my head back and swipes my lips with his tongue so I open to him. The gold of his eyes startled me when he spun around moments ago, but instead of responding with fear of the animal within him, I find that I crave it.

I crave everything about him.

What's wrong with you? I think, even as I let the beer bottle slip from my fingers to thud and spill foam on the soft grass so I can trace the lines of his body with both hands. I recognize the risk I'm accepting by staying with him. This relationship is new, and I've faced more drama and danger in these past weeks than I ever imagined I would. But at the same time, it feels right to be here. Shane understands me better than the people I've known my whole life. He'd stand beside me, so I won't abandon him now. Especially with that haunted look in his eyes.

Running my hands down his stomach I press my palm

against his cock, straining beneath the worn denim of his jeans. The groan Shane exhales against my mouth sends heat pooling in my belly, coiling with anticipation. It chases away any second thoughts I might be having about my choices.

"Let me help you forget," I whisper, sucking his lip into my mouth to coax another moan from him. "Just for a little while, let's both forget. We can figure out the rest tomorrow."

Dropping his own bottle to the ground, Shane scoops me into his arms and carries me toward the cabin. Staring over his shoulder at the blue sky and lush emerald forest, I imagine painting a shadowed couple with the same background. A contented huff escapes me, drawing Shane's attention.

"What is it?" he murmurs with a shy smile and hooded gaze.

"Just thinking that you really might be my muse."

"I'm flattered," he replies with a chuckle, climbing the few steps to the deck, then carrying me over the threshold and pushing the door closed with his hip.

Shane carries me through the small living space and into the bedroom with its cozy quilts and wall of windows mirroring the openness of the front rooms of the cabin. He sets me gently at the end of the bed, then steps back to kick off his boots. I do the same with my shoes, but before he can do anything else, I grab the waistband of his jeans and tug him closer, gazing up at him as my chest warms with desire.

Shane's eyes no longer look gold or hazel at this angle, they're nearly black with need as he watches me unbutton his jeans, and then pull the zipper down so I can tug them off his hips. I stroke him, teasing him through the thin fabric of his boxer briefs so that he tips his head back with a ragged breath. From where I sit it's easy to push his soft cotton tee up to reveal his stomach, then chest. He helps by pulling it over his head with one hand while I explore the planes of his body with my lips and tongue, nipping with my teeth so he hisses and his muscles tense. After a moment his hand settles under my chin, tilting my face up so I meet his hungry gaze.

"What do you want, Kaycia?" he murmurs, running his thumb over my cheekbone and then threading his fingers through my loose hair.

"To make you feel good, Shane," I whisper. "To show you you're not alone."

For a moment, I worry I've ruined the mood. His eyes are glassy and far away as he swallows and cradles my head gently, but I proceed to trail open-mouthed kisses down his stomach, slipping off the edge of the bed to kneel before him and pull a heavy sigh from his lips. He tightens his grip on my hair as I smile mischievously, biting my lip and meeting his gaze while I pull his boxer briefs down. When I take him into my mouth, he closes his eyes and tips his head back with a moan. I echo him with a little whimper of my own as I tease him and slide him farther into my mouth, chasing my lips with one hand wrapped around him and letting him guide the speed with his increasingly rough grasp tangled in my hair. The dichotomy of his gentle sadness earlier and the pleasurable roughness makes my stomach flip and my core heat with desire. With a growl Shane suddenly pulls me away from him and to my feet.

"Don't you want—" I start, but his lips crash against mine, his hand clutching the back of my neck as our tongues dance and breath becomes one.

"Not yet," he groans into my mouth. "I want to get lost in you, Kaycia."

I don't answer. I don't need to as I wrap my arms around him and our mouths meet once more. Shane turns so he sits on the bed, pulling me between his bare thighs and stripping my shirt and bra off. My breasts feel heavy with need as my nipples pebble from the cool air, then from his attention, as he runs a thumb over one while taking the other into his hot mouth. A rumble of approval ripples through him when I gasp at the sensation of him nipping at my flushed skin.

Moments later he lays back, pulling me atop him until all either of us can think about is the pleasure we find in the other's embrace.

Laying together after, I watch Shane's lashes flutter while he dozes. Although he's sleeping, his lips are tense and his brow is furrowed as if the worries of the day haunt even his dreams. Moving slowly so I don't wake him, I cuddle up against his side and stroke his hair, easing the longer strands from across his forehead. His breathing pauses momentarily, making me hold my breath, fearing

I've woken him, but his face quickly relaxes and he seems to drift deeper into sleep.

When his breathing evens back out I whisper softly, "I may be a fool, but I think I love you, Shane McKinley."

I tell myself it's far too soon for me to admit this to him. I'd never speak the words out loud if he was awake, embarrassed by how swiftly I've fallen. But something about our connection has deepened even more after today, and I can't stop myself from confessing it to him. Even if he can't hear me.

Especially, because he can't hear me.

I stroke his hair once more before rolling onto my side to watch the birds on the feeder hanging from the big tree behind the house, mentally compiling a list of supplies to request from the city.

Chapter 33
Shane

I'm glad Kaycia rolls away from me after she secretly whispers that she loves me. Or at least thinks she does it in secret. That way she can't see how hard I fight to hide the smile on my face, or hear the pounding of my heart. I'm fairly certain she would see it beating through my chest if she looked close enough.

Because I love her, too.

I already knew it but didn't want to scare her off by confessing it to her so early in our relationship. After today I didn't want to tell her because I didn't want her to feel obligated to stick with me in the face of the destruction that's chasing me down. But now I'm just a chicken shit for not opening my eyes and replying to her outright. I only held back because she whispered it so softly, obviously thinking I was asleep. If she's not ready to tell me when I'm conscious, I don't want to make her feel more vulnerable than she already does. Just knowing she feels the same way is enough for me.

After about twenty minutes, Kaycia quietly rolls off the bed, her bare footsteps are hardly audible as she tiptoes toward the bathroom. After about five more minutes she slips out of the bedroom and the sounds of pots and pans carefully being removed from the cabinet echo through the quiet of the cabin. Soon after, the scent of cooking drags me from the bed. Standing before the windows along the back wall, I stretch and smile as the sun sinks behind the tree line. Though Kaycia and I both love the stars, I can't help but think of sunset as our time of day now. Slipping into a pair of jeans, I make my way to the kitchen to find Kaycia in my discarded tee and a pair of panties, stirring a pot of marinara while spaghetti boils.

Leaning against the pantry door I clear my throat with a smile. "Getting domestic for me?"

"Hey. Did I wear you out?" she teases, spinning to face me. "Nice little nap?"

"Probably the best of my life," I murmur, wrapping her in my arms and burying my face in her loose hair. She grins against my shoulder but doesn't realize that I'm referring to her whispered confession, not the sex beforehand. Chuckling, Kaycia pulls away and turns off the little kitchen timer.

"Grab us something to drink while I finish this up. I hope it's okay that I snooped in the pantry and cooked whatever I could find."

"Anything you do is fine with me, baby girl. I'll have

Max pick up some groceries on the way out, too. We can grill out while he's here. Text me your list and I'll have him bring it out."

Sharing space in the small kitchen is a different kind of dance than I've performed before. I make a pitcher of iced tea, while Kaycia stirs the pasta and heats the sauce. The casual domesticity is its own kind of seduction. It's the kind of thing a man dreams about, but doesn't ever fully admit to wanting until the right woman comes along.

Each time I brush against her, moving between the cabinets, the fridge, and the table, sends little lightning bolts shooting through me. She smiles when I spill the tea, pouring it while distracted by her bending over to find a colander and I laugh in return while soaking it up with a dishtowel. We avoid the heavy topic of our damaged apartments, making small talk and flirting over our pasta.

"Did you use the entire container of parmesan?" she asks with mock horror.

"Hey, I am who I am, okay?"

"Of all the things I've learned about you, I never expected such a thing."

I wink and reply, "I'm sure I still have surprises for you that will top this." She blushes and smiles, but no further retort follows.

After our meal, I pile the dishes in the sink and pull out a box of boozy popsicles that were left after a long holiday weekend. Despite the slight freezer burn, I can't deny the appeal of watching Kaycia enjoy hers. I kiss the sticky remnants from her mouth before we retire to the chairs around the fire pit. The weather is starting to offer the barest hint of autumn, turning cool in the evenings this far north of the city. Kaycia wraps herself in one of the quilts from the couch and stares into the fire.

"I want you to teach me how I can defend myself," she finally says after long minutes of silence, surprising me with the topic.

"Kaycia, shifters are stronger than humans. Even if I taught you how to throw a punch, your best bet is to not be in their crosshairs at all." I sigh, readying to remind her that she should get out of town instead of trying to fight back. "I can have Max bring you a bag. He can take you to the airport."

"*Stop.*" Kaycia's voice is harsher than I've ever heard, even when she was upset earlier. "I'm not *going* anywhere. I'm *not* leaving you. So, stop thinking you're going to send me away or that I'm going to run. Even if that isn't a good enough reason for you, which it should be, I still have the gallery to answer to. I'm not risking my reputation with Kelly or ruining my exhibition by disappearing. Plus, I'm broke. I can't afford to just hop on a plane or check into a hotel for an extended vacation." She pauses, taking a deep breath before meeting my eyes. "Look, I know I can't physically overpower them, but I want you to help me improve my chances. Something."

"Have you ever shot a gun before?"

"I have. Not in a long time, but I shot BB guns and pistols when I was a kid at my grandpa's farm."

With a deep pull on my beer, I relent. "I'll teach you

how to use the shotgun I keep here and see how you do with one of my pistols. I'll ask Quel to come out with Max. She's strong because she's a shifter, but she's also lived alone as a woman in the city for a long time. She can give you some tips on how to get out of trouble if it comes down to it and you don't have a weapon. Especially if they send another of their human buddies."

"Thank you," she whispers. Her tone pulls my attention from the fire to her face where I find tears welling in her eyes.

Shit.

"Kaycia, what's wrong?"

"I..." She takes a steadying breath and wipes at her eyes. "I'm just really glad we met and...well, I'm just a little scared. Are they going to hurt you?"

"Come here," I whisper, pulling her from her seat to join me in my lap. "I'm glad we met too. If they hurt me, it won't be anything that I can't handle, okay? But I'll be damned if they hurt you."

Kaycia tucks her head against my chest and I hold her close. "Shane..." she whispers again, hesitating as her heart rate increases subtly and her scent shifts enough to tell me she's anxious.

"Yeah?"

"I...well...I..." She toys with the hem of my shirt, not meeting my eyes.

"I know, baby girl." With a squeeze I sit back so I can see her face before I continue, "I love you, too."

Now, with the tension broken, her tears are accompanied by a smile. I chuckle as she playfully smacks me on the chest. "You weren't sleeping earlier, were you? You sneak!"

"No, I was not. But I do love you, Kaycia. I will give my life to protect you, even if loving me is what puts you in danger in the first place. Do you understand? They're *not* going to hurt you."

"I love you, Shane. Even if you turn into a fur ball and have brought more drama to my world in the last month than in my entire life."

"Living in the city will do that, huh? Never a dull moment."

"Ha. Ha. Let's go inside now?"

I brush a soft kiss across her brow, tilt her chin up with my index finger before placing a soft one on her mouth to match, then let her pull me to my feet and lead me back into the cabin.

———

Two days later, Max and Raquel roll into the driveway, Max's truck loaded up with canvases, an assortment of paints and brushes, and various art supplies, along with bags of groceries. Kaycia skips off the front deck and wraps each of them in a hug before helping to carry some of the bags into the house.

"How's playing house in the woods going?" Max teases, handing me a couple of canvases to carry up the stairs.

"Just fine. Any news?" I question.

I've had him monitoring our apartment building, but the likelihood they would return, especially with his scent lingering is slim. Max's keen falcon eyesight makes him the best for spying, and I appreciate his willingness to help, but I can't keep asking him to miss deadlines for work because of my past coming back to haunt me. The best thing would be for me to track them down and end this myself, but I can't bring myself to abandon Kaycia.

"Nah. Except the lady on the first floor threw her boyfriend out. Other than that, no one's been around. I went in yesterday and the doors are repaired, except for the claw marks. When I peeked through the windows nothing else had been messed with." Max's affable nature still shines, even when discussing possible threats. He gives a slow smile as he looks between Kaycia standing on the deck with Raquel, then to me. "Sure does seem like things are working out between you and your girl, though."

"I can't complain about the time together, but I wish it were under different circumstances. Thanks for making the drive out."

"No problem, man. Kaycia's a doll, none of us want anything bad to happen to either of you."

"Hey, Shane!" Raquel calls from the deck. "You ready to do this or what?" She's tagged along to show Kaycia some self-defense tactics like I'd promised. In a tight black sports bra and leggings under her black leather jacket, Raquel looks like a goth yoga instructor next to Kaycia's ripped jeans and loose tee.

"Yeah, you two go on out behind the house. Max and I will be out once we get the groceries unloaded."

"You sure that's a good idea? To let Quel loose without supervision?" Max goads while grabbing the final three grocery bags and slamming his truck door.

"She'll be good," I answer confidently.

When the groceries are unpacked, Max and I head around back and I eat my words.

Chapter 34
Kaycia

Raquel cracks her neck and strips off her leather jacket so she stands in just a black sports bra and leggings. Before tossing the jacket aside, she reaches into the pockets to pull something out. For a minute I panic. Even though I've watched Raquel shift into an adorable raccoon that begs for belly rubs and marshmallows, I know that she's tough and much stronger than me. Seeing her back and arm muscles flex under the dark tattoos that curl across her tan skin only reminds me of that fact and makes me wonder how the hell I think I'm going to be able to defend myself if *wolf* shifters come after me.

My nerves ratchet up even higher, sending sweat tingling under my arms and slicking my palms when Raquel turns around to reveal a handful of zip ties and a roll of duct tape.

"You ready?" she asks with a devilish smile.

"Uhhh…what?" I glance between the supplies and her raised brows.

"Shane told me you needed some instruction on defense. I figure you need to know how to get out of a bind just as much as how to throw a punch. What do you want to start with?"

"Walk me through my options," I say nervously.

Ten minutes later, I'm lying on my side on the grass with my hands zip-tied and my mouth taped shut.

"What the fuck, Raquel?" Shane's shout echoes across the open space near the pond while Max's guffaws add harmony.

"And you weren't worried about Raquel! When has she ever 'been good'?" Max chortles.

"Watch and learn," Raquel insists, arms crossed over her chest as she studies me.

Within a few moments, I've scurried to my knees, lifting my arms overhead and swiftly bringing them down so that my wrists are in front of my stomach with my elbows flared at my sides. The force of the movement breaks the zip ties and I rip the tape from my mouth with a wince.

"Can we *not* do the tape again, please?" I ask, rubbing my raw skin with my fingers. "Ever."

Shane approaches wearing a deep frown. He takes my hand and tenderly traces the red lines around my wrists from the zip ties. We've practiced several times and my skin is sore, but my confidence is higher than before we started.

"What next?" I ask.

"Let's do a couple of defense moves in case someone grabs you. Now that the guys are out here, they can help. Max, come up behind me and grab me like you're going to abduct me."

"Nope," Max replies. "Not just nope, but fuck no. I'm not giving you a chance to kick me in the nuts or bust my nose."

"It's for practice, you dick," Raquel insists. "Fine. Shane, you man enough to do the honors?"

Stepping out of the way, I watch as Shane nods. Within a blink, he's moving quicker than I thought possible. He charges toward Raquel, wrapping an arm around her waist and forcing her arms against her sides. He grabs her ponytail tightly in the opposite fist. Raquel growls and her eyes briefly flash gold before she bends her knees, dropping low as she slams her head backward into Shane's nose. He grunts but holds on as she wiggles and drops her weight to loosen an arm, striking back with her elbow into his stomach, then his groin. To finish, Raquel lands a brutal stomp to Shane's instep. If he wasn't wearing boots I'd worry more, but he lets go and holds his nose which drips with blood. Just as Max had anticipated.

"Gods damn it, Quel," Shane groans, tipping his head back. Crimson coats his lips and chin before he can staunch the bleeding.

"You wanted me to show her!" she retorts with a sly grin, smoothing her hair and re-tightening her ponytail.

"You could have just walked her through it instead of beating the shit out of me."

"Told you," Max says with a sideways look at me.

"Are you okay?" I ask, swallowing my nerves. Everything happened so quickly. I fear that my mind will go blank as soon as someone grabs me in real life. Raquel moved so fast, like her muscles knew exactly what to do, instinctually adjusting for Shane's moves.

"I'm fine," Shane answers, wiping the back of his palm across his bloody face. The flow has stopped, his shifter healing kicking in to mend him quickly. "Quel, walk her through it."

For the next half hour, Raquel explains the movements and reasoning behind each one. How to know when to hit with an elbow and when to dig in with fingertips and nails, when to drop your body weight, and when to risk a head butt. She shows me how to use a hammer strike with my keys wrapped tightly in my fist, and how to hit the weak points of the human body.

The entire time I wonder, *How can I possibly defeat a* shifter *with any of this?*

After the verbal lesson, Raquel tells Max to try it out with me.

"Don't go easy on me," Max tells me, not worried about a broken nose or sore groin like he was with Raquel.

"Back at ya," I answer, sounding far more confident than I feel.

When Max's arms circle me, pinning my arms to my sides as Shane demonstrated with Raquel, a low growl disrupts my focus. Shane's eyes are an unchanging, luminous gold, and his teeth are bared at Max. Forcing myself to ignore him, I try to break loose, elbowing and stomping, but Max holds tight. His hot breath tickles my hair and panic begins to set in when I can't get free.

"Remember what I told you!" Raquel shouts. "What do you do when they come at you from behind?"

Heart hammering, I try to remember the movements Raquel showed me. I'm embarrassed by the whimper that escapes me as I struggle, thrashing around while Max's grip holds firm. I continue to wriggle, my confidence eroding. I'm not convinced he's even using his full strength. After another few seconds, Shane slams into us, dragging Max off me and tossing him aside like a rag doll. The guttural snarl that explodes from him as he stares at Max has me taking a step back, eyes wide.

"Fuck, Shane!" Max shouts. "*You* asked us to help!" He stands, brushing his hands on his jeans and shaking out his hair.

"Shit. *Shit*," Shane mumbles, looking chastened and running his hands over his face. "Max, I'm sorry. I didn't mean to do that."

"You good?" Raquel asks me. She stands close to my side with her body positioned between the guys and me. Shane breathes deeply, calming as he approaches us, but Raquel is focused on me instead of him.

"Yeah. Yes. Yes, I'm fine." Breathless and frustrated, but fine.

"You're in deep, aren't you?" Raquel whispers to Shane when he's close, eyes still on me. Shane just nods.

"Shane, you good, man?" Max asks, approaching slowly and not making eye contact.

"Yeah." Shane answers. He swallows and inches toward me, eyes on the ground in contrition. "I'm sorry, Kaycia."

"What happened?" I ask, still confused by his outburst. I look between each of the shifters, but no one seems to be as surprised as I am.

"He's bonded to you now. He won't be able to stand seeing you in trouble, no matter who's doing it," Raquel explains. "It happens to most of us when we fall in love, but it's worse in wolves. Territorial bastards." She looks between us with a mischievous smile. "Sorry if you haven't discussed the big 'L' word yet, hope I didn't ruin the romantic moment."

"We have," I say to Raquel, but ask Shane, "Why didn't you tell me this might be an issue?"

Shane takes my hand, stroking his thumb over the back as our fingers entwine. He still looks like a child who's been scolded. "I didn't realize it would be. I haven't experienced anything like this before."

Max and Raquel pretend they're not listening, picking up Raquel's jacket and the supplies she brought, but they're entirely too quiet to be believed.

"Okay, then you teach me," I tell Shane.

"I think we need a break. Let's have lunch and then we can work on something else."

"Deal."

Chapter 35
Shane

We are halfway through our lunch—burgers that Max and I grilled on the deck while I apologized again for tackling him—when my phone rings. The area code is from back home, but I don't recognize the number. I'm already keyed up from what happened with Max and this call does nothing to alleviate my tension. I feel like shit now that my head has cleared. Max is a good friend. I didn't hurt him, but he didn't deserve that hit, even if he keeps telling me not to worry about it.

Excusing myself from the table, I step onto the deck with a backward look at my friends. "Hello?"

"Shane? Is that you?" a female's voice replies. It's familiar, the tone similar to my mother's.

"Who is this?" I demand, realization settling in my gut.

"Brother? It's Lana."

Lana. My sister. I was stupid to think she would have

let it go after mom refused to tell her who she was talking to.

"Lana. Why are you calling me? You know it's forbidden. Are Mom and Dad okay? Is it Aubrey?"

"They're all fine, I just needed to find out who Mom was talking to. It was eating me up after she was so cagey the other day." Her voice is a whisper when she asks, *"Brother,* how are you?" I can hear restrained emotions in her voice.

My strong little sister would rather die than admit she has feelings, but I struggle to keep mine in check listening to her. Calling my mother opened the incision that I'd managed to stitch shut. Now the threads that kept my emotions at bay are pulling loose with each word Lana speaks.

"I'd be a lot better if I could see you, all of you, and if these Ross assholes weren't looking for me. But Lana, you can't call me again. I miss you all so much, but you can't get wrapped up in this."

"Shane, we're already wrapped up in it. Dad took Aubrey on a camping trip across the country. They left this morning and are talking about being gone for months. Who goes camping that long? I'm not stupid, he's getting him out of town until things settle down and Colton isn't looking for a McKinley son to even the score. If you would just come back and challenge him you could end all of this."

"You know I can't do that. Just crossing into the territory would set me up to be hunted, and if I lost, they'd punish all of you. This exile is *my* punishment. If you welcome me back, it's yours, too."

I remind her of the rules of the pack, the ones that kept me from being killed all those years ago. The ones that keep them safe from retribution for my actions.

"You think the last ten years haven't punished all of us? You won't lose, brother."

"I can't do this, Lana. I love you and I miss you, but it's best for everyone that I stay gone."

"Where are you? You said they've been after you. You don't think they'll find wherever you've run?"

"It's better if you don't know that, little sister."

"Don't you want this to end?"

"Lana, I have to go. I love you, but don't call me again."

"Damn it, Shane—" she starts, her voice rising with frustration, but I don't hear the rest. I hit the end button before she can curse me more.

———

"L et's call it a day," Kaycia offers when I make it back into the house. She's studying me closely while Raquel and Max give each other concerned, furtive glances.

"You wanted to practice more," I remind her, trying to ignore the curious stares.

"I think I just want to set up to paint for a bit, if that's okay? We can target practice tomorrow."

"I need to get to the shop for a bit. My boss is going to

be unbearable if I don't get some work done," Raquel jokes, but her heart isn't in it.

"Give me a ring if you need me to bring anything else out," Max adds, standing and gathering his keys and phone from the kitchen counter. "Your exhibit still in a week, Kay?"

"As far as I know. I'm supposed to call the gallery tomorrow to iron out the details since I won't have the last two pieces I expected. Unless something wild happens"— she looks at me with a worried frown— "everything should be in order."

"Jamila's catering gig is slated to do the bar for the event," Raquel interjects. "So, she and I will both be there for you."

"I'll be there too," Max concludes, giving Kaycia a quick side hug and clapping me on the shoulder. "See y'all soon."

———

"**A**re you okay?" Kaycia pointedly asks once Max's truck is out of sight.

"I'm fine."

"Who was on the phone?"

She's gathering some of her art supplies into a bag to carry out with a small canvas but stops when I hesitate.

"You jealous?"

"Don't be a jerk." She purses her lips in annoyance. "You were already being grumpy after that shit with Max, and when you came back in you were even worse. I know we haven't been together long, but I can read you, Shane McKinley. You're upset."

Blowing out a deep breath, I sit on the leather sofa and cradle my head in my hands while she waits for an explanation. How can I explain pack politics to her so she doesn't think we're no better than wild animals?

"It was my sister."

Chapter 36
Kaycia

I listen as Shane tries to explain the intricacies of pack dynamics while growing increasingly worried about him as he paces the floor.

"Lana said our dad took my little brother on a road trip to get him out of town. If he's still figuring out the shift, that's best. But it just leaves her and my mother at the house. I don't know whether the Rosses will come looking for me here or try to lure me back there. Either way, it looks like the only way this is going to end is if I challenge Colton and win, or he kills me. I don't think I can run from this anymore."

"Let me get this straight. If you fight this guy and win, you what? Take his place as their leader? And he just *lets* you do it?"

"I doubt it would be that simple, but on paper, yes. A pack alpha can be challenged by anyone, and if the challenger wins, they become the new alpha. But this is a blood feud. He's coming for me over his brother's death. I think I'd have to kill him. And he will try to kill me."

"But since you were exiled, you could be executed anyway just for going back?"

"Technically, yes."

I let out a deep exhale, steepling my fingertips over my nose and closing my eyes. "What are you going to do?"

"I don't know. I don't want to kill anyone else. I have enough blood on my hands." He looks up at me, his eyes sorrowful. "I don't want to leave you or the life I've spent all this time building."

"Nothing says you have to."

"Me killing Logan ten years ago says I might. Plus, Lana is more like a bloodhound than a wolf. I guarantee she's going to track my number to Argent and find my shop. She's not going to just give up on this because I hung up on her. I'm honestly surprised Colton's trackers haven't already trashed the shop by now. Although, they might be steering clear of Raquel to stay under the radar while they try to force me to respond to the damage at our apartments."

"What do we do in the meantime?"

"*You* need to focus on preparing whatever you need to for your exhibition. Get your head in that space, not this bullshit. We can target practice tomorrow and you can stay with Jamila and Raquel the night before the opening. I need to figure out my next move."

Reluctantly, I listen to him, accepting his kiss on my forehead before I take my canvas and paint to overlook the pond out back, leaving him to pace on the deck. The peaceful setting does nothing to ease my mind. All I manage to get on the canvas is a splash of carmine against the soft white fabric.

The color of blood pervades even my art.

———

The next day Shane surprises me with not only a shotgun, but a hunting rifle, a semi-automatic pistol, and a revolver. He shows me the proper way to handle each one, raising fond memories of shooting with my grandpa until I discover that the shotgun and rifle kick a lot harder than the BB gun I used to use.

Massaging my sore shoulder, I take the first handgun from Shane. "Okay, what do I do now?"

"Take off the safety and pull the slide back," he advises. He shows me the motion, but I struggle to mimic it.

"Should it be this hard?"

"It can be. But give it a shot."

I shoot the target until the clip is empty, not doing a terrible job, but not winning any awards either.

"Not bad." Shane is encouraging, but I'm disappointed.

"Not good either."

"Try this one, maybe it will be a little easier?" He hands me the last pistol, a revolver. It's lighter and smaller than the other handgun, and the results are pleasing.

"Oh, that was much better!" I'm tired, but happy with the small circle of holes in the target.

"If you were aiming for the shoulder, it was great. If you were aiming to kill someone it might be lacking," Shane jokes, but wraps an arm around me and offers a squeeze. "I'll pack up here if you want to head on in."

I leave my safety glasses and ear protection with him before heading to the cabin. *I don't want to kill anyone,* I think, glancing back at the target before I'm too far to see the little holes in the torso outline printed on the paper.

When Shane reaches the deck, I'm sprawled on the porch sofa with a glass of water and my phone so I can call Kelly. "I'll make this call and be in in a minute."

He nods and retreats into the house to give me my privacy. Glancing down at my phone I cringe at the missed calls from my mom and texts from Meg. It's been a few days since I've spoken to either of them.

Opening my phone I read over the messages.

MEG

Hey girl! Any new stories about Hot Neighbor? How's everything going? Are you ready for your show?

MEG

Remind me of the gallery you're having it at again, please? I'm so bummed I can't make it.

That one is followed quickly by a photo of her toddler holding a sign that reads: *We Are Proud of you Aunt*

Kaycia, written in Meg's bubbly handwriting in different colored crayons along with colorful drawings of stick people and flowers.

A text from my mom follows, it's been longer than usual since I last touched base. I feel a little guilty, but not guilty enough to call her to explain that I'm in hiding in the woods.

I shoot quick messages back to both of them, apologizing for the delay, answering their questions, and asking how they are before calling the gallery.

"Red Lark Gallery," Kelly says briskly when she answers.

"Hey, Kelly. It's Kaycia."

"Kaycia! How are you? All set for your big debut? They've started hanging things like you advised."

"Thanks so much. I'm so bummed I couldn't be there today to check it out and bring the final pieces like I'd planned. Unfortunately, someone broke into my place this weekend and trashed it."

"Kaycia! That's terrible! Are you okay?"

"I'm physically okay, it's just a mess. Several pieces were damaged beyond repair and I have to stay somewhere else for a bit until they get it all repaired at my building. I'm not sure I'll have anything else to add except one piece that wasn't damaged." I give a little lopsided smile in the direction of the cabin when I think of the painting of Shane's profile.

"What assholes! But don't worry, I can have the installers move things a little to adjust for it," Kelly offers. "I'm so sorry that happened."

"Thank you. I think that will work great. I'm out in the country regrouping, but I'll be back in town before the exhibition to check in and make sure everything is squared away."

"Perfect. See you then. We're looking forward to it, I have several buyers already interested from our mailing list! Take care and we'll talk soon."

My heart soars as the call ends. The excitement over people interested in my work is almost enough to make me forget about the last few days, but not quite. I had Max bring the sunset painting with my canvases, so I can add the final few touches. Nothing else would even be remotely ready in such a short time.

In the time it takes for the sun to dip below the trees, I decide that anything I create out here will be the start of something new. I'll focus on the single piece to round out the collection and then worry about the others once we are clear of this mess. Speaking with Kelly and having a firm plan helps me feel more confident than I have in days, leaving me in higher spirits by the time I join Shane back inside the cabin.

Chapter 37
Kaycia

"Ugh! I can't seem to get started on anything today!" I toss my brush down in frustration after staring at the canvas with red blooming across it for over half an hour. It's reasonable for me to still feel shaken up after everything that's happened over the last week, but nervous energy courses through me this morning. The call with Kelly reassured me that the number of pieces I dropped at the gallery are enough, but even though I decided that I didn't need to create anything else for the exhibition, I can't help but feel lazy by not creating to make up for what was damaged. I've spent so much of my time since I arrived in Argent creating and focusing on work that taking a break feels like I'm wasting valuable time.

"What's wrong?" Shane asks, walking in through the front door after a series of beeps from the keyless entry pad. He told me earlier he was going to scout around his property, just in case anyone was snooping around, and made me promise to keep the doors locked until he got back.

"Nothing. I just can't focus."

"Anything I can help with?" he asks, nuzzling against my neck while the few pieces of hair that have fallen from my bun tickle my skin. The scrape of his grown out stubble on my sensitive skin is electric.

"I just have all these jitters and can't seem to clear my mind. Ouch!" I laugh and pull away, rubbing the spot near my collar where he's nipped it with his teeth.

"I could help you focus on something," he whispers against my ear, raising goosebumps when he slides his hands beneath the fabric of my shirt, slipping them through the oversized arm holes to caress my skin and cup my breasts. "Maybe getting out in the forest would help you."

"Are you suggesting a hike? Or something more physical?" I tease, but my smile fades when I turn my head and see his eyes flash golden. My tummy flips and my skin flushes as he runs that hungry gaze over me.

"Have you ever been chased, Kaycia?" he rumbles, pulling his hands free of my shirt.

"*Chased?* Is this some Little Red Riding Hood/Big Bad Wolf fantasy?"

"Do you want me to eat you up?" Shane answers, nipping again at my neck and making my core go molten. My mind scrambles a little and I can only answer with a breathy chuckle. "How about I give you a head start? If I win, I get to do whatever I want."

"And if I win?" I ask, staring up at his dark eyes. Only a slim ring of gold surrounds the dilated pupil.

"I always find my prey." His voice is a low growl as he begins pulling his shirt over his head. "Better get moving."

I scramble to my feet with a giggle and dart out the front door.

The sun is warm on my face as I look around the yard, trying to decide which part of the tree line to enter. We've hiked around Shane's property a few times, but always on a deer path with him leading the way. *Do I follow the same path or make my own? How serious is he about this?* Glancing over my shoulder I can see him through the glass, unbuttoning his jeans with a wide grin, the gold of his eyes glinting through the pane.

I fight the squeak rising in my throat as I round the back of the house and head through one of the less-groomed paths through the tall trees at a brisk jog. The leaves rustle on the wind and smaller creatures run for cover as I dash down the trail, doing my best to avoid loose rocks and tree roots. Sweat beads on my brow as I run, looking over my shoulder under the dappled light of the forest. A howl from the cabin floats on the breeze and my heart rate ratchets up with excitement as I try to run faster, my breath coming quick as I decide which way to turn.

A smile creeps across my lips when another howl rises on the wind, my heart pounding harder in response. But then, that thrill turns to panic as I wonder, *What exactly does he plan to do if he catches me? Will it be in his human or animal form?*

My heart stutters as my steps stumble on the uneven ground and I look over my shoulder again. Gray fur darts between the heavy trees as Shane weaves through them in the distance. My breath hitches again when the flash of gray appears in my periphery faster than I anticipated. Then, Shane is there—a huge wolf with its tongue lolling—standing in front of me on the path, giant paws sinking in the soft earth.

The sight steals my breath for a second, fighting my natural human instinct to flee at the sight of a predator. I step to the right and the wolf moves to block me, matching my movements as he prevents me from escaping. I swallow, apprehension and anticipation warring within me as Shane's wolf forces me to walk backward toward the trees.

A gasp involuntarily escapes my lips when the rough bark of a tree bites into my back unexpectedly. Before I've caught my breath the wolf is close enough that I can feel the tickle of his fur on my bare legs. In a blink, he's shifted, standing in front of me in his naked human form, sweaty and panting with a grin stretched across his handsome face. The happiness in his expression is etched in the crinkle of his eyes as he leans toward me.

"Told you I always find my prey," he murmurs through rapid breaths, the tone making my heart flutter and my thighs clench in anticipation. Shane takes another step forward, inhaling deeply as he places a palm against the tree near my cheek. "Mmm...your scent tells me you're excited that I did."

Shane inhales once more and then I'm pressed against

his warm body, arms wrapped around him as I pull his mouth to mine in a rough kiss. He holds me close, pressing his thigh between mine, and grinds against me. Capturing my moan with another heated kiss, Shane runs his hands over me, reaching under my shirt to caress my back and breasts.

"Come on," he says against my lips, leading me down the dirt trail toward a clearing.

"Are we hiking? You're not wearing any clothes."

"Maybe you're just wearing too many," he replies, squeezing my ass cheek when I catch up. "I'll be fine, it's not a long walk."

Once we exit the tree line, I'm breathless for reasons beyond running through the woods. The clearing opens to a bubbling creek bed with a small field of yellow, pink, and purple late-season wildflowers that overlooks the mountains beyond. It's beautiful.

In the center of the field awaits a blanket, extra clothes for Shane, and picnic supplies.

"*This* is what you've been doing all morning! How did you know I'd run this way?"

"I didn't." He shrugs. "I figured you'd either run and play along or that I'd just bring you on a hike. I had much more fun this way." He cuts his eyes to me, licking his lips.

His lightly tanned skin gleams with a sheen of sweat in the warm sunlight and heat radiates from him where our arms touch. Turning toward him, I pull his mouth back to mine and jump up to wrap my legs around his bare waist so he can carry me to the blanket.

Laying me down on the thick fabric, Shane settles between my thighs and draws a contented sigh from me when he drags open-mouthed kisses down my throat. When he raises up, holding himself above me on his palms, I wiggle enough to pull my shirt off, tossing it aside along with my bra, and pulling him back down to lavish kisses against his lips. His stubble scratches my skin, leaving me tender where his lips have touched and marking a map of his adoration on my flesh.

"Shane," I pant, arching my back to get more friction from his naked body.

"What is it?"

"Take my shorts off," I whisper. His chuckle is soft against my throat as he kisses lower and lower.

"Always so impatient," he teases.

I whimper in response when he grinds against me. It doesn't take long before he's unbuttoned my shorts and pulled them and my panties off, leaving us both bare in the warm, golden light.

"Gods, Kaycia. You're beautiful," Shane breathes, his hands tracing my curves and exploring the places he's learned make me gasp and melt under his touch. "I..." He pauses, looking down at me with blown pupils. The soft expression on his face makes my heart race and heat flushes my cheeks. "I've never felt like this before. It's like I can't get enough of you," he confesses.

"I know," I admit. "I feel the same way. Is this what Raquel meant when she said you were bonded?"

"Kind of." Shane breathes against my throat, trailing

kisses down to my collarbone. "When shifters fall in love we tend to fall hard. Bonding is just one step further. When we bond to someone we're more attuned to them, more protective. Like she said, it's stronger in wolves."

"Ah, I see." My chest tightens at the explanation. I may not be a shifter, but whatever I feel for him has to be just as strong.

"Come here," he murmurs, then surprises me so that I let out a little shriek followed by a round of giggles as he rolls on his back and pulls me atop him. "I want to watch you. I want to see what I do to you."

In the past, I might have been nervous or covered up more, but with Shane, I know he's not going to judge me for what I desire or make me feel like I'm not sexy enough to be with him. Instead, I slide against him, relishing in how he feels when I tease him. Watching him lay his head back with a groan makes me feel powerful knowing that I can make him feel as good as he makes me. I plant kisses across his chest, licking and teasing him, coaxing a laugh as I drag my fingernails across his abs until the laugh turns to a moan when my hands reach his cock and circle it, stroking over him.

Satisfied at the amount of teasing he's endured, I straddle him and slide against him while my need coils low in my belly. Each time I circle my hips, I slide my clit across his length until I feel my pleasure nearing. Shane watches me with hungry eyes, biting his lip and letting me seek what I want. Tension coils low in my belly until I come undone without him even entering me. I bite my lower lip, a breathy laugh escaping as I lean forward trembling.

"Someone liked being chased, too, huh?" Shane teases, sliding his hands over my hips until they wrap behind me and grip my ass.

"Apparently, so," I agree. "Your turn."

Rising up, I guide him to my entrance, then slowly ease him inside me. His grip on my hips tightens and his breath comes quicker as I tease him, sliding him back out until he's practically panting with want. When I finally seat myself completely, he moans, fingers gripping so tight they might leave bruises. I smile at the thought of his marks on me. As I ride him, his eyes glow gold, watching my body limned by the golden hour light. He slides a hand up my belly, teasing my breast while I cup the other, teasing my nipple with a shuddering breath as I rub my clit.

"That's right, show me what you like," Shane murmurs, gaze intense. "I want to watch you come before I fill you up."

His words are almost my undoing, unleashing a feral moan from me as I drag his hand from my breast, bringing it to my mouth, and sucking his index and middle fingers between my lips while I continue to ride him. Being with him seems to unlock some instinctual part of me, allowing my body to take what it wants without second guessing anything. Shane's gasps and moans send liquid heat coursing through me as my muscles tense. When I shatter around him, head thrown back with pleasure, he pulls his hand free of my lips. Grabbing my hips he takes control, moving them for me and speeding our rhythm so that I brace myself with my palms flat on his chest until he reaches his own climax.

"Gods damn, baby girl," Shane's voice is low and raspy as he holds me close to him, arms wrapped around me gently. My head is tucked against his shoulder, but I can feel him nuzzling my neck and hair. "I love you, Kaycia."

"I love you, too," I reply.

Warmth surrounds us on the blanket even as the sunlight fades. I can't tell if it's the residual late summer heat or just the emotions between us that make me feel so comforted. We spend the rest of the evening laying on the blanket, exploring each other's bodies, nibbling on the picnic, and watching the fireflies dance for our last evening together before I return to Argent.

Chapter 38
Shane

"Is this inspired by what I think it is?" I ask, grinning at the multi-hued painting on the table. Kaycia started it yesterday, and now that I'm looking at it closely, the dabs and dots of colors are obviously the wildflower clearing from yesterday. I can't fight my smile, remembering how eager Kaycia was for me to yank her shorts off and fuck her amid their blooms. The memory of her riding me, her scent mingling with the flowers, has me hard just thinking about it.

"It was pretty memorable, don't you think?" Kaycia's voice drifts from the bathroom where she's finishing packing her bag for her return to the city. We decided it would be best if Jamila picks her up in her hatchback. As a human, she's the least likely to be followed or traced to me.

"You promise you're going to make it back in time for the exhibition?" Kaycia asks, this time standing behind the couch with her backpack. She bites her lip from nerves.

She's been getting antsy about her opening night. I'm not even sure she slept last night.

"Of course. I'd never miss it." I try to force as much warmth and confidence into my smile as I can before pulling her into an embrace. "Jamila's here."

Kaycia looks around me toward the window with a furrowed brow. "There's no car in the driveway—oh!" Jamila's silver hatchback pulls around the bend in the driveway just as she's questioning me. "Wolfie ears?"

"Yep," I reply, tapping one of my ears before holding her close again, resting my chin on top of her head.

She holds me tight, then abruptly steps back with her head cocked and eyes narrowed. "Wait a minute. If your ears are that sensitive...what else have you overheard?" Her eyes widen and cheeks flush when I bite my lip and give her a sideways smile.

"I'll head out early tomorrow morning just to be sure. I can hang out at Max's beforehand." I avoid answering, stepping out of her arms to grab her bag.

"Shane McKinley!" she gasps. "This conversation is *not* over."

"Jamila's waiting." I fight my grin when I see her glare.

We walk out front to meet Jamila, who hops out of the driver's seat to pop the hatch for us to stow Kaycia's bag and the painting she's taking back to the city. She's finished the eponymous "Sunset Daydreams" in time to add to the exhibit.

"You excited?" Jamila asks, smiling at Kaycia. Kaycia's

excitement overrides her nerves and shines through when she grins back and nods.

"Yep! Just gotta drop this at the gallery and take a peek at what they've done. Then it's almost time! Love you," she adds, turning in my arms and kissing me. Jamila's brows shoot up when she hears, but she just smiles at me and climbs in the car waving to me from the rolled-down window.

"I love you, too. I'll see you tomorrow." I press my forehead to hers, memorizing her scent. With one last embrace, I release Kaycia and step back up onto the deck to watch them drive away.

———

While watching the sunset with a cold beer on the patio, my phone buzzes. It's another area code from my hometown, but an unfamiliar number.

If Lana gave my number to anyone else, I'm going to lose it.

"Hello?" I answer gruffly.

"Well, well, well..." A deep, masculine voice responds. "How the fuck are you, Shane McKinley?"

I'm fucked.

"Colton. How did you get this number?" I grind through the tension wrapping around my ribcage like a steel band. I listen hard, trying to see if I hear something familiar—the city, traffic, anything. The sound of a woman struggling in the background stops my heart. Suffocates me.

Is it Kaycia? I strain to listen.

"I have someone special here who gave it up."

"Let me talk to her. Now."

Colton chuckles, his nonchalance stoking my rage as the sounds of struggling get closer and louder.

"Let me go, you stupid son of a bitch! Shane? Shane! Don't tell them where you are!" I'm relieved and terrified within a single breath.

It's not Kaycia.

But it *is* my sister.

"Lana?" Her name rushes from my lips, but before she answers or I can say anything else, Colton is back on the line. The noise in the background makes it clear someone is dragging her somewhere they can keep her under control, her spits and snarls fading rapidly the farther they get from the phone. Colton must have several men keeping her bound or has drugged her somehow. Otherwise, she would have already shifted and taken off a hand, or more.

"So, McKinley. Are you going to do this the easy way and tell me where you are? I know you aren't at your apartment. Where did you sneak off to with that pretty little human I hear you've been fucking?"

"So, it *was* your cowards who trashed her apartment and left me threats. Couldn't just come find and face me yourself?"

"You're the one in hiding. If anyone's the coward it's *you*," he snarls. "Here's the offer. You tell me where you are and let me give you the punishment you deserve for what you did to my brother. Or, you can listen while I cut pieces off your pretty sister. Or maybe I'll visit the little slut you've been seeing? One of my guys said she has an exhibit at that fancy gallery she's been in and out of so much recently. Tomorrow, I believe? Kaycia Durand, right? Says on their website that it starts at 6:30. That's convenient, even includes appetizers and an open bar. Is she with you right now? Think you can keep her safe?"

My mind spins. If Colton or his pack bust into the gallery there's nothing I can do. I can't risk them ruining her exhibition or reputation. I certainly can't lose control or kill someone in front of a group of highbrow art collectors. If I tell him where I am and just face this, I can negotiate to leave her out of it. Lana's already involved, but I can still protect Kaycia.

"Fine. I want to know you've pulled your guys from watching her. I want you to agree to let my sister go as soon as you see me. Then I'll tell you."

I can't risk offering to meet him back at my parents' place. If I did, then *I* would be the one breaking the exile and would be put to death. Plus, he can't bring an entire pack with him if he comes to me.

At least this way I have a fighting chance.

Regret choking me, I sigh and think of Kaycia.

"Deal."

Chapter 39
Kaycia

I toss and turn on the pull-out sofa in Jamila and Raquel's cramped living room trying to get comfortable. I fail miserably at fighting the anxious energy that fizzes through me and end up staring at the overstuffed bookshelves in the streetlight that shines through the cracks in the blinds. Even though I checked in at the gallery and everything is hung perfectly, I worry that no one will show up.

What if it's just my friends, me, and a disappointed Kelly?

What if they've all been telling me my work is great to make me feel better when it's really trash?

Stop it, Kaycia, I scold myself.

I know my work is good. If it wasn't I wouldn't have this opportunity. Strangers aren't nice to you for no reason, and when I first reached out Kelly *was* a stranger. She invited me to her gallery based on the merit of my work, not my personality. She wouldn't risk her or her gallery's reputation for an unknown if she didn't believe in my talent.

Adding to my nervousness, Shane has been exceptionally quiet this evening. He texted to say goodnight hours ago with very few words, and I worry that being forced into close proximity so quickly was a mistake. What if he's regretting the speed of everything now that I'm not underfoot and he's had a chance to breathe?

Stop. It. He's probably tired. And he has his own problems, you insufferable worrier.

It's true. Shane has a lot to deal with now that his past is resurfacing, the remorse over everything that happened is like a fog dimming him. I wish I could be there with him tonight, but I get the impression that he's used to working things out on his own. The added pressure of letting me in on all his secrets might be adding even more of a strain. With a heavy sigh, I roll around for another hour or so before finally falling asleep shortly before dawn.

Aromatic, dark roast coffee drags me off the sofa bed around nine o'clock. Raquel is in a tank top and boxers sitting on the countertop next to Jamila who wears a romantic, silky nightgown while scrambling eggs in a bowl. Raquel holds out an empty mug from the little mug tree so I can pour a cup of the enticing coffee before speaking.

"Good morning," Jamila greets with a raised brow. "Rough night?"

"Oh gods, do I look that bad?" I question with a grimace, pushing my hair back to try to straighten it a bit.

"I could hear you tossing and turning," Raquel offers.

"I'm sorry."

"No, no. I'm up late all the time. Practically nocturnal." She crinkles her nose in jest. "You didn't keep me up. You okay though?"

"I'm just keyed up about tonight. I'm not sure what to wear or how to do my hair or how to act. It's nerve-wracking to talk to strangers about my paintings and that's exactly what I have to be prepared to do. And Shane was weirdly quiet last night," I blurt in a single breath. "Sorry, I'm spiraling a little. I sound like some high school girl worrying over her crush." I cup the coffee mug between my palms, wishing I could drown myself in the bitter depths.

"Enough of that," Raquel snaps. Jamila gives her a stern look before pouring the eggs into a hot skillet. Raquel shrugs, then adds, checking points off on her tattooed fingers, "Your art is amazing and you're a bad bitch. You're going to kill it tonight regardless of what you wear. And Shane would crawl across broken glass on his hands and knees for you, you don't have to worry about his feelings. He's just a moody fucker sometimes."

"That's true," Jamila chimes in, simultaneously scrambling the eggs and popping sliced bagels in the toaster. "On all counts."

Reassured by Raquel and Jamila's pep talk, my mood shifts from worried anxiety to a manic hum of excitement. We combine my packed clothes with some of Raquel and Jamila's to perfect my ensemble for the evening. I pack my backpack with sneakers, a t-shirt and jeans, and my riding jacket to keep in Jamila's car so I can change after the show and ride back to the cabin with Shane. The leather pants, flowing floral silk blouse, and heels I selected for the event won't cut it on the back of his bike for a couple of hours.

As I'm blow-drying my hair, a text from Shane pops up. Short and sweet, it relieves the tension that's crushed me all morning.

SHANE

I'm so proud of you and I love you, Kaycia. Don't ever forget that.

My reply text is left unread—a quick selfie in the full-length mirror blowing him a kiss—but I can picture him on his bike heading back to the city. He wouldn't risk checking the message on the road. I have so much to do before I catch a ride to Red Lark with Jamila that I ignore the tickle of worry and get to work on my makeup.

For now, my focus is on the exhibit. It can be on Shane later tonight.

———

Jamila and I sing along to her radio the whole drive to the gallery. She's wearing her all-black catering uniform but has a hint of glitter highlighting her eyelids and cheekbones to add a little flair to the otherwise muted look. Her playlist is a mix of upbeat tunes that put me in an excellent mood although I still haven't heard anything more from Shane.

Kelly is already directing the set-up of the refreshments when we enter Red Lark. She gives me a warm hug before the main phone rings and she glides to answer it, leaving me to look around the gallery alone. With Jamila setting up, I don't have much to do with a little over an hour until the exhibition opens. My phone buzzes in my pocket and my heart leaps into my throat hoping it's Shane telling me he made it to Max's.

Instead, Meg's name fills the screen. When I open the text, I'm greeted with her smiling face in front of a familiar location. The sign for Red Lark Gallery hangs over her head. "What in the world?" I whisper to myself, striding from the back of the gallery toward the front windows.

A laugh escapes me when I see Meg standing out front. Her smile is bigger than I've ever seen and I squeal as I rush to open the door as quickly as I can in the heels I borrowed from Jamila.

"Holy shit! What are you doing here?" I cry wrapping my arms around her.

"Well, Tyler surprised me with a free weekend," Meg answers. I release her to grin and take a look at my best friend in the flesh. Her brown hair is sleek and straightened with a fresh blow dry and she looks trendy in a pair of jeans, heels, and black blouse. It feels like forever since I've seen her in person and I can barely contain my tears at the surprise. "Are you surprised?"

"So surprised! I can't believe you're here!" I hug her again, holding on a little longer than normal.

"Are you excited? Do you have a little time so we could

go grab a coffee or something, or do you have big things to do here to get ready?" Meg asks, her eyes taking in the gallery.

"I have time! We can go around the corner. Let me introduce you to a friend first and see if she needs anything."

I drag Meg to meet Jamila, making introductions and seeing if she wants us to bring her anything back before we head out to the café around the block. In all my excitement I almost forget that I still haven't heard from Shane.

Chapter 40
Shane

Guilt nearly suffocates me as I leave Kaycia's reply text unread. I can see part of her response on the screen along with a photo, but I can't bear to open it. If I do, I'll confess that I won't be there tonight, and I can't risk worrying her enough that she'd consider missing her exhibition. This night is too important for her, I won't be responsible for ruining it any more than I already have. I can only hope she'll be so wrapped up in work that she won't be able to worry about me until things are finished. As long as she stays safe it will be worth it.

I send a message to Raquel, begging her to keep Kaycia focused and telling her that I need to deal with some family stuff before I head to Argent. I pace through the living room, running my hands through my hair and checking the time on my phone screen. I need to keep my wits and stay in control of my temper tonight. Around six-thirty, I start to text Max to give him a heads-up about what's happening but pause mid-text when gravel crunches at the end of the drive. My heightened hearing alerts me to two vehicles approaching.

I wait inside, watching through the front windows of the cabin as a black SUV and a dark gray, heavy-duty pickup pull in behind my motorcycle. I could still get around them, but it wouldn't be easy with the way they've blocked me in. They were already a day's drive from their pack's territory and heading toward Argent when Colton called me last night. I knew they'd reach me by late afternoon.

I'm not going to run again. I'm sick of looking over my shoulder. It's time this ends.

Either we squash this feud tonight, or one of us dies and takes it with us to the grave.

Colton Ross gets out of the truck, another wolf following close behind from the passenger side. Two more exit the front of the SUV when I step onto the front deck. My claws and fangs threaten to shift with so many strange wolves nearby. I have to dig my fingertips into my arms when the back door opens and a third wolf pulls a woman from the back seat. She's tall and lanky, wearing a burlap sack over her head with her arms bound behind her.

Even though it's been ten years, I recognize my sister. The way she staggers and has to be supported confirms my suspicion they've drugged her. Nevertheless, she struggles between two of her captors, trying to free her arms from their tight grip. The clumsiness of her movements sends a wave of remorse crashing over me, followed by a rising tide of anger at Colton Ross.

"I'm here. Let Lana go." The resignation in my voice surprises me.

I haven't given up, but I sure as hell sound like I have.

"Nice place you've got here, McKinley," Colton sneers, ignoring my demand while strolling around like a prospective buyer walking through an open house. I note the pistol he wears in a shoulder holster but see no other visible weapons on his companions. His dark brown hair is buzzed close to his scalp and his light blue eyes shine when he pushes his sunglasses up on his head. Their bright color doesn't match the black heart he's grown over the decade since Logan's death.

His cocky attitude is the same as it always was, but he's filled out since I knew him. He's no longer the slim little brother to the Ross pack heir. This is an alpha wolf in his full glory, even if he's sinking to deplorable depths by threatening the daughter of a high-ranking member of a neighboring pack. If my father knew he had Lana, he would have already started a war.

"Shane?" Lana mumbles behind the hood. "Brother, don't turn yourself over to them. They'll kill you."

"Lana, this is between us." I allow my anger to seep into my words, eyes never shifting from Colton.

"He killed himself when he killed Logan. Old man Cameron was a fool to think I would let that debt go with an exile," Colton goads with a growl at my sister. To her credit, she doesn't shrink or cower at his tone.

I step down onto the grass, scanning the men as they array themselves on the lawn. I don't recognize three of them, instead thinking of them by their distinct characteristics: Ball Cap, Ripped Jeans, and Tattoos. A fourth, the one wearing a beat-up leather jacket, however, is familiar. "Caleb Davidson," I call to the young man. "Have you changed pack allegiance? You'd dare lay hands on Sean McKinley's daughter?"

He cuts his eyes to Colton before frowning and answering, "My mom remarried. The Rosses are our pack now." Caleb stares at his feet and flinches when I spit on the grass.

I don't offer any further response to the youth who once followed my brother and me like our own personal fan club, addressing Colton again, "Your father agreed to the exile. Logan was his son and heir. If old man Ross agreed all debts were paid, it's your responsibility to abide by it."

"My father was weak and too easily influenced by his desire for loyalty and peace. The old fool always wanted the packs to work together."

I make a sound of disgust in my throat at his disparagement of his father. "Nice way to speak of the dead, Colt. We were friends."

"Fuck that childhood shit, McKinley. What you did to my brother would never have happened if we *were friends*."

My anger surges. "Logan brought it on himself and you know it. He fought dirty and died with his hands soiled."

Colton growls low in his throat, his eyes flashing with rage. "I'm the alpha now and my wolves agree with me. It's time for you to stand a real trial for what you did."

"Challenge him, Shane!" Lana shrieks on her knees, her voice muffled from the sack still covering her head. "Gods damn you, challenge him!" I can only imagine the fury on her face.

Ripped Jeans lands a backhand across where her cheek should be, sending her sprawling across the lawn, unable to cushion her fall with her hands bound.

"Shut up, you bitch!" he snarls.

I reach the wolf before he knows what's hit him. We roll into the gravel of the driveway, claws forming in my anger as I throw punches, ripping clothing and tearing flesh as we growl and wrestle. A gunshot silences us and I still, holding his shirt as I kneel on his chest heaving angry breaths.

"There's the temper that got you into trouble before," Colton chuckles, holding his pistol in the air. "Boys, get him and hold him with his sister until I'm ready for him."

They drag me to Lana's side panting and bloody. I don't resist. I'll bide my time for the moment. My cell phone remains in the driveway, the screen broken on the rough ground.

I spit blood on the grass as I stare at Colton. "At least prove to me that you've pulled them away from my girl, you prick. If you're going to break your word about freeing Lana, show you have an ounce of dignity and keep that one. I kept my end of the bargain, at least honor part of yours."

"Okay, okay." He replaces his gun in its holster and pulls out his cell. Dialing, he places it on speakerphone and approaches so I can hear the ringing.

"What's up?" a gruff male voice answers.

"You and the boys can back off the artist," Colton orders. "I've got him."

"You sure? Looks like a good time in there. It's getting started now. They've got an open bar and those fancy snacks they pass around on trays for rich people. She's a pretty little thing, too. You know I like blondes."

I snarl, chest heaving and eyes gold with my anger. My wolf claws in my chest to shift.

"Leave it. Head back home. We don't need her, and we don't need any attention from the cops if you two fuck up."

"All right, all right. We'll head out. She's been eyeing us. Thought I might have a chance to pick her up later if McKinley doesn't show up for her. Maybe I can soothe her broken heart," the fucker jokes, knowing I'm here listening.

Misery coils in my gut knowing she *will* have a broken heart soon when I don't show up with Max. I should have been on the road hours ago. Not much time now before she realizes I'm not coming.

Colton hangs up, then returns his glare to me. His lips curl into an eerie smile as he approaches me. "Okay, McKinley. Let's have a little heart-to-heart."

Chapter 41
Kaycia

When Meg and I return to Red Lark carrying our to-go coffees, I notice two strange men who look far too weathered to be in this part of town hanging out across the street. In my excitement to see her, I didn't pay attention to whether they had been there earlier, but their leers make me feel uneasy, a twisting sensation taking the place of my happiness.

I casually glance at my phone while Meg asks me about mundane aspects of city life, but still no texts from Shane.

Punching the key code, I let Meg inside the gallery and follow quickly behind, looking over my shoulder to observe the strangers. I lead her through the open space, pointing out my work and some of the other artists featured in nooks off the main floor.

Red Lark is one of the smaller galleries in the art district, but Kelly has built a loyal clientele after years of working in some of the larger galleries. She steps from her office as we near the refreshments, elegantly attired as always, in a navy sheath dress, complete with nude pumps and minimal, but expensive, jewelry. Her gallery is just as sleek as she is, the walls white and exacting, with no scuffs or blemishes to detract from the exhibition.

"Kelly," I call to her, waving her over. "This is my best friend from home, Meg. Meg, this is Kelly. This is her gallery."

"Nice to meet you, Meg. Is this your first time in Argent?" Kelly asks with a warm smile.

Meg shakes her hand and nods. "It is! Your gallery is beautiful. I'm so excited to be here."

The sunset is just barely visible over the buildings outside and the golden hour light filters through the tinted front windows. By the time people begin filing in it will be perfect. Jamila waits to serve drinks at one of the bars with another bartender, and the caterers have set out charcuterie and hors d'oeuvres in preparation for guests.

While we wait, Jamila and Meg make easy small talk, discussing everything from Meg's flight and kids to Jamila's favorite restaurants and theater performances. I smile, nodding when expected, but my heart is slowly sinking.

"Did your parents call to wish you luck?" Meg asks. Jamila tries to mask the grimace that takes over her face, focusing on pouring glasses of wine in preparation for the influx of visitors to the bar. She hands me a glass of pinot grigio and Meg takes a flute of champagne.

"No. Did you think they would?" I retort bitterly.

"They're the worst." Meg directs her comment to Jamila, but wraps an arm around me. "Well, I'm here and we're going to celebrate!" She clinks her glass against mine, but the smile I offer is forced.

"You're definitely more fun."

"You'll have to introduce me to this new man of yours, too. He'll be here, right?" she asks with an eyebrow waggle.

I swallow and nod. Meg may think my somber mood is due to my parents, but Jamila gives me a searching look before I turn my attention back to the door hoping for Shane's arrival.

———

I can't shake the feeling that something is wrong. I hide my worries behind a glass of wine and blame it on the normal nervousness that comes with an exhibition, chatting with patrons and introducing Meg to people I've become acquainted with in the gallery scene.

Fifteen minutes after the official start of the exhibition, Raquel strides through the doorway. She's a striking figure in the bright white of the gallery, tucking her helmet under her arm and making a beeline to join us. She's friendly to Meg, but something about the wariness in her eyes when she repeatedly scans the crowd puts me ill at ease. Neither of us mentions Shane and the omission makes my stomach twist with nervousness.

The gallery steadily fills with patrons and curious pedestrians who saw the sign and open door—free drinks and appetizers will lure humans no matter what. The milling bodies negate my worries that no one would come. I shake hands with patrons and make small talk, accepting their praise with as much grace as I can, even if my eyes constantly drift to the open door and darkening sky beyond. As I'm chatting with someone about the inspiration for one of the paintings my heart drops.

Max strolls through the front door.

Alone.

"Excuse me for just a moment, please?" I ask the kind older man and his partner. They wave me away with a smile and continue browsing while I walk briskly to kiss Max on the cheek, pretending nothing is amiss. Kelly steps in to pick up the conversation, glancing at me with a little furrow pinching her brow.

"Hey, darlin'. You look great!" Max smiles, the consummate flirt.

"Where is he?" I ask, foregoing pleasantries.

"Who? Shane?" Max replies, looking around confused. The easy smile vanishes when he doesn't see his friend. "He's not here?"

"No. He said he was coming to town early to hang out with you and then come to the exhibit. I haven't heard from him in hours."

"He never came over," Max answers. "I figured he was just coming straight here and was already on the road once I realized the time. I waited as long as I could, but I didn't want to be too late." Raquel makes her way through the people as Max pulls his phone out. He dials Shane's number, but I can hear it ringing and then going to voicemail.

"This isn't right." I'm beginning to panic. My hands are sweaty and shaking as I look around to make sure no one notices my impending meltdown. Chest tightening, I set my wine on a nearby counter. "He wouldn't do this to me."

"No," Raquel agrees. "He wouldn't."

She and Max share a meaningful look.

"What? What are you both thinking?"

Thunder rumbles ominously outside and the twilight sky darkens even more with incoming clouds.

"I think you should focus on your show and let Max and me go check on Shane," Raquel soothes, but tension coils tight in her shoulders and clenched jaw.

"I'm already on it," Max replies. "I'll meet you out there."

"What are you doing? What's happening?" I ask Raquel. Max briskly walks back out the front doors. When my eyes meet Meg's across the room, she gives me a curious look of concern. She takes the fresh glass of champagne she was waiting on and mouths 'Are you okay?'. I have no idea how I'm supposed to explain any of this to her, but I hold up a finger to indicate I'll be right over.

"I'm worried the rival pack may have found him. He texted me earlier with a cryptic message about family business, but I didn't want to worry you. I thought he meant he'd be late. I'm sorry, Kay. Max and I will go check it out. You stay here."

"Like hell I will." Anger and fear cancel out clearer thinking, and my years of being cautious go by the wayside. "I'm coming with you."

"Kaycia, you aren't a shifter. You don't heal like we do. If this gets ugly you could get hurt. Badly," she says, her voice low and pleading.

"That's why I had you teach me."

"It's one thing to practice in case some creep grabs you in a parking garage, it's another if it's a pack of wolves out for blood."

She's right. Of course, she is. But my resolve is set.

"I don't care."

Sighing deeply, Raquel doesn't fight me. "Fine. Let me get your bag."

Within a few minutes, she's back with my backpack from Jamila's car. I snag it from her as I hurry to Meg's side.

"This is so fun, Kaycia! People seem really excited about your work," Meg gushes, gesturing around with her glass. Her smile fades again when she sees my face up close and looks between it and the backpack. "What's wrong?"

"I'm so sorry, but something has come up. There's been an emergency with my boyfriend. I have to go."

"Oh no! What happened?" Meg looks alarmed and glances around for somewhere to set her glass. "Do you need me to come with you?"

She has no reason to doubt my excuse. The Kaycia she knows is the epitome of responsibility. *That* Kaycia would never run out of an important event because of a guy, let alone get wrapped up in the mess I've found myself in. But I can't dwell on that now. I have to make sure Shane is okay.

"No. Raquel can take me. I'm not sure what's happened. I'm so sorry. I'll text you later. We can do brunch tomorrow. Let me know where you're staying." I rattle off the platitudes without giving her time to respond with a strained smile. "Thank you so much for coming."

I hope I'm not lying. I hope I get to see her tomorrow. I can't dwell on the risk I'm potentially facing; I have to hug my best friend goodbye and get changed.

"Come with me, I'll tell Jamila and she can help get you back to the hotel, okay?"

Meg lets me drag her back to the bar where I leave her, pulling Jamila aside to whisper, "Please help her get back to her hotel. I feel terrible leaving her, but I don't know what's going to happen."

"I'll take her myself. Be careful." She looks between me and Meg, then catches Raquel's eye walking back through the gallery with a spare helmet, worry clouding her face.

I leave Jamila with Meg and Raquel, then rush to Kelly's office to pull on my jeans and sneakers, shoving my backpack under Kelly's desk. On the way out, I snag Kelly's arm.

"Kaycia? What's wrong?" she asks, looking over my hasty wardrobe change and the jacket in my hand.

"I'm so sorry, there's been an emergency. I have to leave."

"Okay, don't worry!" she says in the calm, efficient tone I adore her for. "I hope everything's okay. I'll handle everyone and keep you updated. Just let me know if you need anything." She pats my shoulder in farewell and I rush to meet Raquel. She hands me the extra helmet and leads me to her bike out back.

"Oh, crap. Okay," I whisper to myself and shake out my hands, trying to clear my nerves when I spy the shiny sport bike. It's much faster and very different than Shane's. My adrenaline spikes and I tremble knowing how fast she rides on a normal day. I can't imagine what this is going to be like.

"Don't freak out, hang on to my waist or hips, and lean *with* me. I'll keep you safe, but we have to fly, yeah?" Raquel reassures me with a tight smile, then mounts her bike. I hop on behind her and wrap my arms around her waist with my eyes squeezed shut. I can barely hear the thunder as she revs her engine and pulls out onto the street.

Chapter 42
Shane

Twilight has faded to full dark, except for the soft glow of the interior lights of the cabin and a strand of decorative string lights over the deck. I'm still at an impasse with Colton and his pack members while the sky rumbles with encroaching thunderheads. He inspects my cabin, riffling through my belongings while his boys keep me standing in the yard seething, one on either side to keep me in line. The scent of the storm tickles my nostrils as lightning flashes its warning. Before long the rain will begin. By the time this is over any blood spilled will have washed away.

Lana lays quietly on her side in the grass. They removed the hood, but the fight has left her since I haven't challenged Colton. Her hazel eyes, the same color and shape as my own, plead with me, pupils blown from whatever they drugged her with to keep her calm.

I know what she wants me to do. She thinks if I challenge Colton for his rank as alpha, I'll win and take his place. It would effectively end the blood feud he's pursuing. But I'm not interested in killing anyone else. It broke something in me when Logan Ross stopped struggling against me that night years ago. The rage that blinded me over Ethan's death immediately faded with Logan's last breath, and all I felt was regret and misery. I've felt it ever since.

"So, what's the plan, Colt? I know you didn't kidnap my sister and drive for a day and a half to chat on my lawn. What do you want?"

I try to focus on my enemy, but my eyes flicker to the darkened driveway where I watch helplessly as my broken phone screen illuminates over and over with incoming messages. It's late enough that my absence at the gallery is noticed. My chest aches thinking about how badly Kaycia will be hurt waiting for me to show up. But I couldn't risk putting her in harm's way.

"Seems like you've done real well for yourself, McKinley. Nice little place here in the woods, fancy apartment in the city, well known cycle shop. Found this"—he holds out one of Kaycia's shirts that she left behind, holding it against his face and inhaling dramatically. "From the looks of things you've even been playing house. Doesn't seem like you're still mourning or being punished at all. I don't think that's fair, do you boys?" Colton directs his rhetorical question to his buddies. "I've been missing my brother and his murderer has been having a grand time in the big city."

"Are you going to monologue some more, or get to the fucking point?" I snarl.

"I'm taking you back with me." Colton grabs me by the collar and shakes me like a wayward pup. "The pack wants a piece of you, and I want to show Cameron that the truce between us is over. I'm going to get the justice that should have been had years ago." He releases me, pushing me sideways in an attempt to knock me off balance and raise my hackles.

"Fuck you. I'm not going back. As soon as you take me into the territory, I'll be violating the exile, and it will make it legal in both packs' eyes for you to kill me without repercussions."

I give a vicious grin. I'd suspected his scheme, but he's just confirmed it. No matter how much he wants to take his revenge, he's still trying to keep his hands clean as the new alpha. He knows by seeking me out and pursuing me, he's violating the terms of the exile as much as I'd be if I went back home.

"You're too big of a pussy to just handle it yourself, aren't you? What did you think? You'd toss me out on the side of the road near the hollow and say I'd returned?"

Colt's jaw flutters, but his sneer hides any hint of further emotions. I press on with a scoff, "Is my sister, right? Do you think I'd win? You've already shown your lack of honor by not letting Lana go when you said you would. Afraid to tarnish it more in front of your boys when you get your ass handed to you?"

"Your bitch of a sister would just as soon attack us if we

let her go as anything else," Baseball Cap remarks, on guard closest to Lana. She gives a lazy grin in response, her eyes hateful but growing clearer as she watches.

"She's twice the wolf you are, and she scares all of you, doesn't she?" I respond, then turn to Colton. "I'm not going to challenge you, but I'm sure as fuck not going home with you either. So, sounds like you have a choice to make about what happens next."

I take a few steps back toward the deck as thunder echoes again. Caleb tenses as the first drops of rain begin to pelt us in the twilight. He's not the only one of the Ross men who looks nervous. They'll all be complicit if I'm dragged back, and they're already guilty of abducting my sister. If they're questioned after dragging me along it would be my former pack's right to punish them all. My father and mother would be allowed first blood.

It would end violently.

"You and your boys are going to have to man up and deal with me here. Or else you better leave my sister and get the fuck off my land."

"Have it your way," Colton snaps, eyes flashing as he dips his chin.

The two shifters closest to me spring, Tattoos grabs at me while Caleb blocks me from running the other way. I land a punch to Tattoos' ribs, grabbing his hair and pummeling his gut until Caleb grabs me from behind. The rain soaks through my clothes and causes me to slip on the wet grass. The three of us go down in a mass of bodies, wrestling and clawing in the rain. If I shift, I could slip through the woods and come around the other side to attack, but shifting in the middle of a fight is tough and risks precious moments of vulnerability.

Time passes in snarls and punches before Ripped Jeans joins the fray and pulls me up by the back of my shirt. Between the three of them, they knock me to my knees, landing a few blows to my jaw and kicks to my ribs and gut, while Colton watches with a smug smile. When blood drips from my face, pooling on the grass at my knees, Tattoos and Ripped Jeans hold my arms, preventing me from getting to my feet.

"It's been a while since you've fought hasn't it, McKinley? You look a little rusty," Colton gloats walking toward me as the rain cleanses the blood from our already healing wounds.

Breathing hard, I struggle for a moment, my fangs threatening to break free as the shift calls to me. It always does when there's blood and violence. But the urge dies as soon as I hear a shout from the bottom of the drive.

"Shane? *Shane!*" Kaycia shrieks over the storm as she runs up the driveway wearing the jacket I gave her.

Where the fuck did she come from? How did I not hear her or scent her?

"Kaycia, no!" I struggle harder, trying to make her understand. Tattoos twists my arm harder behind my back. My shoulder threatens to dislocate and the searing pain steals my breath. "Run!" I croak.

"Well, look here. A little leverage to encourage you. Grab her," Colton says, directing Caleb to retrieve Kaycia with a pointed nod. Ripped Jeans stalks behind him, his scent telling me he's excited for a chase.

Before I can get free, hell breaks loose.

Chapter 43
Kaycia

The thunder and wind get worse the farther we get from the city. I cling to Raquel, telling myself to breathe and lean with her as she weaves through traffic. She accelerates and zips between cars without flinching, while I can't tell if my stomach is in my throat because of worry for Shane or the ride. If she knows I'm terrified she doesn't let on, driving through the night and drizzle like life depends on it. Which, it might.

As we pass through the blinking red light near Shane's property, the bottom drops out of the black clouds and the rain goes from a mild drizzle to a full-on storm.

Can you even ride a motorcycle in the rain? I wonder, blinded by the water on my helmet's face shield. Raquel slows, her headlight illuminating Max's truck parked on the side of the road about a hundred yards away from the base of Shane's gravel turn-off. Raquel parks behind the truck and we both dismount, standing in the downpour.

My legs shake when I stand, quivering from adrenaline spiked by the speed and my fear for Shane's safety. Once we pull our helmets off, we approach the truck, but Max is nowhere to be seen except for a pile of clothes on the front seat.

"Damn, he hauled ass," Raquel mutters, then shouts over the rain to me, "He had enough of a head start he must be scoping it out." She presses a hand to the hood of the truck, "It's still warm. He hasn't been here long."

I rub my hands over my arms, shivering from the rain and worry when a bedraggled falcon flies into view and shifts back into Max. He grabs his shirt from the front seat and holds it over his crotch for my modesty more than his own, then shouts over the storm, "Shane's at his cabin. There are five wolves, six if you count a woman that I assume is his sister. It's not looking good." He continues to give details to Raquel while I rub my hands together and stare toward the driveway.

"Okay, I'll go in on foot. You take to the sky. Is the rain going to be an issue?" Raquel asks Max, leaving me out of the equation.

"It's not ideal. I won't be as agile. But I can handle it. I'll take the guy holding Shane's sister and create a distraction for you."

"Okay. I'll try to surprise a couple of the others to give Shane a better shot. He can take two on his own, I'm sure."

"One's an alpha. You think he can take him?" Max questions.

"I think so," Raquel answers, but her expression says otherwise.

"What about me?" I interrupt, hoping the patter of the rain hides the panic in my voice.

"You need to stay out of the way. We already talked about this, Kay," Raquel answers. She's already stripping off her jacket and bundling her wet hair into a tight bun.

"I can shoot. I'm not useless. Let me help."

Max and Raquel look between me and each other before Max opens his door and leans across the seat to the glovebox. When he returns, he holds a handgun. I'm relieved that it's a small revolver, similar to the one I used when I practiced with Shane.

"It's only got five shots," he reminds me as I take it from him. "Don't use it unless you have to. Don't get yourself hurt."

"I've got mine too," Raquel adds, adjusting a small pistol holstered at her lower back. I hadn't realized she was carrying it, but I shouldn't be surprised with all the trouble brewing. "You and I will go through the woods. I'll circle behind them while you go straight up the driveway. The rain should keep our scents hidden and give us the advantage of surprise. I just hope you being here doesn't get Shane into trouble. You saw how he was with Max that day he grabbed you."

"Maybe that's exactly how he needs to be," Max mutters.

With those final words Max shifts, his shirt falling to the wet street and his falcon form taking flight. I lose sight of him quickly in the stormy night sky. I have no idea how he's flying, but that's not my concern as Raquel and I slog through the water pooling in a ditch on the side of the road, and climb the mud and gravel toward Shane's cabin.

Halfway up the drive, Raquel grabs my wrist. I'm panting from exertion and nerves, cursing myself for letting my old exercise routine go by the wayside. I walk enough in the city; how would I anticipate needing to run up a muddy slope to rescue my supernatural boyfriend?

"This is where I turn off," Raquel whisper-shouts close to my ear. "Run on up the driveway and get their attention. Max and I will take care of the rest. Take care of yourself first and don't let them get their hands on you."

I think back to the playful chase through the woods that got Shane so excited last week. He caught up with me so easily, and *he* had no intention of harming me. What will happen if one of these other wolves decides to make me their prey? Swallowing hard, heart hammering, I squeeze Raquel's hand and watch her dark outline race into the tree line. After a second's hesitation, I shake my hands out and take a deep breath, then continue up to where a big truck and black SUV block the view of the cabin.

Shane's fighting against three men in the yard, the rain has washed away any evidence of blood, but how can he possibly win against all of them? One man wearing a base-ball cap that keeps the rain from his eyes is standing guard next to a woman sprawled in the grass. I can't make out much about her except long hair, but I assume like Max did that she's Shane's sister. She sees me first, eyes going wide and alert. A big man laughs, watching until a man in a tattered shirt and ripped jeans pulls Shane back from the fray, forcing him to kneel in the mud. One of the ones he was fighting, arms covered in tattoos, wrenches Shane's arm behind him and the grimace of pain that crosses Shane's face sends a slice of misery through me.

Without much thought as to what to do next, I shout, "Shane? *Shane!*"

He jerks his head toward me, wrenching his arm further where the tattooed wolf holds him in submission. Even in the dim light of the string lights his fear and panic are obvious. Dark blotches color his wet tee, remnants of blood spilled—*what have they done to him?*

"Kaycia, no! Run!" I can't hear what the cruel man standing in front of him says, but whatever it is sends two men stalking in my direction.

Before I can turn to run, the cry of a falcon jerks everyone's attention to the sky. The man guarding Shane's sister looks up, reaching for a weapon at his back when Max comes flying down. His talons slip under the brim of the baseball cap, sending it to the ground as he tears at the man's face before he can fight back. Within moments, the wounded man recovers from the surprise and pain. He grabs at Max with clawed fingers, but Max has already taken to the sky. He circles, wings flapping against the storm, before making a stunning dive toward his target once more. This time his attack is anticipated, and the man snags Max's wing, ripping him away from his face before he can inflict more damage with his sharp talons and beak. Max shrieks once as the man he attacked crunches his wing and flings his limp body away. Free of the raptor, the injured man cradles his dripping face in his palms, still distracted as he heals.

Max's efforts weren't in vain. The distraction was all Shane's sister needed. She no longer reclines on the ground. Standing at her full height, she surprises her captor by giving him a wicked head butt to his already injured face. His nose bursts with blood that washes over his lips and chin, sending him to his knees shaking his head. She runs toward the trees while the men who are supposed to be after me hesitate. One takes off after her, while the man in the leather jacket refocuses on me.

Seeing Shane's sister flee reminds me of my own escape and sends me sprinting toward the trees. I feel guilty leaving Shane behind but remember Raquel's order: do not let them catch me. Behind me, Shane's voice turns into a guttural growl, blending with the storm as he struggles, but I can't make out what he's saying over my panicked breathing and the heavy rainfall. I try to hide in the trees but snag a foot on the roots and slip, coming down hard on my knee. Pain radiates up my leg as I wince and bite down on a gasp. It's enough of an error to give my pursuer the edge he needs. I cry out when he grabs the back of my jacket, pulling me backward.

"Come here, little human," he orders, yanking on me like a poorly behaved dog on a leash. I manage to get the front zipper down and slip from the sleeves, leaving him holding the jacket in his fist while I slip and slide on the muddy forest floor. Within seconds, he's on me again, pulling me with my hair tightly gripped in his fist this time.

All I can think about is Max's pistol in my waistband. The metal is warm from my body heat and I think over and over: *Please don't search me, please don't search me.* As though he can read my mind, the big man pauses and runs his hands over me before he yanks the gun from where it was hidden under my shirt. He carries it in his opposite hand, dragging me along as I stumble and limp at his side.

When I'm led back into the clearing, Shane is still restrained on his knees, forced to stare in defeat at where Max, in falcon form, lays silent against a tree. Max's feathers are splayed and bent causing me to wonder how badly his wing was injured during the scuffle. Red slashes from Max's talons heal rapidly on the shifter's face, but one eye is swollen shut from Shane's sister's surprise hit. The cruel man gloating before Shane, the one I can only assume is the alpha who's responsible for this nightmare, stands smirking with his arms crossed over his chest as I'm tossed into the yard. I come down hard on my hands and knees, wincing as my injured knee hits the ground, but at least its spongy from the rain.

"Good job, Caleb," the alpha tells my captor. The man at my side just dips his head in response.

Shane's sister and the shifter who followed her are still missing. Raquel is nowhere to be seen. But I feel the creeping sensation of eyes on us from within the trees.

"Look how romantic. Your human trying to come

rescue you, huh, McKinley? Maybe now that you have a little incentive, you'll be more receptive."

The alpha steps closer as Shane struggles against the man who restrains him. The tattooed shifter wrenches Shane's shoulder viciously, and he hisses in pain. I fear what injuries he'll sustain if he struggles anymore. The shifter in the baseball cap stands ready to intercept should Shane get free.

"Not just a human, you dipshit." Our attention swings to track the sound of breaking glass. Raquel stands next to the SUV holding a shotgun she's used to bash in the passenger window. She pumps it once and the threatening sound sends a shiver of fear over me.

"And what are you? Another useless beast?" Colton gestures toward Max's limp body, then at Raquel and me. "You've collected an interesting group, haven't you? A pest, a parrot, and a weak human woman. But haven't you realized none of them can stand against a wolf?"

"Your wolves are out of practice." A raspy voice drags everyone's attention to Shane's sister, unfettered and alert, drifting from behind the cars. "It took three of them to take me down in the first place. One alone didn't stand a chance." Her hands are clean, but her shirt is bloodied. Her vicious smile tells me it's not hers. "You sure you're in any better shape, Colt?"

Colton pulls his pistol from his holster, passing Shane to approach me. My breath hitches.

Why did I not listen to Raquel? What was I thinking trying to be a hero?

"I can kill her before either of you reach me. And you'll fill your friends with buckshot with a shotgun at this distance," he directs to Raquel when she swings the barrel in his direction. "What's it going to be?"

"I challenge you." Shane's voice is hoarse as his eyes meet mine. He roughly shakes off the man holding him, but neither shifter offers to stop him. Both of them step away wide-eyed at his words. Shane stands, rolling his shoulders with his teeth bared.

"Gods damn you, Colton. I challenge you."

Chapter 44
Shane

ow did I get here?

H I watch as Kaycia is roughly pulled to the side of the yard and guarded by Caleb. I could tear his throat out for his blind loyalty to Colton. She's crying, but her tears blend with the rain as she favors one leg. She's hurt. Her soaked blouse is torn and dirty as she shivers. I'm certain I'd smell the tang of her fear if the rain wasn't masking it.

This is my fault. All I want is to wrap her in my arms and comfort her. But I can't go to her. Not until this is over.

Tonight, the guilt will fuel my rage.

I've done everything I was supposed to. I honored my exile. I've suffered without my pack for a decade. I've tried to forget what it was like to lose control. I learned on my own how to channel my emotions—good and bad—into more productive pursuits. And for what? To be facing off against another Ross wolf on a night that can't possibly end well.

But I can't dwell on the past. I lost my family once; I'm not going to let Colton take my new one away from me.

Max remains in his falcon form and still hasn't regained consciousness. Concern for him tugs at my attention while Colton circles me, removing his holster with the pistol still in it. Raquel is at Max's side, stroking his feathers and whispering while Lana stands guard, her eyes glow golden and intense as she watches me. Caleb still guards Kaycia, his expression somber when he glances at her crying on the ground. The remaining Ross pack members observe Colton and me with interest, but they won't interfere now that the gauntlet is thrown. Raquel and Lana won't intervene either.

The rules of a challenge are ancient. Any wolf can challenge any alpha for their place. Whoever wins, whether through death or surrender, is the new leader. No questions. It's one-on-one and the strongest wolf wins.

Colton may have a grudge to settle, but he's also the one with the most to lose. If I take his place, he loses more than his pride. He loses his feud, his family, and his pack.

If I lose... I look toward Kaycia, my sister, my friends.

I won't lose.

I strip off my soaked shirt and unbutton my jeans, then let the shift take me. Colton does the same, dropping his holstered weapon along with his shed clothing. Our eyes glow in the stormy night as we snarl, lips curling from fangs. Our decade of pent-up rage rivals the thunder.

Tattoos stepped forward as Colton's second, just like I did for Ethan ten years ago. Tonight, I don't claim a second, but Lana's canny gaze is fixed on me. Max is the only spectator not in human form.

With one final growl, the challenge begins.

I let Colton circle.

Wear yourself out trying to figure out an angle, fucker.

Despite being an alpha and having more bulk on his frame as a human, Colton is still slightly smaller than I am in his wolf form. I ignore the jeers from his men and the higher-pitched shouts of encouragement from Lana and Raquel through the rain as I watch him, waiting for a tell or an opportunity to strike. Colton makes the first move, leaping forward in an attempt to latch his jaws around my front leg. I avoid the snap of his teeth just in time. As he passes me, I bite into his flank and the metallic taste of blood coats my tongue before he pulls lose with a yelp.

With first blood drawn, the shouts around us rise higher. I wonder if Kaycia is handling it well, but I can't risk looking away from Colton as he lunges again and again. His third strike is unavoidable; he sinks his teeth into my shoulder and knocks me to my side where I slide across the muddy ground. I fight it, but a harsh whine escapes from the searing pain.

"*Shane!*" Kaycia shrieks.

Struggling under Colton, I manage to free my shoulder with a snarl, fur and blood flying as I snap and lunge repeatedly at his throat. He retreats, giving me time to regain my footing, but he was right earlier. It's been a while since I've sparred. And after everything that's happened this evening, I'm tiring quicker than I'd hoped.

My only option is to win. I'm under no illusion that I'd walk away from a surrender. Just because I'm not in this to the death, doesn't mean I'm naive enough to think he's playing by the same rules. Colton will happily rip out my throat and say he won the challenge fair and square if I yield.

Somehow, he's gotten behind me. As I twist to find him, I'm knocked off my feet again. Blood runs freely from the bite on Colton's neck, but he's not flagging as much as I had hoped.

"I'm going to kill you, you sorry son-of-a-bitch. I'm going to make your bitch of a sister and little human slut watch while you bleed out." Colton's voice comes through loudly in my mind, cruel and full of excitement at the prospect of my pain. *"Your girl sure is pretty, McKinley. Maybe I'll lick her wounds after you're dead. She's obviously developed a taste for wolf."*

"Fuck you," is all I have time to think in reply before he's torn into my shoulder again, ripping fur and flesh as I struggle and bite back a whimper.

This can't be it.

He can't have bested me. I struggle, panic starting to set in as I scrabble on the slick ground. The storm has let up and only a faint drizzle falls now, but the blood and mud prevent me from gaining purchase to throw him off. For a moment, I consider shifting back. It would surprise Colton to find me in human form and it might give me an advantage, but he doubles down, releasing me before biting down harder into my shoulder.

A pathetic whine echoes in my ears before I realize it's me making the sound.

"Gods damn you, brother. If you die tonight, I'll never forgive you." Lana is in my mind, pleading in her own way. She's never been one for tenderness, but I can sense her fear even in her thoughts.

I manage to look toward her, finding her in wolf form at the edge of where we fight, her whine reaches me as the rain eases. Next to her, Kaycia is on her knees sobbing, her blouse ripped and her hair plastered around her face. She looks so pitiful that Caleb isn't even looking at her anymore. My gaze continues around the clearing quickly, Max is finally back in human form, covered with Raquel's jacket, while Raquel eyes the enemy shifters warily.

If I lose and they decide to attack my friends, Raquel and Lana could do some damage. But not enough to protect Kaycia or Max with his injury.

Meeting Kaycia's panicked gaze once more, I inhale sharply and surge to my feet, throwing Colton off me.

This ends now.

Chapter 45
Kaycia

How are they all just watching?

Adrenaline floods my veins, making my head swim with panic as I kneel trembling and cold to watch the giant wolves circle in the center of the clearing. They're lit by what is normally a romantic glow from the string lights, but now it feels sinister. Like I'm watching some sordid cage fight. Colton's goons blatantly disregard Raquel and me as any kind of threat, focusing on their alpha and Shane preparing for battle.

From the corner of my eye, I watch Raquel across the clearing trying to wake Max. Even though he's large for a bird, he looks small and broken lying there in the rain. How can someone hold this many worries at one time? It feels like my chest is going to burst.

The man who took my pistol stuffed it in one of the pockets of his leather jacket, too risky for me to try to reach even if I were brave enough. I assume Raquel still has hers.

None of Colton's men have gotten close to her, especially since she has the shotgun propped against the tree next to her and Max. They're all too focused on the challenge.

I'm useless. Just like they warned me I would be.

I watch Shane's sister staring intently at the fight. When Shane bites Colton her eyes flare gold and she leans forward before one of the men grabs her shoulder. She shrugs him off with bared teeth and he steps back. Hope springs forth at the sight of Shane gaining the upper hand, but it fades just as quickly when he's attacked. I can't help the panicked cry that tears from my throat.

When Colton pins Shane on the muddy ground I begin to shake harder. I'm already cold from the rain, and my adrenaline has faded after the chase and being roughly handled. I worry that I'm going into shock. Will he kill him?

With a terrifying snarl, Lana shifts. She never even takes off her clothing, just tears through it as she changes into a light grey wolf, gold eyes glowing while Colton's men stare at her. She focuses on Shane, before he tilts his head toward me, then over to Max and Raquel, continuing to struggle. It's a small relief to see Max back in his human form, naked and shivering under Raquel's jacket. Any comfort his condition offers dies when I look back to the bloody mess in the yard and hear Shane's plaintive whine.

Shane meets my gaze again, letting out another whine of pain that cracks my heart in two. Then, with a sudden inhale, he twists his body and throws Colton off him.

"That's right! Get him, Shane!" Lana is screaming,

cheering in her destroyed tee and jeans, fully human once more. She gives a meaningful glance to Raquel, then refocuses on her brother.

Raquel is standing now, her body taut like she's ready to fight or flee. She cuts her dark eyes toward the man standing next to me, looking between me and the jacket pocket he shoved the pistol in. She can't possibly think I can get it back from him. I furrow my brow in confusion, but her only communication is to dip her chin once before she reaches toward the shotgun.

Snarling, followed by a shiver-inducing squeal, snap my attention back to Shane and Colton. Shane has Colton pinned, blood running down his shoulder and dripping onto Colton's fur. He grips Colton's throat between his jaws and his rival's eyes roll with terror.

The man at my side is still and silent, wholly consumed by his alpha's struggle with no ability to help. The others seem to be paralyzed, too, all eyes frozen on the fight. No one but me notices that Raquel is no longer a spectator, or that I have started to creep closer to my captor.

Now that Shane has taken the upper hand, teeth still clamped on Colton's throat, Colton stops moving. Shane isn't biting down though, the only blood I see is what's remaining on their fur from earlier wounds that have begun to knit together. As I edge closer to the man in the leather jacket, taking advantage of his focus on the fight, Colton shifts back to human form.

"I yield," he rasps, still pinned under Shane's massive wolf form. Then, louder, he repeats, "I yield."

Colton's men deflate at those words. They each take a knee, bringing the shifter next to me close enough for our shoulders to brush against one another.

Shane steps back and shifts, grabbing the wet jeans that Lana tosses to him. He has ragged healing marks on his skin, pink and angry, but there's no fresh blood anywhere on his naked, bruised body. A relief after watching him and Colton tear at one another so viciously. The men keep their heads bowed while he struggles to pull the wet denim over himself.

But Colton doesn't.

He has retreated to his clothing as well, and I watch in disbelief as he pulls the pistol from the pile and aims at Shane.

Without another thought, my hand is in the man's pocket next to me, pulling the revolver from it, scrambling to my feet, and aiming at Colton.

"Shane! Watch out!" I cry. He snaps his attention to me, then pivots toward Colton as I fire.

A second shot echoes through the trees a breath later and I can't hold back my scream.

Chapter 46
Shane

Colton was pinned.

It would have taken nothing for me to end his life right here in my front yard, but I couldn't bear to taint this place like I did back home. I already knew before the fight started that if he surrendered, I would allow it and would face the consequences of my victory. Even if returning home to be the Ross pack alpha is the last thing I want for myself. I worried that Colton would be too stubborn to surrender, forcing my hand.

His broken voice saying, "I yield," was a relief.

Colton had to know I would kill him if I had to. I let him up to grab his clothes as Lana tossed me my jeans.

What the fuck am I going to do now? I wonder, my muscles aching and my mouth foul with the taste of Colton's blood. I spit, trying to clear the taste, grimacing as I yank on my wet jeans. Even if my wounds are healing, they still hurt as I bend to struggle with the wet denim. Kaycia's sudden movement catches my eye as I stand, but her shout has me spinning on my heel before I can button my fly.

I was a fool to think Colton would surrender. I should have known he'd have no honor.

As I turn, Colton raises his gun. The steel is slick and shiny in the cool, lingering mist of rain. Staring down the barrel, I freeze for a split second before bending at the waist, preparing to tackle him. Before I launch myself toward him, two shots pierce the silence of the forest and Colton jerks back once. Twice.

He falls as I stagger forward in confusion, barely catching myself before I stumble over him. When I kneel at his side, he coughs, dark blood bubbling between his lips and staining the stubble on his chin and jaw. A bullet has gone through his left shoulder, exactly where Kaycia repeatedly hit her targets during our practices. The other landed perfectly in his chest, right where it would be fatal. Even shifter healing can't repair a heart that quickly.

I palm Colton's gun and look over my shoulder to find Kaycia shaking with a revolver dangling in her hand. Her lips are parted as if she's stunned. Lana stands silent and still, Raquel's familiar pistol held firmly in her grip, poised to take another shot. Raquel hovers near Kaycia, one comforting hand on her shoulder with the shotgun ready at her side, watching the shifters on their knees.

The wolves Colton brought still kneel, unsure who their loyalties now lay with.

Me, who won the challenge against their alpha.

Or one of the women who killed him.

"Shane!" Kaycia is crying, pulling away from Raquel and stumbling toward me, dropping the revolver at Raquel's feet. I shove Colton's pistol in my waistband and hold my arms open for her. "I thought he shot you." She sobs against my chest as I fold my arms around her.

"I'm okay," I whisper into her hair, holding her close. "Are you all right?" She doesn't speak, just nods and clings to me with trembling arms.

"He won't heal from that," Lana murmurs when she reaches my side, lowering her gun. She nudges Colton's side with a bare toe, but he doesn't move. He won't move again.

"I didn't kill him, did I?" Kaycia hiccups.

"I don't think so. I think—" I start.

"I did," Lana interrupts. "Stupid bastard. I didn't want to kill him, but he didn't give me much choice." Lana's lips are set in a hard line, but her chin trembles slightly as she looks down at Colton's body. "No one uses me or threatens my family." She meets my stare as she adds, "I'll always be your second, big brother."

Kaycia steps back and I wrap Lana in a hug just as a tear falls from my sister's eye. She grips me fiercely in return, then pushes away. Scrubbing her eyes with the back of her hand, she wipes any lingering evidence that she has any tender emotions. But the sad little smile she gives tells me she's hurting worse than she lets on.

"Thanks, little sister."

"Can I get a hug like that?" Max jokes from the tree line. He's holding his arm, as though the wound from earlier is still painful, but I can't help but snort a laugh seeing him with Raquel's jacket tied around his waist to cover his lack of clothing. One pale thigh is revealed, as though he's wearing a biker-themed sarong. Raquel tosses him a pair of sweatpants from the cabin. She must have raided the place while we weren't looking. She also offers a dry quilt to drape over Kaycia who stands trembling and crying softly.

I take a step toward her, but I don't get to soothe her frayed nerves before Caleb stutters, "Uh... Alpha?"

He looks between Lana and me. All three shifters who remain—minus the one who thought he could recapture Lana in the woods—still kneel on the muddy ground, bound by the rules of the challenge. They must honor their new leader with submission until they're recognized and released.

The problem is, who is their leader?

"I don't want it." Lana steps back with her hands held up. "I was protecting you *after* the yield. It's all you."

"But the final words hadn't been spoken. The transition wasn't complete," I argue. "I don't want it either."

I look at Kaycia, disheveled and muddy, white knuckles clutching the quilt. Regret knots in my gut. She should never have had to deal with any of this. I can't possibly return home to be alpha *and* continue my relationship with her. I wrap my arms around her, chafing my hands on her arms before holding her close and laying my cheek against the top of her head. "I'm so sorry about this, Kaycia."

"Well, someone has to get rid of him and tell the packs what's happened," Raquel states, gesturing to Colton's body.

I turn Kaycia toward the cabin, stepping away from Colton and drawing my friends along with me. "Ross pack members, to me," I order. The three men rise from where they've knelt and stand in front of us. Baseball Cap and Tattoos seem indifferent, while Caleb drops his gaze with sadness as they glance at their former alpha's cooling corpse.

"This is done," I say to them, a growl of authority seeping into my tone. "The blood feud that Colton Ross brought you here to settle is *finished*. We fought and he surrendered under pack laws. His choice to attack me afterward was met with defense from my packmate. Your other pack member lost his life in combat with a wolf he directly threatened. Do you agree that this vendetta is over? We have all paid enough."

The men nod, murmuring variations of, "Yes, Alpha."

I clench my jaw, rattled by the title I never desired. But for now, I'll embrace my authority to keep my friends safe.

"Wrap him up and put him in the back of the SUV. Find the other one to do the same," I command. "We'll be heading out tonight back to Woodbine Hollow to deal with this. I'll allow their families to give them a proper burial.

Lana, you're coming with me. We have to take this to both packs."

The men break apart, following Raquel to grab tarps and blankets from the storage shed.

"You're leaving?" Kaycia steps away, hurt contorting her face. "That's it?"

"I don't want to. Believe me. But, I have to. Just for a little while. I understand if this changes things," I answer, my voice catches but I fight the urge to drop to my knees to beg her to stay with me. "I understand if you don't want me after seeing what life with a wolf can be like."

I imagine she will need some time to process everything and my remorse over her being present tonight weaves its way deeper into my heart.

"You could bring her," Lana murmurs.

"*What?*" I snap.

"Bring her. Mama will love that you're coming home. If you bring a girl with you, it will be even better."

"Lana, I haven't been home in ten years. We have no idea what's going to be waiting when we get there with the fucking body of the neighboring alpha."

"Don't I get some say in this?" Kaycia asks, crossing her arms over her chest and making me notice once more that some buttons have ripped off and I can see quite a lot of what's underneath.

"Of course you do."

"Well, then okay. I'll come with you."

"You want to come back home with me?" I ask, barely

containing my surprise. "You're sure? Even after I ruined your exhibition night?"

"If we can wait to leave until tomorrow afternoon, then yes. I'll come to meet your family." She shudders as the men pass by her with the blankets. "I didn't go through all this to run away from you now, Shane McKinley."

"Sorry, if I hurt you, ma'am," Caleb addresses Kaycia, stopping at my side with his eyes downcast. "I was following orders." He offers her a dry sweatshirt, looking ashamed that her blouse is torn. It takes all my remaining patience to not snarl at him, remembering how he dragged her from the woods.

Kaycia merely melts against my side, casting him a scornful look and refusing the shirt. He hangs his head and continues past us to help his packmates. My wolf swells with pride at her bravery.

"I think it's time we all had a stiff drink if you don't mind," Max says as he walks up to the group. He rotates his shoulder and flexes his elbow testing how it's healed.

"You going to be okay, pretty bird?" Lana asks with a sideways smirk, eyes traveling over Max's bare chest and down over his—*my*—sweatpants.

"That depends on whether you're going to stick around to have a drink with us or not," he replies.

"There's a fucking body behind you, Max. Can you *not* flirt for five minutes?" Raquel chides, taking her jacket back from where he holds it out for her. She holds her phone to her ear filling Jamila in and reassuring her of our safety.

"He deserved it." Kaycia surprises me with her remark as she scowls at Colton's body being wrapped in a blanket, then tarp. "He would have killed you," she amends more softly as she leans against me.

"I think Max is right. We all need a drink."

Chapter 47
Kaycia

We rode home before dawn. The misty remnants from the night's storm washing us clean as we reentered Argent. Lana agreed to drive Colton's truck back, while his pack members carried both Colton and the other shifter's remains in the SUV this morning. Shane and I will leave to follow after I say goodbye to Meg.

Kelly didn't ask many questions when I called to check in this morning. She just asked if Shane was all right and told me to take a break after the excitement and bad luck I'd had over the last few weeks.

I expected Meg to be more difficult to convince. But making excuses for rushing out of the show was easier than I anticipated when we met her in the lobby of her tourist-filled hotel mid-morning. She was grumpy at first, lamenting about our lack of girl time, but perked up when I introduced Shane and said he was going to pay for brunch —including bottomless mimosas—to make up for ruining the night. If she noticed how haggard Shane and I look, she doesn't mention it.

"It was a misunderstanding," he says smoothly, taking a sip of his mimosa. "I was supposed to come with Max, but my bike broke down. I could have fixed it with a few things from my shop but I was in the middle of nowhere without cell service, so everyone started panicking. Max picked me up walking back to my cabin and Kaycia and Raquel showed up shortly after. I'm sorry if she had you worried."

Smiling, I roll my eyes and shake my head indulgently, as though to say "men!", masking the traumatic night we actually dealt with.

"Motorcycles are so dangerous. Kaycia, I can't believe you actually ride on that thing with him," Meg fusses in jest while she looks out the window at Shane's bike parked at the curb.

"I promise I drive safe with her." His hand finds mine and squeezes.

"You better. And you better be good to her, or I'll come up here and kick your ass." Meg laughs and pours another glass of champagne with a splash of orange juice before our overpriced plates of eggs benedict, fruit, and pancakes arrive.

"Don't worry I'd never let anything happen to Kaycia."

If Meg knew the chaotic truth about last night, she would be screaming at Shane and dragging me onto the plane home. Maybe I should let her, but I just squeeze his hand back and smile up at him.

"So how did the exhibition end up doing?" Meg asks, waving over a bartender for a refill.

"So much better than I could have imagined! I spoke with Kelly this morning and she said that there were only two pieces that weren't spoken for. And a few people left their contact info for commissions, too! I should be busy for a while. She even mentioned a potential residency opportunity."

"That is so amazing! People seemed to really love it though," Meg gushes. "You can do anything, friend."

If she only knew.

Shane slides his hand up my thigh, squeezing gently with a soft smile and pride in his eyes. "Yeah, she can."

It feels strange to be so excited and happy about my artwork and my future when a man died last night, even if he would have killed Shane without a second thought. I haven't had time to really parse through my feelings yet. I can't imagine how I'd be handling this morning if Lana hadn't stopped Colton from shooting Shane. I certainly wouldn't be pretending I was doing well over brunch.

I wish I could share everything with Meg, but I know she'd never believe me if I told her Shane and his friends are shifters. Let alone that he was involved in a deadly battle for pack alpha last night and that's why I had to run off. I'd be getting dragged home for an entirely different reason then.

Brunch passes smoothly. Shane answers all of Meg's questions with concise answers, and he comes off as polite, if not a bit shy. Very much how I viewed him before I hit him with the canvas and started this fever dream of a relationship.

Meg and I wait while Shane pays the tab and she squeezes me and laughs, the last mimosa making what she thinks is a secretive whisper more like a shout. "He's so cute, Kaycia! Way to go, you!" She manages to tone it down when Shane huffs a laugh behind us, asking, "You think this is the real deal?"

Glancing over my shoulder, I smile at Shane. I know he can hear every word with his wolf senses, even if we whisper. Turning back to her, I reply, "Yeah, Meg. I really do."

"I'm so happy for you, Kay. Be sure to drag him down to Summerville for the holidays, okay?"

"I will. And I promise that the next time you visit we'll have more time to show you around."

"It's no biggie! I should have let you in on the secret. My flight home is this afternoon anyway. I've got to get to the airport soon."

We say goodbye in the lobby, and I watch Meg get on the elevator. She blows a kiss as the doors close, waving and grinning until we can't see her anymore.

When we turn to leave, I tug Shane back toward me so he stands at my side in the reflection of the mirrors that line the elevator lobby. He's just as handsome as the night of our first date, even if his hair is longer and his eyes are deeply shadowed from our late night. A shiver runs over me when he slides a finger down my spine, his eyes flashing the gold of his wolf in the reflection. My hair hangs loose, the blonde waves fluffy from the residual humidity in the air, but instead of having trouble recognizing the slightly wild-looking woman staring back, I simply see myself. The person I've always been underneath the people pleasing and overthinking.

I lean my head against his shoulder for a moment, like we're posing for a picture, then, we walk hand-in-hand to the curb where Shane hands me my helmet. Within minutes we are heading to the apartment where our bags are packed and waiting. Max agreed to let us use his truck for the drive to Shane's parents' house since a multi-state trip on the back of a motorcycle is where I draw the line for adventure. Max hands off his keys after Shane tosses our bags into the backseat of the truck.

"Be good to her," Max says seriously. "Don't wreck my shit or I'll hunt you down."

"I'll take care of your truck, Max. You keep an eye on our places, yeah?"

"I'll water your plants," Max says, winking at me. I don't have nearly as many as I should now, but I appreciate it anyway. The little pothos I gave Shane managed to make it unscathed through the ransacking of his apartment—I'll take that as a good sign.

Raquel and Jamila pull up in Jamila's hatchback to give Max a ride back to his condo.

"Be careful with the wolves, Kaycia. They're all a bunch of moody fuckers," Raquel advises, but her grin spreads quickly as she chucks Shane on the shoulder. "Stay out of trouble."

"And hey, Shane?" Max calls as Shane shuts my door for me. "Tell your sister to give me a call. I'm happy to show her around the city if she comes to visit her big brother."

Shane rolls his eyes, then clasps hands with Max, pulling him in for a hug complete with back pats. I wave to Jamila and Raquel as Shane slides into the driver's seat, then laugh when Max and Raquel argue over who has to ride in the compact backseat.

Before he starts the truck, Shane turns to me, a serious expression on his face. "I promise, once we get through with this, I'll make it up to you for missing your exhibition."

"Oh, I know you will," I reply with a sly smile. He just chuckles until I add, "I managed to pack a little something extra. I figure we can take advantage of the night at the hotel away from other wolfie ears. I believe it might be what you heard through our thin walls."

His cheeks flush and he gives a sideways grin, but swiftly changes the subject, exhaling and turning the key in the ignition. "You ready for this?"

"To meet the parents? Sure! Parents love me. I'm sweet."

Shane laughs, reaching his hand behind my seat to rest his palm on the headrest before leaning over to kiss me. "Yeah, you are, baby girl," he whispers, then kisses me once more, nipping at my lower lip. With a final deep sigh, he puts the truck in drive and pulls away from the curb, heading home.

Epilogue
Shane

Two days in the truck, one exceptionally enjoyable night in a hotel, and hundreds of miles later, we pull into the driveway at my parents' house outside Woodbine Hollow. The ridge of mountains standing guard on the horizon are unchanged, but other things are different. Me, more so than anything else.

The trees lining the driveway have grown, arching overhead now, but the crunch of the rough gravel drive induces a wave of nostalgia, sending my heart sprinting with each yard we drive through the shade.

Two motorcycles are parked next to a beat-up farm truck in front of the main house, and four people await our arrival on the wrap-around porch. Staring through the windshield, I take a shaky breath.

My mother and father look the same, if a little greyer than I remember. Lana rocks on the porch swing, and a young man I barely recognize stands up from where he sat next to her to walk down the steps. I get out of the truck, round the front to open Kaycia's door, and offer her a hand to step down, then turn to face my family who have all gathered at the foot of the stairs.

My mother's eyes are full of tears, but like Lana, she wipes them away before they fall as she smiles. My father steps forward to take my hand, starting to shake it before he pulls me into a tight embrace that makes me hold tight to my own tears.

"Welcome home, son." His voice trembles with restrained emotions and he holds me at arm's length as if to inspect me. When he releases me, I turn to my mother who cradles my face in both palms with a smile.

"My sweet boy," my mother says, wrapping her arms around me and resting her head against my chest. She seems smaller than she did before I left, even if her strength is evident in the tightness of her embrace. "I'm so glad you're home."

I can't hold my feelings back any longer as a desperate sob escapes me, and I cling to my mother. The last time I hugged my parents was when they hastily wrapped my bleeding arm and handed me a rucksack and duffle with my entire life held within. My father's large hand cups the back of my head as though I'm still a child while I breathe deeply to regain control over my emotions.

With a steadying breath, I turn to the young man. "Aubrey? That you, little brother?"

"It's been a long time, Shane," Aubrey answers, voice

thick with emotion. His voice is deep, and his shoulders are as broad as mine, even if he's still a few inches shorter. Nothing like the boy he was when I left.

"Too long," I agree. Aubrey rushes forward to hug me, still as exuberant as always.

Lana clears her throat. "Now that all these emotions are handled, let the man introduce his girl. Poor thing is just standing there," she remarks, waving her hand to where Kaycia waits quietly behind me. Lana smiles wide at Kaycia, their friendship forged in the rain on the lawn of my cabin.

Kaycia has held back, waiting in front of the truck with wide eyes. I scrub away my tears and take her hand in mine with a reassuring smile.

"Mama, Dad. This is Kaycia Durand," I announce, pulling Kaycia forward to meet my parents. "And this is my little brother, Aubrey. You already know Lana."

Lana wrinkles her nose with a smile and a wink at Kaycia, while Aubrey dips his chin and offers a little wave, as though afraid I might react poorly if he were to shake her hand. Even if Kaycia may not realize it, I know that my family can scent our bond without my need to announce the seriousness of our relationship.

"Oh, come here, sweetheart!" my mother exclaims, not worried in the least. Her open arms greet Kaycia as though she's an old friend. "Thank you for taking care of him," she whispers while she hugs her, then holds her out at arm's length with a wide smile. "Welcome to the pack, honey."

Kaycia smiles and returns my mother's embrace

without hesitation. My father smiles at me with a hint of familiar sparkle in his eyes, dipping his head in approval.

I'm unexpectedly overwhelmed by emotions watching Kaycia be welcomed by my family. I never thought I'd get to see them again, let alone introduce them to the family I've built after being torn from them.

Before that happiness can root too deeply though, my father interrupts. "Let's get the two of you settled. Aubrey can carry your things to your old room. I assume you're both fine with sharing a bed?" Kaycia blushes deeply, but I just nod my approval and Aubrey heads to the truck to grab our bags. My father continues, "A council of Ross pack members will be here tomorrow evening. We need to discuss your plan first thing in the morning, Shane. But for now, let's have dinner and hear how you've been spending your time."

He opens the front door for Aubrey to carry the bags in, holding it for my mother to pass through with Kaycia. With a backward glance, he enters behind them, leaving Lana and me on the porch.

We used to spend hours out here together, playing games or doing homework, while my mother fussed over Aubrey. I inhale deeply, the scents of home and Woodbine Hollow comforting me despite the knowledge of what awaits.

Lana clears her throat, pulling me from the pleasant memories as she nudges my ribs with a pointy elbow. "So, what are we going to do now, *Alpha?*"

———

Continue *The Wolves of Woodbine Hollow* in Book 2:
Neon Elegies

Afterword

Thank you so much for reading Shane and Kaycia's story.

If you enjoyed this book please consider leaving a review on Amazon or Goodreads (or any of your other favorite review spots).

Reviews and word of mouth are the best ways you can support your favorite indie authors, and I appreciate every review! The more people who read my stories, the more I can continue to write and share them with the world!

xo,
LB

Acknowledgments

First and foremost, thank you to my wonderful husband and daughter, who put up with me being glued to my laptop for hours when an idea hits, and who love and support me no matter what.

My alphas and betas: Holly Ann, Jess, Rhiannon, Krystal, Kristen, and Lauren. Thank y'all so much for listening to my rambling voice notes and chaotic texts. Some of you have been with me since *The Bartered Soul* was just a draft, and without your encouragement, I might not have made it to this series! (An extra shout-out to Kristen for telling me to write this book after sending her a random reel, I did it!)

Kelly, my editor and friend. Thank you for helping me to tell this story the way it needed to be told and for hyping me up when I had moments of self-doubt.

Sam Rueter: Thank you for answering a random DM and offering me insight into an artist's process so I could make sure Kaycia and her show were realistic.

To my ARC Readers and Instagram friends: Thank you for supporting me on this author journey, you mean the world to me.

About the Author

L.B. Benson is a native Texan and a lifelong reader. She formally immortalized her love of books by earning a Bachelor of Arts in English from the University of Texas. While she primarily writes romance, you can find her engrossed in almost any genre.

L.B. spends her spare time dreaming up stories in the Texas countryside where she lives with her family.

———

Stay up to date by following along at https:// lbtheauthor.com or on social media (@lb_the_author).

 instagram.com/lb_the_author